Praise for One L

"With Suzanne Park's irresistible humor and lovably relatable characters, *One Last Word* is a breezy, clever romp through the tech world. I can't count the number of times I laughed out loud!"

—Rachel Lynn Solomon, *New York Times* bestselling author of *The Ex Talk*

"With pitch-perfect humor, endearing insights, and wonderfully relatable characters, *One Last Word* is a smart and breezy read about taking hold of the life you want and refusing to let go. An absolute delight."

—Allison Winn Scotch, bestselling author of *Take Two, Birdie Maxwell*

"*One Last Word* is the best kind of novel: laugh-out-loud funny, bittersweet, and so darn relatable you wonder if the author's been hanging out inside your head. Suzanne Park has written another absolute winner."

—Camille Pagán, bestselling author of *Good for You*

"What a pleasure to dive into *One Last Word* by Suzanne Park, a smart, contemporary, and laugh-out-loud novel about taking chances and making amends. With a clever plot twist that leads to deep storylines about love, friendship, and family ties, Park draws us in with relatable characters and sharp dialogue. The overall effect is a satisfying tale of a modern woman choosing to live life on her own terms."

—Lian Dolan, author of *The Sweeney Sisters*

The Do-Over

"With depth and warmth and wit, *The Do-Over* is a beautiful, hopeful portrayal of second chances in life and in love. The carefully executed portrayal of anxiety, as well as the wonderfully engrossing love story make this a pitch-perfect read. I absolutely loved every word. Suzanne Park is a hidden gem in the romance world, and *The Do-Over* is her best book yet."

—Christina Lauren, *New York Times* bestselling author of
The Soulmate Equation

"A satisfying story of overcoming your fears about expectations—other people's and your own—and figuring out your own worth. Second-chance romance meets all the other second chances we need to give ourselves."

—KJ Dell'Antonia, *New York Times* bestselling author of
The Chicken Sisters and *In Her Boots*

"A fantastic, empowering second-chance romance that combines wit and charm with an always insightful commentary on imposter syndrome, anxiety, and the challenge of finding ourselves. Suzanne Park wrote a true gem!"

—Ali Hazelwood, *New York Times* bestselling author of
The Love Hypothesis

So We Meet Again

"Funny, romantic, and a real-world novel. It centers on Jessie Kim, a young Korean woman who is laid off from her finance job. . . . It tackles sexism and racism in gripping ways."

—*Today* on *So We Meet Again*

"Some books just feel like an old friend, their first pages embracing you with an instant familiarity and warmth you can't help but sink into. Suzanne Park's *So We Meet Again* is that kind of book. . . . A cinematic, charming heart-squeeze-of-a-book that has found its way to my Ultimate Comfort Reads shelf."

—Emily Henry, #1 *New York Times* bestselling author

"A laugh-out-loud comedy with a warm heart. Jess's journey of finding her way amid the noise of the world's expectations will make you smile and sigh and want to chase your dreams."

—Sonali Dev, award-winning author of *Recipe for Persuasion*

Loathe at First Sight

"*Loathe at First Sight* bursts with humor, heart, and great energy. I loved it! Park is a hilarious new voice in women's fiction."

—Helen Hoang, *USA Today* bestselling author of *The Kiss Quotient*

"Park gives us the story that only she could create. It's hilarious, smart, and the rom-com we need!"

—Alexa Martin, ALA Award–winning author of *Intercepted*

"Park has created a wholly original, smart, fierce heroine (with a hilarious inner voice) who takes on an industry hell-bent on underestimating her. . . . Just like the 'entertaining, fresh, snarky' video game she conjures in her novel, Suzanne Park has written a fast and fun debut, putting females in the lead."

—Amy Poeppel, author of *The Sweet Spot*

Also by Suzanne Park

The Do-Over
Loathe at First Sight
So We Meet Again

One Last Word

A NOVEL

SUZANNE PARK

AVON

An Imprint of HarperCollinsPublishers

ONE LAST WORD. Copyright © 2024 by Suzanne Park. All rights reserved. Printed in the United States of America. No part of this book may be used or reproduced in any manner whatsoever without written permission except in the case of brief quotations embodied in critical articles and reviews. For information, address HarperCollins Publishers, 195 Broadway, New York, NY 10007.

HarperCollins books may be purchased for educational, business, or sales promotional use. For information, please email the Special Markets Department at SPsales@harpercollins.com.

FIRST EDITION

Designed by Diahann Sturge-Campbell

Art throughout © shmel/Shutterstock

Library of Congress Cataloging-in-Publication Data has been applied for.

ISBN 978-0-06-321609-9

24 25 26 27 28 LBC 5 4 3 2 1

To my found families who have kept me afloat

Chapter One

Some days don't go as planned.

For example, today.

Today, I dribbled hot coffee on my lap during my commute to the office, leaving me to decide if spit-cleaning my dry-clean-only pants would make the stain even worse.

Today, I discovered that the new red whiteboard marker was leaky, staining my hands as if I'd stabbed someone.

Today, I found out that the product I'd been working on all year—the career-defining app I'd been toiling away on during workdays and weekends—was simply nonfunctional.

And yet, I was scheduled to present this nonworking app wearing brown-speckled pants, with noticeably bloodied hands, in an important meeting, while the founders of the company sat and judged me.

Casey, my favorite interface designer at the company, hovered over my shoulder as I tapped my finger on the tablet, trying once again to make the app work. I exhaled hot air from my nose like a pissed-off dragon. "Nothing's working. Why is nothing happening?"

He explained, "Sara, these are the storyboards you can use as visual aids this afternoon. See? That's an image of the app icon. Swipe right and you'll see the welcome message and the drop-down menus. Honestly, we'd be on schedule with a working prototype if it hadn't been for this meeting." He shrugged. "The design team did a good job though showing how it *will* work."

Swipe. Swipe. Swipe. The still images were nice. The diverse template gallery offered designs ranging from simplistic to high octane. An easy-to-use font selector with smart pairing recommendations for headline and copy was something other apps didn't offer. Themed photos based on content theme, mood, and personality type were all cutting edge.

Despite all the day's earlier mishaps, I'd be walking into that meeting with a sure thing. For months I'd happily geeked out on developing these features. The level of customization for this messaging app was unparalleled.

I took off my glasses and rubbed my eyes. "I'm sorry I freaked out. The meeting is in ten minutes, and then I hope it'll be back to business as usual." My brain was out of sorts from caffeine overload and fatigue. I could barely see straight. When my boss came back from vacation, I'd need to talk to him about taking a long overdue sabbatical.

"No worries, if I was working long nights like you, I'd be a barely functioning zombie with draggy feet too. With saggier flesh."

I couldn't help but notice he'd said *too* and *saggier*. Saggier . . . compared to whom?

He clarified. "Maybe a little hydration and some fresh air would help." He hesitated before adding, "And some expensive under-eye concealer." I'd worked with Casey for nearly five years, and we'd been friends for almost as long, so I knew the drill. He came with an excellent work ethic, beautiful aesthetic sensibility, and slap-in-the-face directness. On the weekends, he frequently wore a T-shirt with the word "Sasshole" on the chest. Casey didn't hold anything back, especially when it came to his favorite topics, such as dating, fashion, and under-eye puffiness.

"We can go to Sephora and get you some caffeine-infused cooling eye gel later this week. It works wonders. But not tonight. It's gym day, and it's kettlebell Tuesday." Casey unzipped his jacket to reveal his other favorite shirt, the one I bought him for his birthday. A black tee with "Kettlebell King" screen-printed in large white letters. He was the strongest person I knew, which came in handy when I needed to rearrange furniture, move apartments, or make an IKEA trip.

"Sounds good, thanks Case."

He jutted out his chest, then closed the door behind him.

After I rearranged a few photos on the tablet, my phone alarm rang, startling me. It was my five-minute warning to head to the meeting. I grabbed my tower of devices—laptop, tablet, phone—and arrived at the executive conference room with time to spare. But this was one case when punctuality didn't matter: the session before mine ran over. When the door finally opened, a large group consisting of mostly men shuffled out of the conference room in complete silence, heads hanging low. What happened in there? It was almost lunchtime, and there wasn't even chatter about the brand-new bacon bar in the cafeteria. The entire floor smelled like bacon, which to anyone who loved meat, namely the exact demographic who worked at my company, was the world's best air freshener. You'd have thought they were walking out of a funeral.

I raised an eyebrow at my friend Dave when he exited the room. My shorthand for "WTF." He muttered, "Brutal," and shuffled past me.

The moment I walked in, alarm bells went off. I wasn't the type of person who believed in burning sage to clear out evil spirits or bad juju, but the only way to describe the room's energy was "severely fucked up."

My manager was out of the office, so my skip-level boss, Seth, took his place as his proxy. He and I sat across from the Color Wheel

Communications founders, Marcus and Bryce, both of whom were speed-typing on their laptop keyboards, side by side, virtually in sync. Bryce was faster. Marcus hit the keys harder. Neither of them welcomed Seth or me, or even bothered to look up when we plunked down in the squeaky boardroom chairs.

I flipped the projector's power switch, connected it to the tablet, and waited for my first image to appear on the white wall. Noting the lack of engagement in the room, I resigned myself to flipping through features quickly and then, if needed, diving into the numbers in the appendix. That was assuming the meeting would even start—they still hadn't looked at me.

Clearing my throat, I spoke with gusto. "The app we're releasing at the end of the year is currently unnamed, but the project is internally called UMD. Upon My Death."

Bryce stopped typing and slapped shut his laptop. Marcus continued to look at his screen but had at least stopped pounding the keys.

Seth nodded at me, his glasses sliding down his nose. *Go on, while they're paying attention.*

I jumped straight into the product description. "Upon My Death allows users to send messages to anyone they want after they pass. It sounds a bit morbid, but we're seeing a ton of social media activity about the critical need for individuals to own their narrative before they die. Early research suggests that *controlling the conversation* has strong appeal in a wide range of ages. The uses for an app that gives you the last word could include confronting bullies, getting closure on personal matters, and offering goodbyes to loved ones."

No one was typing or talking. That could be good . . . or possibly bad. They also weren't smiling or asking questions about where I had gotten this idea. Truthfully, off the record, I'd gotten it from an action movie where an evil mastermind had rigged an entire metropolitan infrastructure to blow up if he was killed. If he didn't "check in" and confirm his well-being by midnight every night, chaos and destruction would ensue throughout the city. On the record, I told people this concept derived from a popular competitor's app that let you tell coworkers and colleagues that they had BO. It ranked #5 in the Apple app store and had held the #1 spot for many months.

My idea was so much better.

The ongoing silence creeped me out. I moved on to their favorite topic: money.

"Let's talk about the company's financial gains from developing this app."

Continuing to the fiscal projections, I laid out the forecasts for user growth, ad revenue, and lifetime value. My voice remained firm, but I could feel my body temperature rise by the second, which meant profuse sweating would soon follow. Forehead perspiration first, and then a sweaty upper mustache area would come next. After that, it was like body-part roulette on what would be subsequently drenched.

I needed to get through this presentation fast.

Once I started speaking about global opportunities, Bryce cut me off. "We've seen enough. Bottom line: this project is too small to pursue. It might be profitable, yes, but we need big ideas to invest in now. Not this small peanuts shit."

Seth jumped in, seemingly on my side. "Sara has a track record for discovering revenue streams, and she can walk you through some projections. They've been vetted by Finance and are on the conservative side, but are hardly, as you say, small." But then he looked at me and shrugged. Had he really looked at the numbers? Was this an expression of doubt?

Marcus sighed. "I don't see the point of this exercise. We should deploy our engineers elsewhere. Something worth their time."

A fire lit within me and I raised my voice. "You don't think my app is worth anyone's time? But you see the point in your existing app that only makes Bubble-Wrap-popping sounds?" This was Marcus's first project at the company and it had never turned a profit, yet was still well-funded.

Surprisingly, Seth backed me up. "Sara's project is a brand-new opportunity for the company, and it's gotten so much buzz internally."

Marcus said, "I see it as less opportunity, more opportunity *cost*. We have other projects we'd like to focus on, and we're lucky this idea didn't go into development yet. We've barely invested resources, so it's an easy one to cut. Maybe we can defer the project instead of cancel it outright, since you're being so pushy."

"Pushy?" I asked, biting back my seething anger.

Bryce chimed in. "Bossy. Pushy. Bullish. Whatever. We can table this for next fiscal if you still want us to consider it."

Seth could sense I was a powder keg ready to kaboom. He used his calm kindergarten-teacher voice. "Sara, let's regroup and come back next year when we have our thoughts together."

I scooted my chair back and stood so I was temporarily the tallest person in the room. Before speaking, I took a calming breath. "I *do* have my thoughts together. I've been working on this an entire year and worked hard to pull these numbers and images together. And you looked at it for what, three minutes at most? I've been at this company for over five years and I have a good understanding of your products. You've gotten complacent and you're letting all the interesting and creative ideas get shelved, and smart, passionate people are leaving here in droves." I kept my tone composed and professional, like I'd rehearsed all day. My exhausted body was running only on pure adrenaline and all I really wanted to do was go home and crash on the leather sofa in front of my TV, but I needed to push through.

Bryce rolled his eyes. "I disagree. We have tons of good people here. Though maybe some are not a good fit here because they're cut from a different cloth than us. There are two types of people at this company . . . idea generators and doers. All we're saying is, right now we need fewer of the former and more of the latter." He looked at Marcus. They both crossed their arms in sync.

Marcus focused his attention on his laptop screen. "Are we done here? If we are, we can end early and then we won't be behind with the rest of the afternoon meetings."

I looked at Seth. No way. I needed the final word. "Actually, one last thing. I'm an idea generator *and* a doer. I'm looking for more strategic opportunities, because I've done a ton of nonpromotable work for this company, a disproportionate share, I might add, and I want to grow. When I started at this company, I thought the best way to get established was to offer something this place was missing: efficiency and order. I created processes. Workstreams. Collaboration tools. It's thankless work that no one wants, and it continues to get dumped on me, because you all think I'm *only* a doer. I'm also creative and passionate. I'm ready for more responsibility. I've already gained whatever knowledge and skills I was going to, so now I need to move up and out. It seems my only option is to leave this company and take my idea with me."

"Sure. You can have it, no problem." Marcus scoffed. His tone quickly changed when he saw my face and knew I was dead serious and not bluffing. "We're not against *you*, you've got drive and ambition. You seem like a hard worker. We just don't see you as an idea person. We're looking for big, scalable ideas. Not . . . this."

Remain calm, Sara. Centered. Give the impression you're willing to have an open strategic discussion without an ounce of pettiness, because that is what a senior leader would do.

"Unbelievable." I used all the strength within me to swallow the remaining words teetering on the tip of my tongue.

When I didn't respond as he expected, he said, "Let's not get hasty. You're overreacting and letting your emotions take over."

I . . . what?

I was most certainly not doing that. I had taken great care to mirror their body language. To match their tone. All while being careful to respond the way a confident leader would.

No. This was not okay. I refused to work at a narrow-minded company that threw around microaggressions like it was Gen Z influencer slang. "Pushy? Overreacting? Really? Would you even say these things to *men* in the office?"

I leaped to my feet and scribbled "I will be leaving the Color Wheel Communications with two weeks' notice. —Sara Chae" on the whiteboard behind the founders' chairs. I took a photo and emailed it to Seth and cc'd HR. It was then that I noticed the projects for the company were scribbled on the board, most of which had been stricken with thick black marker. The few with green checks were presumably ones they wanted to pursue. One they greenlit was "Cupcake Bubble Popper Ultimate Exploding Edition."

I smothered a scream.

Clenching my fists, I announced, "That whiteboard note serves as my resignation letter. Thanks for your time and feedback. It was illuminating." I grabbed my belongings and opened the door for Seth to follow me out. I added, "I think I wrote it with a Sharpie, not a dry-erase marker."

Hand sanitizer from the reception desk would probably get that right off, but I wasn't going to tell them. That would be yet another nonpromotable task for me, no thank you.

As the door closed, we observed the founders gaping at the whiteboard together, the mood of the room shifting with the power dynamic change. Instead of bursting into tears, I wanted to punch, kick, and yell, further validating that getting the last word, especially for people like me, was empowering and necessary.

Now I had motivation to turn this idea into a reality. Exactly what I needed.

Chapter Two

*T*wo weeks postemployment and I was doing okay, considering. Yes, I'd lost track of time and was showering every other day. Maybe every other other day. And I'd given up my cool downtown loft, put everything in storage, and moved in with my sister. But still, I managed to get dressed in a fresh outfit every morning, even if it was mainly athleisure couture. I had applied to a few jobs and even had a few video interviews . . . but honestly, my heart wasn't in it.

I wanted to work on my app.

I didn't want to give up on it.

I had honestly thought this idea would finally get me out of mid-level management purgatory at Color Wheel Communications, rising above bug tracking and project management, and finally into a director role. When I joined the team, it was after a massive industry shake-up, with all the big companies giving out pink slips at once like they were bulk candy on Halloween. Although I had needed the break, I wished my departure back then had been on my terms. The experience of getting laid off en masse, knowing it wasn't reflective of my performance, hit me hard. When I started at Color Wheel, I didn't want to make any waves, so I played it safe. Maybe too safe.

My "roll up my sleeves" reputation made people think I was the one on the team to dump work on because they knew I'd do it. Do it well, in fact. I'd been in my same position as a senior product manager for far too long, and only managed to make horizontal shifts to other projects, taking on more unpromotable, thankless responsibilities, but never moving up or getting pay bumps any bigger than inflation rates and cost of living adjustments. And thus the never-ending cycle of mundane middle-management minutiae continued.

Something inside me begged me to see my app through. A spark of passion. A flicker of hope. I hadn't felt this before. Could I even launch this myself?

While sending out résumés, I also researched entrepreneurship funding opportunities in Los Angeles, and to my surprise, I discovered that the esteemed Silicon Beach VC Pitch Warriors Competition was still open for submissions. It was a three-month contest during which selected companies battled head-to-head to move on to the last round, and there, contestants had an opportunity to appear in front of California's top VCs. Millions of dollars in funding were up for grabs.

But the deadline to enter Pitch Warriors was that same day. No exceptions. This left me only a few hours to upload all my financial projections and submit the final application before midnight.

The whole uploading process was maddening. The servers were slow, likely because everyone else was filling out the same forms at the exact same time. And surprising for a tech-centric organization, these glitchy online documents were the kind that you couldn't skip ahead on to check out the remaining questions without risking losing all the data you'd already filled out.

Infuriating.

After filling out most of the form fields, I was faced with a dilemma: Should I choose the well-known, cutthroat pitch competition or the fairly new three-month mentorship program? The sheer volume of materials and information they requested for the competition—questions about product build, running experiments, early user feedback—left me wondering if I was even ready for a competitive challenge of this scale. The previous winners had classy branding, video demos, and elaborate pitch decks. I had a few pretty pictures and some basic PowerPoint slides. Practically child's play.

My sister, Jia, came out of her room and stared over my shoulder, watching me type.

"Uh, this is private," I muttered while shifting in my seat, tilting my laptop screen down.

She laughed. "If you're rooming with me for free, I have the right to know if you're watching or reading any shady Trojan horse virus-y shit that's not suitable for work on *my* internet plan."

I shrugged and pushed the screen back up. She'd offered to house her older sister in a pinch, which was generous. After helping me move into her rent-controlled apartment in Venice, she said I could stay for as long as it would take to find my next gig. Jia had taken a new job at a brand consultancy firm on the Westside and had recently moved into a one bedroom with a large walk-in closet that fit a twin air mattress, so I'd spent the last few nights sleeping under a canopy of light jackets and ski coats. I did the laundry, dishes, and shopping in exchange for room and board. By LA standards, this was a good deal for someone just starting out and taking their training wheels off their big-girl bike. But maybe not that great for someone like me who had just turned thirty-four.

She commented, "You should use a more reliable and safer browser." I expected her to say more, since she always had a lot to say about everything I did, but she was on her way out, dressed to the nines, at nine P.M. Jia was always the fun, social one in the family. Maybe it was because she was the youngest and I was the oldest. Or because she was eight years younger than I. Or because she had made the decision a few years ago to not be a workaholic and enjoy life, and I hadn't. She was always out with friends or on dates, while I frequently had intimate nights with an over-nuked leftover Chipotle burrito or a Lean Cuisine spaghetti with meat sauce.

"Maybe you could come out and join us when you're done with whatever it is you're working on late on a Friday night?" she asked while sliding into sparkling strappy sandals.

"I'll probably be right here in this very spot till midnight at least. Have fun." I sighed and went back to typing. I did want to have fun and go out, in theory. But I had a lot on my mind, and I wasn't as carefree and fun as Jia when I was saddled with stress.

Jia jangled her keys as she shut the door behind her, then locked it from the outside. She still hadn't gotten used to having me as a roommate, since I could have easily helped out by locking the door behind her to save her time. She continued to do things as if she were living alone: leaving the door open when she was using the bathroom, talking on speakerphone while shouting out her personal business, or eating ice cream straight from the pint. It was fine though, I'd practically raised her, so I was used to seeing the good, bad, and ugly of Jia.

Anyway, my goal wasn't to stay here, if I could help it. Casey from work had said I could stay at his place in Playa Vista, and my friend Olivia from college said I could crash on a pullout couch in the apartment she shared with her roommate, but she was all the way in Rancho Cucamonga. I chose Jia, because it seemed weird to accept either of those offers if my very own sister lived in the same city in a desirable, walkable location, and had a perfectly good air mattress in her closet.

I had a solid plan. Actually, two. To get into the competition or the mentorship program. I still hadn't decided yet. Backup plan: to find a job at another tech company. Lots of recruiters hunting and fishing on LinkedIn needed product managers. As for the backup to the backup plan . . . I didn't want to think about that. If I ended up needing a third choice, it was time to consider a complete life overhaul. A pre-midlife crisis. The sky would be falling, and I'd be Chicken Not-So-Little running around with my head cut off.

Memories of past presentation blunders, meeting faux pas, and awkward executive encounters from previous jobs flashed through my head, making me groan out loud. *Stop it, Sara. Turn off the cringe compilation reel and get focused on finishing this application.*

Maybe going out with Jia later would be a good idea after all. Get a load off my mind.

Or maybe this was all a waste of time, and none of this was worthwhile. Why did I think that running a company on my own was even a possibility? It was so out of my comfort zone that it was practically in another universe.

I scrambled to my feet and began pacing around the apartment. This was a bad idea. I needed my old job back.

The light in the hallway flickered and made a popping sound. The corridor went dark from the burned-out LED light, most likely an electrical problem instead of a bulb issue. When I went to investigate, I banged my right pinky toe into a medium-size brown box sitting on the floor near the foyer. Pain shot through my foot as I hopped around, but I was distracted because the mystery package was addressed to me.

Peeling the shipping tape, I pulled out a wrapped box with a card attached nestled in packaging peanuts.

I opened the envelope. The front of the note read "It's boring here without you!" Inside, my former work teammates had written warm wishes and farewells, and sent along a going-away gift.

My eyes welled with tears as I read their words.

*Who am I supposed to bitch about management with
if you're gone? Wishing you all the best! Let me know
where you land, I'd love to work with you again. —Myles*

*I know you'll kick ass in whatever you do next.
Remember the little people when you're at the top.
Love, Kass*

*Where will any cool new ideas come from? You will be
missed. Sincerely, Derrick*

*Whoever gets to work with you next is so lucky. I know
I was. —James*

*You were the best product lead I've ever worked with. I
hope you go far. —Nick*

Your work husband misses you already. xO, Casey

*Thank you for not downloading anything shady the
5.25 years you were here! Take care, Chase (your
favorite IT guy)*

Inside the small wooden box was a green succulent in a small red pot that read "Hope your new place doesn't succ!" I barked a laugh and smiled as I read the instructions: "Light optional. Water when you remember. Nearly killproof!"

I placed the plant on the white bookcase wall in the living room, on the shelf that housed Jia's growing candle collection. Lavender. Sandalwood. Rosemary. Jasmine. And the favorite one that she lit every evening, lemongrass. The churro-scented one I'd bought her as a thank-you for letting me crash there was still in its cylinder tube.

There was more spring in my step despite my busted toe, which was a little swollen and forming a bruise. I barely felt it though, too wrapped up in happy thoughts. My old team believed in me. Now it was time to believe in myself.

* * *

At 11:50 P.M., I reached the final page of the application, the terms and conditions. By submitting, I would be agreeing to seven pages of tiny-font legalese. I couldn't risk missing the deadline by reading all the fine print, so I hit the submit button at 11:59 and watched the circle swirl as the word "uploading" flashed on my screen. My hand trembled on the mouse, my index finger threatening to left click and resubmit, but I used all my willpower to wait.

Uploading.

Uploading.

Upl—

"Congratulations!" the new page read. "We've received your application. Please check your email for a confirmation."

Ding! My inbox highlighted a fresh new message. Subject: "Thank you for your submission to Pitch Warriors!"

I fell back into the couch, my shoulders temporarily relaxing the continual scrunch.

It was done. And the rest, as far as I could tell, was out of my hands.

Even though parts of my shoulders and neck were releasing tension, my stomach was still clenched. Partly from stress and nerves, but also because I was starving. That one Lean Cuisine I'd had around lunchtime wasn't enough to keep me satiated through the late evening.

Jia's kitchen was more like a kitchenette: it had basic appliances such as an oven and stove, but Jia had to rent a refrigerator and she didn't have a dishwasher. There was a large faux-marble island smack in the middle of the room where she'd placed a few bar stools, and this doubled as a dining table since she didn't have any room for one. It was certainly an odd use of space on this side of her apartment, and even stranger was how huge her bedroom was in comparison.

Although Jia had rented a fairly nice fridge, it wasn't stocked with anything. In fact, it was the opposite; it resembled the bottled water and toilet paper aisle at Target soon after the pandemic hit. She had various take-out containers in her fridge, but with no indication of how old they were. Even when I lived alone, I wrote down dates on boxes and plastic lids with a Sharpie, to make sure I wouldn't accidentally poison myself at a later date by eating something past the acceptable consumption time frame. But maybe Jia had her own system. I left everything as it was and closed the refrigerator door. In the freezer drawer were ice trays and two Lean Cuisines, identical to my previous meal. Underneath the ice and Lean Cuisines were a pint of freezer-burned chocolate chip ice cream, a small bottle of vodka, and another empty ice tray.

Groceries were my responsibility, so I had only myself to blame. Time had escaped me that day and I needed to go shopping soon, but not at midnight.

Jia texted. You done? Nightcap at the new wine bar across the street?

I looked down at my clothes. Black ribbed T-shirt and black stretchy pinstripe pants. Barely passing the threshold of acceptable attire for being seen in public. I'd have to wear one of Jia's nice coats if I made a public appearance, even if it was Venice, where the dress code in most places embraced the quasi-beach culture. Sure, down in 5

As soon as I turned on the light in the bathroom and saw my haggard reflection in the mirror, I adjusted my estimate.

Make that 10.

My God. I'd need time to work on those under-eye bags.
She replied: Great! I'll grab a table and order drinks

I tossed my black-rimmed computer glasses on the marble sink countertop and put on a surface layer of makeup, added caffeine gel for the eyes courtesy of Casey, and dry-shampooed my hair. Running my fingers through my locks to give them more volume, I gave up and spritzed a little hair spray along my partline, hoping for the best. Exactly ten minutes later, I left the apartment and ran down the two flights of stairs, exiting the building onto Rose Avenue. Jia had sweet-talked her way into a reasonably priced rental on one of the most dichotomous commercial streets on the Westside of Los Angeles. The Whole Foods sharing the corner parking lot with the 99 Cents Only Store was one of many examples of the conspicuous contrast of the once-affordable, beach-shabby Venice and the permeation of one-percenter life. Dilapidated buildings were torn down instead of restored, converted to new artisanal eateries and curated boutiques catering to the young and upwardly mobile. Or to those who aspired to be in that demographic.

I jaywalked across the street and zipped up Jia's off-white puffer coat. It was a chilly and gusty March night, and while it was in the upper sixties and sunny during the day, our proximity to the ocean made it necessary to have a few winter weather pieces on after dark. My sister was waiting for me at a small round table, with an extra glass of red wine and an empty seat across from her. She'd found the warmest seat in the restaurant, by the massive stone fireplace with gaslit wooden logs.

She lifted her coat off the stool and gestured for me to sit. "Thank goodness you're here. Three guys have already tried to use this opportunity to sit down and hit on me, like this is some sort of speed dating scheme or I was a damsel in distress who needed them to keep me company." She rolled her eyes while shaking her head.

It was funny how Jia talked about such things as if everyone had the same experience. Guys in bars always gravitated toward her: she had the "it factor" when it came to desirable partnering. Physical magnetism. Primal attractiveness. Whatever it was—pheromones, body chemistry, face symmetry—she always got hit on wherever we went together. At Costco, at the gas station, at the gas station bathroom. Everywhere. In comparison, if I was sitting at a table with an empty chair, nine times out of ten someone would ask, "Is anyone sitting here?" and when I would say no, they'd steal the chair away to another table, usually filled with hotter people. The other one out of ten times, the open chair would then be used to hold coats and purses from the neighboring patrons.

What was the opposite of the "it factor"? The quit factor? The shit factor?

"Cheers to finishing your application!" Jia raised her wineglass and I toasted her. "So now that that's done and you're not as stressed, can you tell me what you applied for?"

Before I could answer, a fidgety server slinked up to our table. "Hi. So sorry to interrupt. The gentleman at the bar would like to pay for your next drinks. Is that okay?" He motioned his head over to the counter, where a silver-haired man in his mid-fifties lifted his glass and smiled. He looked older than our dad.

Jia handled it like a pro. "Please thank him for his generosity but we are respectfully declining the offer. We'll be finishing up soon and we'd be wasting his money and time. And if he asks, we don't have plans for any after-hour activities, for him or anyone else."

Our server nodded and pressed his lips together tightly, smirking a little as he walked over to the bar guy. He handled the news well. So well, in fact, that he pointed to the table of three ladies seated two tables down from Jia and me and sent the server over to them next.

She muttered into her glass, "Wow, he's determined."

I nodded. "It's a numbers game for him. Lots of women in this bar and he's just going table by table until he gets a yes."

Jia sighed. "I wish the people who approached me were guys I'd actually want to hang out with. It's always some creep. In business school I had a tough time finding anyone to date too, even though the ratio was in my favor."

My lips curled into a smile. "I think the saying for that goes, 'The odds are good, but the goods are odd.'"

She nearly spat out her Merlot. "Oh God, yes, and it's so true. Anyway, back to our discussion. What were you applying for again?"

I gave her a quick rundown of the Pitch Warriors VC competition and mentorship program and explained my last-minute decision to apply for both. "I honestly couldn't decide which option would be best for me, so I checked one and requested consideration for the other in the notes and comments section."

Her eyes widened. "Do they allow that? What if they disqualify you for not following their rules? What happened to my rule-abiding sister?"

I shrugged. "Sticking to the rules has gotten me only this far in life. Maybe it's time to try something a little different." I still had plan B. Finding a job at a tech company if this attempt at entrepreneurship blew up in my face.

I signaled to the server to return to our table.

He asked, "Check?"

I shook my head. "I think we'll have one more glass. But don't tell that guy who wanted to send over drinks."

Jia interrupted. "Make that a bottle. We're here to celebrate." She looked at me. "Honestly, this is the first time I've seen you out of my apartment in over a week, you really need to get out more. Plus, I'm getting a fiscal year bonus soon that doesn't even help keep up with cost of living in Los Angeles, but it's enough for a modest, nice bottle at this modest, nice establishment."

The server came over in a hurry with wine and two fresh glasses.

Two clean pours later, and after a few gulps and swallows, Jia tapped on my phone on the table.

"Show me the app you built," she demanded.

I picked up my cell phone and offered a caveat. "It's still being built, so it's buggy and clunky. It barely works."

I clicked on the black stylized "UMD" icon and waited for it to load. Casey had been moonlighting as my app designer and developer, working nights and weekends. Like me, he never went on dates. Unlike me, he spent many hours at the gym when he wasn't glued to his computer. And when he wasn't building muscle, he was gaming or binging Netflix. He had time to spend on my app, and he was kind (and bored) enough to do a good job with it.

"It's called Upon My Death?" Jia laughed as the progress bar moved slowly. "That's so morbid. You need someone who can re-brand that, stat. I can help if you want."

"That would be great," I said, smiling at Jia. I sometimes forgot that she wasn't just my kid sister, she was someone with an MBA and a solid career in marketing. If anyone could help me with an app-naming project, it would be her.

Casey had let me know that in the latest features update, the app allowed syncing to my contacts, which was why it was taking so long.

Finally, a prompt appeared on-screen. "**To whom shall we send a message?**" it asked with friendly purple sans serif font.

Jia giggled. "To whom? Why does that sound so formal? Are some of the options 'Sir' or 'Madam'? Never mind, we can work on that too, along with the branding."

I typed in her name. "You can send canned messages or personalized ones when you pass. See? I can choose the family category, then select 'sister.'" The email field autofilled with her personal email address.

"Hey, that's pretty cool! Do you use machine learning for this? It knew I was your sister *and* which email of mine to use? That's fascinating."

I nodded. "The goal is to have algorithms figure a lot of this out. Right now Casey has the bare-bones app working, mainly for demo purposes. And if by some miracle I'm selected for the competition or mentorship, I hope to find engineers with that kind of expertise. We're also working on creating canned or autofill messages in different styles and voices to match the user based on social media posts and uploaded writing samples."

I chose a prewritten "I wanted to let you know how much you mean to me. You're a wonderful sister" message prompt. As I typed more words and added some custom verbiage, it used predictive technology to suggest additional words, phrases, and sentences.

Jia nodded as I finished my note to her. "So this will send to me . . . upon your death?"

"Yes, it should. You can also customize the settings so the app can send on a certain day in the future. Maybe it can even send out last wills and testaments, since it's always a tricky thing to figure out latest versions when someone dies. We're still working out how to fully monetize this idea. Maybe adding birthday, anniversary, and graduation reminders as a phase two. As it is now, a message service after someone dies, it's more like a feature than a product. If it sends a message out only when someone dies, there's not much of a recurring revenue stream, right? Maybe they can prepay or something, but still, it's not enough. Anyway, as I said, there's a lot to figure out. And everyone will want to know how it can make money."

She asked, "Wait, can we go back a few steps? How does the software know you're dead?"

I smiled. This was something I'd already figured out and was proud of. "Every day it crawls legacy-dot-com and the local paper obituaries for death announcements. Ideally I can have it look for death records too, but that is tricky on a state-by-state level, and international."

Jia took a sip. "I have to hand it to you. Your brain works in strange ways, but I'm digging this app. There are so many people I'd wanna say 'fuck off!' to but wouldn't have the guts to do it." She took my phone and typed out a quick message. "How about this one?"

She turned the phone screen around so I could read it. "Sara, you need to stop being a hermit and put yourself out more. Sincerely Yours, Jia."

I rolled my eyes and deleted it.

She glanced to her right and left at the emptied tables. "I think it's time for us to go."

I turned around to survey the area. "Ah, when they're putting chairs on the tops of tables and turning off the music, it's a universal sign to get the hell out."

"How would you know? You never go out!" Jia quipped.

"I do, sometimes!" I said. Okay, rarely. Or hardly ever. Maybe she had a point.

We chugged our last ounces of wine and settled the tab. When we stumbled out onto the sidewalk, the wine hit me.

Jia tilted her chin up and pointed to the night sky. For the first time ever in all my years of living in Southern California, I observed a supermoon high above our heads.

She said, "I think this is a sign. A full moon is supposed to be a time of clarity and change. And this is a big-ass supermoon."

Maybe it meant it was time for super-size clarity and mega-immense change then. Hopefully it would all be for the better.

Drunk off our asses, we reloaded my app when we arrived home. I wrote long-winded messages to people at work I wanted to tell off, letting giggly Jia read and edit, then dragged the notes to the trash icon. While Jia got ready for bed, I also penned a pithy five-paragraph essay about why my sister was the greatest sibling in the world, complete with an enthusiastic sign-off of "Heavenly Yours," which inexplicably autocorrected to "Heathenly." I stored Jia's email address for a future send after my death but changed my mind and dragged that to the trash folder too.

Other messages poured out of me, to people who I thought needed to hear from me one last time: my old high school (unrequited) crush, my former best friend who ghosted me, and my domineering mom and dad. As the alcohol emboldened me, I crafted pettier messages. To my old landlord who refused to budge on the lease requirement to give two months' notice after living in the same place for four years, and two more pissy notes to Bryce and Marcus, my old company cofounders.

Adrenaline pumped through my body as I wrote. Drafting these letters energized me, and having the last word was empowering. After a lot of typing and a few belly laughs later, I deleted those messages and grabbed a tall glass of water. The rest of the night was a giant blur, with Jia getting a second wind and grabbing the keyboard from me to edit my words and ordering Chinese food from the one sketchy place that was open 24-7.

It was delicious.

*　*　*

I woke up on the couch in the morning with my face pressed on my laptop keyboard. Luckily I hadn't drooled and short-circuited my computer or electrocuted my face. I did, however, end up with tiny keypad squares imprinted on my right cheek, which left an impression reminiscent of corn on the cob. Or a hand grenade.

My fingers brushed the deep square indentations as I muttered, "Shiiiiit."

Jia didn't miss a beat when she saw me rise from the couch and stretch. "Your face . . . the texture looks like an Eggo waffle."

She was already in gym clothes? What time was it?

I croaked out, "Are you headed out?" My mouth felt full of cotton from the night of dehydrating drinking. I was selfishly hoping she'd be away for a few hours, because my pounding head couldn't handle her early-morning teasing and needed complete silence to recuperate.

"I just got back from kickboxing class, actually. Thanks for noticing." She sipped her smoothie and handed me an identical one she pulled from the fridge. "It'll hydrate you. Way better than your morning coffee."

"I like my coffee," I muttered. "It's more my thing."

"You mean bitter?" she quipped.

I narrowed one eye and tilted my head. "Strong and acidic."

"Well, I'm out of coffee, so you'll have to deal with a delicious, healthy smoothie. I should have made you come to the class with me."

This was when I really noticed our age difference. Mid-thirties versus mid-twenties. I couldn't even remember the last time I'd taken morning gym classes and gone somewhere to get smoothies. Maybe five years ago? Ten? Never?

Jia was a chipper morning person who always managed to get a lot done before most people were awake. Society rewarded people who woke up at the crack of dawn. Grocery stores were empty, you could get in a full gym session before work, and parking in LA around sunrise was never an issue. Night owls were a special breed, using their most alert hours on the computer or watching TV. My most productive hours were between ten P.M. and two A.M., way past other friends' bedtimes, especially ones with kids. This was the time Jia was getting her restorative REM sleep.

She swirled her cup so the bottom bits of her smoothie reintegrated with the icy part. "When do you hear back from the competition?"

"Interviews happen soon for the final candidates. Then everyone will be notified by the end of the month." I hoped they would let me down on the earlier side. I had a few other potential job options in play and wanted to move forward if it wasn't looking like this was going to happen. The likelihood of being selected was around 5 percent, so the odds were not in my favor.

Jia handed me a banana. "I've been thinking of other app names. I think you should do some focus group testing, but I'm leaning toward something lighthearted but still somber, like Coda, Postscript, or Denouement. Maybe those are too ambiguous or brainy. Epilogue or something longer like Since I'm Gone or One Last Word could work. Probably best to keep it less obtuse, more mainstream could mean more money."

My head still pounded, but the smoothie and banana helped. "I like those options, they're much more catchy and less . . . deathy."

She barked a laugh, which made my ears ring and my head nearly explode from the volume. "I'll keep brainstorming, but overall I think the less morbid the better."

At first, I'd thought my crashing with my baby sister would cause a whole lot of friction between us. But it turned out I was actually happy to have her around: it was less lonely, and she didn't seem to hate me more with each day that passed.

Not having the structure of an office to go to every day took some getting used to, and because I wasn't an entirely anti-social person, the abrupt move from working in a large corporate setting to working from home—or in my case working from *closet*—wasn't the most suitable for my personality. I liked my office gossip at the coffee machine. I enjoyed the quick coworker lunches. Who didn't love hearing the latest in promotion and firing rumors? I'd recently heard my handwritten whiteboard notice went viral within the walls of the company. It took them days to remove the Sharpie ink, and because they waited too long, the words were still visible even after a deep cleaning. My indelible resignation was there for anyone who booked the executive conference room to see. Friends told me a photo of it circulated on the internal employee message board and my resignation was the most liked post of all time. And it beat out the grand-opening announcement of the new bacon bar.

Jia wiped the counter. "Have you thought about renting a co-working space soon?" It was like my sister and I were on the same wavelength about me needing social interaction. Or maybe she was just a little bit annoyed with how I cramped her living space. And ate half of her groceries plus worked and slept in the company of her dry-cleaned wardrobe. I also took up half of her sink space in the bathroom, making it difficult for her to get ready for work in the mornings. Come to think of it, she said it in a way that was more of a demand than a question . . .

"It's next on my to-do list," I said.

It wasn't. But a coworking space was cheaper than paying rent, and if going to a coworking space for most of the day would help me minimize my sister's discomfort and avoid the expense of finding housing in overpriced Los Angeles, with large security deposits and uncontestable proof of income, then so be it. I could find the bare minimum (cheapest) plan they had—maybe I could negotiate to use the Wi-Fi in a coworking closet a few times a week for dirt cheap. Oh, the possibilities.

"I'm confident you'd be more comfortable working somewhere outside of this apartment." She definitely said it as more of a request than a constructive suggestion.

After she downed her drink, Jia asked, "Do you need the shower? I need to meet up with friends for brunch soon."

"Nah, you go ahead," I said. Didn't bother to tell her I wasn't planning to shower anyway. As soon as she shut the bathroom door, I popped two ibuprofen pills, fired up my laptop, and searched for coworking spaces in the area. Many of them had vacancies, offering compelling rent deals for first timers. Now that my dreaded Pitch Warriors application was in, I could focus my time on finding a new place to be during the workweek.

In the afternoon, I made some calls to set up tours of my top choices, and while I was on hold, I received a notification that Benjamin Green was following me on LinkedIn and other social media accounts.

Benjamin Green. THE Benjamin Green. Holy shit, he was one of the Pitch Warriors advisors I'd researched online before applying! Formerly at Angelshark Ventures and Warner Capital Management, Benjamin had so much institutional knowledge in tech and, specifically, mobile apps. This not only meant that the application had gone through, but that someone had skimmed it and taken time out of their day to find me on social media. It couldn't just be coincidence, right? In a typical week I got maybe one new follower; what were the odds that this was just random follow?

Was I supposed to follow him back? Would that look too stalker-y? He had over a hundred thousand followers and was reciprocating only a small fraction of them.

I decided to wait a few minutes, composing texts to Jia and Casey about this new development. I clicked on who Benjamin was following, hoping to sneakily gain insight into my competition, to see if this sudden interest in me was a sign that my application would be moving forward.

He was following major news channels, other investors, and . . . Asian women. I scrolled past hundreds of names and bios of women of East Asian descent. Searching online, I came across several pages of images of Benjamin dating different Asian women. My stomach lurched as I closed my computer. I'd heard about the rampant racism, sexism, and fetishism in the VC community. But now it was right in my face. The ugly side of tech. I'd trained myself to play ostrich with my head in the sand for many years, avoiding social and networking opportunities that could lead to harassment and discrimination against me, and there were many. Even at my former workplace I'd encountered and managed to avoid men like Benjamin. Racist and misogynistic predators were everywhere in the business world, and they weren't going anywhere. Because the system was built for men like them.

The pit in my stomach grew larger as I deleted the "OMG GOOD NEWS!" text I was just seconds away from sending to my entourage. I hated that something that should have been positive news could be tainted so quickly.

DING!

Another notification, and this time not about a guy with an Asian fetish. This was an email from the Pitch Warriors coordinator, Zach Golden. Subject line: "Zoom Meeting Request—Follow-Up Questions."

A quick Google search revealed that the email sender was an actual normal person in VC, and, in fact, didn't have a social media presence that suggested an affinity toward Asian ladies. Sighing with relief, I clicked on the email.

The committee wanted to meet me. Nothing else was revealed in the generic email other than open time slots over the next two weeks. Yes, it was unsettling that Benjamin Green had a penchant

for women who looked like me, but there were other judges too.
Other mentors. And at this point in my career, I had to be like
Hamilton in the Broadway musical and not throw away my shot. It
might be my only one.

I replied with my availability and hit send.

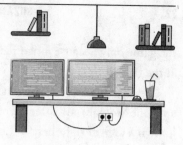

Chapter Three

Two good things about coworking spaces: reliable Wi-Fi and the ability to hold a stable, professional video call with important people. Although my sister's apartment had its charm, with funky art installments, reclaimed wood shelving, and minimalist candles on the bookshelves and side tables, the backdrop didn't exactly scream "Tech CEO." A strong first impression was important for me.

"Wow, your furniture is nicer than ours!" one of the male VCs exclaimed as the call started. I'd gotten to the AtWork office space at seven A.M. so I could book one of their nicest rooms, one with a large window and fancy floor lamps from Design Within Reach. On the wall behind me was a wild contemporary painting titled *Good Morning*, but which should have been called *Nondominant Hand Brushstrokes by Drunkard*.

I fessed up immediately. "Actually, I'm in an AtWork office. But this room is my favorite, I used to own all of these when I was younger." I turned the monitor and gestured behind me to the right, pointing to the bookshelf holding vintage board games.

"A fellow Risk player, I see," one of the older men commented. "I'd like to think it helped me with strategic thinking at a formidable young age. Bravo."

It didn't seem like the right time to mention I'd originally bought the game only because it had red dice, and red was my favorite color at the time.

Luckily, Benjamin Green wasn't there. Instead, it was two men and one woman; all three were from Ultralight Ventures, a well-known VC firm right here in Los Angeles. The two men wore charcoal gray Patagonia Polartec swag vests with a stitched-on logo for AMPLIFY, an annual VC conference Ultralight had recently sponsored in Vegas. Though they shared a penchant for the same "tech dad" wardrobe, they couldn't be more different. One had a distinguished, serious look, with thick wavy black hair highlighted with a few tufts of silver, while the other looked like a cologne model with angry villain eyebrows. The stern-faced older woman had a stylish blunt bob and wore a high-collared blouse and cardigan.

I slid my clammy, trembling hands under my thighs, fully out of the camera's view, while they introduced themselves. I observed their body language, volume, and tone, so I could emulate them when it was my turn to speak.

I'd read a lot about the VC world, and how someone like me needed to instill confidence in my product *and* have the investors stand behind the founder. There was a well-known, widespread disparity in capital raising between male and female entrepreneurs. While nearly 40 percent of businesses in the United States were owned by women, female-owned businesses received less than 2 percent of all venture financing. Two percent! Which was why it was something of a miracle I was even offered an interview. Instead of being proud I'd come this far, I couldn't help but wonder if they had a long list of twenty-something-year-old male Stanford engineers ready for interviews too.

Stop second-guessing yourself, Sara. Once I secured this virtual meeting, Jia and I had practiced my pitch with mock interviews. Not only was I prepared, I was ready to shine. Acing this interview was critical because some of the interviewers, maybe all of them, would likely be biased from my appearance alone, simply because of my double X chromosomes.

"Enough about us, let's get started, shall we?" Amanda, aka Mandy on her Zoom screen, combed her fingers through her shiny helmet hair. "I'll go first. We were impressed by the level of product detail you included in your application." She gestured to the two men next to her. "Them especially."

One of the other VCs chimed in. "We had a few technical questions. Did you want to include your developer on the call, or the CTO at your company? It's pretty nitty-gritty in the weeds stuff. I can email it later, but it's basically regarding feature sets and level of customization."

I leaned forward, as if my laptop were a giant microphone at a Senate hearing and I was the speaker on the floor. "I can answer those. I'm the tech lead."

The younger of the two men smiled. Tom, with the asshole eyebrows. "Okay, then who is your strategic business point person?"

I cocked my head. "That's me too. Did I not include that information in the form?"

All three tittered. The woman said, "Oh, yes. It's all here. We just wanted to know if there was anyone else on board as cofounder, or CTO."

I shook my head slowly, suspicious. Casey was listed on the form, and Jia had said I could include her as the head of marketing, just for optics' sake.

"Very well then," Mandy continued. "We have other business questions about your ad-based revenue projections. I see you've chosen this over a subscription-based model."

I nodded, speaking firmly. "Our research, primarily surveys and attitudinal studies, suggests that the type of actions our potential customers would take are more transactional rather than loyalty-based. I also included a preliminary list of advertisers and partners willing to offer profit sharing or to buy ad space, ones I've already approached. And of course we can always incorporate ad income using a third-party ad platform."

Rapid-fire questions about when we would achieve breakeven, customer retention, and operational setbacks almost rattled me, but I remained calm. Steady. Even . . . charming. When Mandy asked, "Your messaging platform looks limited in scope. There's the risk of other competitors and, of course, the cost of servers and app maintenance would go up as the numbers of users increase. Could you talk about costs and risks?" all of the rehearsing with Jia paid off, and I had attended so many fast pitch events and watched so many videos from TechCrunch Disrupt that I knew what types of questions to expect.

And because I anticipated what they'd ask in the interview, I steered the conversation to be more forward-thinking, explaining where I saw the market going. "Our company can potentially penetrate lucrative markets such as wedding registries, graduations, elder care, and domestic law." Okay, admittedly, some of it was talking from my ass, but what I didn't want was for them to get stuck on limitations and not focus on the big picture.

After I finally stopped nervously spouting off plans for feature refinement, Mandy said, "One last question, and it's one that we're asking candidates these days who are smart on paper but haven't spent much time off their computer . . . how are you on camera?"

My jaw fell open in surprise. I couldn't help it. Did she mean video or, like, broadcast TV or news show interviews? I mean, we were on Zoom, which was on camera . . . did that count?

She explained, "You're clearly well-spoken and passionate, which we're happy to see. In this business, for early-stage companies, the *who* is maybe more important than the *what, how, and why*. Your business is interesting to us, not like some of the female-driven lifestyle brand founders or toddler healthy snack companies looking for funding." Mandy oozed disdain, with her narrowed eyes and slightly scrunched nose. What was her deal? As an executive in venture capital, she was a unicorn in the industry, and you'd think she could (and would) help support other women, yet Mandy showed bias against earnest businesswomen in nontech sectors looking for funding. She reminded me of some of the women in senior leadership I'd crossed paths with at the last few companies I'd worked at, the ones who cut other women down in meetings and didn't believe that a rising tide lifts all boats. Mandy was the type of person who would use her unicorn horn to poke holes in all the other boat bottoms. The type who embraced and thrived in competitive—not cooperative—environments, looking down on other women instead of mentoring them.

I responded, "I've spoken on camera at various Silicon Valley and Silicon Beach tech conferences. Those were recorded and you can find them on my old company's YouTube channel if you'd like to see them."

The three of them looked at one another, nodding. Stan, the older of the two men, explained more. "We're asking this because we saw your request about being considered for both the mentorship and the pitch competition. If we chose you for the competition, the top three finalists will be doing something different this year. They're all going on *The Bullpen*."

My stomach lurched. *The Bullpen* was a new show similar to *Shark Tank*, but more confrontational, and mostly tech-focused. It was a Web-only show but still had a subscribership of over a million and was streamed live. The show had a reputation for being belligerent and brutal, which was why it was so popular. Those who didn't get voted off and went on to receive funding were indoctrinated into a special esteemed group called the Bulls. To date, no woman had achieved this level of notoriety. I accidentally mumbled "Oh shit" under my breath, which caught on microphone just as one of them received a phone call.

"You'd be okay with that?" Stan asked. "It was in the terms and conditions on the final part of the application process."

I nodded, remembering I'd skipped that whole section so I could submit the form before the deadline.

Tom muttered, "You'd need a likable stage presence. Less ice queen. Maybe less quiet too. Show that you're different from other Asian female founders cropping up all over Silicon Valley. Smile more, for example."

I let out an exasperated breath. *Did he really just say all that out loud?*

My blood pulsed so hard I could feel the pressure in my fingertips. My tipping point had been reached. "I need to say something, and I'm not going to preface it with 'I'm sorry' first, which women are prone to do. Ice queen, Tom? I'm not an ice queen, nor am I fake. That is offensive and I don't want to work with people who think what you just said to me is permissible." It was people like Tom who gatekept this industry. No matter how hard I worked or how far I'd come, I always felt subordinate to these jerks. Tom and others like him outright stereotyped women like me. What else did he think, but not disclose? That I'm a pushover . . . quiet and demure? Or prickly and sharp-elbowed?

Why did I even bother trying to instill change in the way business was done with its old boy network, when clearly the industry didn't want to progress? Did I even have a place in an industry like this? Did I want one?

Stan jumped in before I could really lay into them. "Sara, I want to apologize on behalf of my colleague here. Thank you for saying something, and your passion for doing the right thing is admirable. Frankly, we would be lucky to be able to work with you. If you'd be so kind, I'd like to have a discussion with my teammates here about what transpired today. To set clear expectations and do better. Someone will be in touch with you soon." He paused and said, "For what it's worth, my mother is Japanese. I'm white-passing and my last name is McGuinness, so my colleagues might not even know I'm hapa with Irish-dominant genes. I wanted you to know this so you understand where I'm coming from. I'm appalled by what transpired today."

The other two shifted uncomfortably in their seats as we said goodbye. Logging off, I had time to be self-reflective. Had I done the right thing? I'd probably blown my chances, but I had to believe that it wasn't my only opportunity. Playing back the conversation in my head, it wasn't just this one isolated incident that had made me snap. It was all the hostility, biases, and uncomfortable situations in the workplace that had weighed so heavily on me over the years, and this interaction during which I felt under attack was the straw that broke the camel's back. The only way things could change was by standing my ground and using my voice. If I didn't speak up, who would?

Chapter Four

A week later, two emails hit my inbox nearly at the same time.

The first one was from the committee . . . I'd been accepted into the mentorship program! My stomach flipped as I scrolled through the requirements to continue the process. Without any hesitation, I clicked all the "yes, I agree to sign over my life for a three-month duration" checkboxes and submitted the agreement.

The second email was from Stan, who had spoken up on my behalf during my panel interview. It was a short personal note letting me know he was impressed by my conviction and had requested that he be my official mentor, should I choose to participate. He would assign his superstar VP to oversee my day-to-day, someone he thought would be a good match given my personality and strong skill set. Deep down I wondered if this VP would be my handler, because Stan was concerned about my hotheadedness and brashness, which warranted a babysitter. This hotshot was probably a numbers whiz with the EQ to keep me in line. Maybe even coach me. But most importantly, it was someone Stan trusted. In any case, I appreciated the special attention, and wrote him back to let him know I was thrilled to be his mentee.

DING!

A third unexpected email, which I thought was a confirmation of my admission to the program, vibrated my phone. But it wasn't. This one canceled out the two good-news emails with a two-word subject line: "WE'RE FUCKED."

Casey didn't even bother to write anything in the body of the email. It was a screenshot from the admin view of our app dashboard. I didn't see what he was referring to at first, until I zoomed in on the image.

New user profiles: 1 (me)

Average number of messages created per user: 8

Average message length: 75 words

Unsent messages: 2

Undeliverable: 1

I read the stats over and over again before it clicked in my head. Dread flooded my body as I tried to figure out what happened.

Some of my messages had been sent?

Oh no.

I logged in and clicked on the unsent mail folder. The two messages were missing recipients. One was "Test #1" with the words "I fart way toooooo much," which I vaguely remember Jia writing while crying with laughter. "Test #2" was simply a poop emoji. Another drunken Jia creation.

I called Casey. "Are you saying that the messages . . . some of them . . . but they weren't supposed to . . . what the hell? What does this mean?"

He groaned. "From what the data's showing, your messages, the ones you drafted to your mom, former best friend, and high school crush, et cetera, they were all sent out in one big batch from the two categories you created, 'Family and friends' and 'Shitheads.' We didn't enable timestamps so I don't know when exactly. I can dig in the code to find out more."

I cried out, "How is this even possible? We have safeguards in place, there are checks and balances implemented to verify my death!"

"Safeguards? Yes, we do. Well, we did. I updated the software to allow the messages to sync with iOS or Android email contacts, and we had the AI crawl the obits late last night. They also scour public social media accounts for death announcements now. I mean, if you look at it from a tech standpoint, it's impressive that it worked. It synced to your contacts AND had one hit from a Sara Chae in Flushing, New York, who passed away last week and was publicly memorialized on Facebook. She's apparently in your address book too. With these two occurrences both being requirements for the software to move to the next step, your messages released to recipients' emails."

I didn't know the other Sara Chae. Not really. A million years ago I'd met her at an Asian American college leadership conference and we exchanged numbers but that was it. According to her obituary, she was a year older and an accomplished New York district attorney. Stanford undergrad. Yale Law. A very accomplished Sara Chae, probably closer to one my parents would have wanted. The kind of Sara who didn't live in her little sister's walk-in closet in her mid-thirties. I went down a Google rabbit hole: Cause of death, stroke. Married, no kids. Donations to brain stroke research in lieu of flowers were requested by her family.

How incredibly sad. Poor other Sara.

Falling onto my couch, laying splayed out, I held the back of my hand on my eyes. *Please say this is all a bad dream.*

Seconds passed, and my reality sank in. "Our app picked the wrong Sara. Shit." This meant my app had mistaken one Sara Chae across the country for me. Yes, I'd lived in New York a few years, but the app was supposed to conduct basic identity verification, including secondary photo facial recognition confirmation from the obituary, which was one of its most unique features and differentiating capabilities. Was my app racist? Thinking all Asian women looked the same? SHIT. We needed to figure this out immediately.

I bolted upright. "Casey, we can't get funding if the app is fundamentally broken." Pressure mounted in my chest, making it harder to breathe.

Casey said, "I'm on it. It's never misfired like this, so I'm especially invested. I don't want you to lose out on funding because I'm not a good enough programmer to set this up right. On the bright side, you have proof that the messaging part works. But until I figure out what happened, I'd lay off writing drunken *eff you* emails and leaving them sitting in your outbox."

"It was a prototype with a *fake* and *nonfunctioning* outbox," I cried. "I didn't think it would WORK, and then go LIVE." This was a drunken mistake, one that could be the spiraling, fiery death of my career and personal life. My heart raced as I clicked through all of the mail folders.

"Well, I guess we're officially in beta now with a viable but buggy app. Congratulations, you're a tech genius and I'm an outstanding app developer."

"Fuck me," I muttered.

Casey sighed. "I hate to say this now, but there's more. It's not a major problem but one you should be aware of, if you end up talking to or emailing the people who received messages from you. The header of the email looks like personalized stationery."

I let out an audible breath. "That sounds like a good thing."

"Well, um, I put in a placeholder that says 'From the coffin of Sara Chae.' It was a joke I was going to show you later. Please know that I didn't think messages would be sent out anytime soon from our platform. And what's worse is that it has a skeleton jumping out of the casket and I thought you'd find it funny. Everyone who gets a message from you will think you're dead. I'm really sorry about that."

Rubbing my temples, I said, "I love you, Case, but right now I also kind of hate you. I'll need some time to process this shitstravaganza and figure out what to do. Oh God, I think I wrote messages to Bryce and Marcus . . . with coffin stationery. Shiiiiiiit!"

"I'm sorry, boss. I honestly didn't think it would play out this way. When we hang up I'll look into a notification step so that mail that's about to be sent can be blocked by the sender. If it helps, your high school crush's email was AOL-dot-com. If he's our age, there's like a zero percent chance he's still using that email account."

"And how about the others?"

"Your mom and your former BFF? No, they're Gmail. Same with the one to your landlord. And the ones to the cofounders were the company email. But maybe you can unfuck this situation and turn it around somehow. You've got grit and you're a master at being resourceful, I believe in you."

Of all the recipients, the least likely person to respond would be my ex–best friend, Naomi. She was lowest priority compared to the others: the whole reason we'd had a falling-out was that she flaked on me one too many times and eventually ghosted me. The probability of her replying after getting my death notice with any kind of "oh no, this can't be true!" message was zero. Unresponsiveness was the very reason we weren't friends anymore. But this time, I had the last word. Well, technically, with her ghosting me I'd always had the last word.

After my friendship breakup with Naomi, I learned to move on without having a BFF, though regret still lingered in my heart even after so many years. This app reopened the wound.

"I'm such a failure," I said. "Maybe I should just trash the whole idiotic start-up idea. There's too much to fix."

Casey softened his voice. "We'll keep trying. We'll fail again probably, maybe bigger and better next time. This app is built on your vision, your tech, and your hard work! We've come so far, so let's take this idiotic idea of yours all the way."

I cracked a smile. "Thanks, Casey."

My phone buzzed with an incoming call.

"Shit, it's my mom," I groaned.

Casey said, "Good luck! I'm rooting for you!" and hung up, leaving me to deal with the aftermath on my own.

I took a deep breath and answered the phone.

Chapter Five

On speakerphone, Umma launched into Korean expletives.

BLEEP! BLEEP! BLEEP!

"Why you send me this email?"

BLEEP!

"This is how you say thank you to parents? We sacrificed so much!"

BLEEP!

"You don't call us for a month to check on us and you send this?"

BLEEEEEEEEP!

The only good things to come of this mishap were that my app messaging clearly worked, and the recipient had opened the communication. That was it.

This was the angriest I'd ever seen my mom, including the time I was three and took the brand-new Clinique lipstick she got in a promotional gift bag from Macy's, swiped my mouth with it, and pressed my lips all over the hallway walls, leaving deep red kissy marks on the off-white Sherwin-Williams matte paint. I actually thought she might murder me that day.

And now there was a good chance she would murder me for this.

"You make me so mad! We did so much for you!"

There were a lot of deeply emotional sentiments I'd expressed in that letter, but I didn't remember much because of my high degree of intoxication when I wrote them. Regardless, what struck me was my mom's instinct to yell at me, when, in theory, I was supposedly "dead" and she expressed little or no concern over this.

Her vocabulary didn't include words I'd learned in therapy, such as "intergenerational trauma" or "internalized guilt," and in my letter I had tried to explain these things in a way that she might understand. Things that as a thirty-four-year-old woman I was still working through on a daily basis.

I skimmed the letter that was sent to her, surprised by my drunken eloquence.

> For my whole life, I believed that Appa and you had sacrificed so much so I could be successful, but was this fair to me? To pin all of your hopes and dreams on your oldest child? When you came to America, you didn't have children, so did you really move here for my future . . . or for yours?
>
> It's sad to admit I couldn't talk about my real thoughts with you while I was alive, but there is some comfort knowing you'll be aware of them when I'm gone. Maybe I should have done more for myself, done what I wanted with my life, without worrying I would be a disappointment to you. And now that I'm no longer here, I wanted you to know I felt I needed to sacrifice my own happiness to preserve yours. Three and a half decades of deep regret and I'm only now telling you how I feel. Please know that I love you, but it was not an easy love . . .

To make matters more cringeworthy, in addition to the coffin and skeleton on top, it ended with one of the default canned email sign-offs, "Best, Sara."

My mom and dad were not "feelings" people, which became clearer as my dad joined my mom on the phone, creating a disharmonic duet of yelling, cursing, and blaming, my mom in alto soprano, my dad grumbling in tenor.

He complained, "No respect for your umma and appa! What kind of message you send to your hardworking parents? Why you don't care about us?"

I cut in. "Actually, I visit every month and bring you groceries."

My dad replied, "When you get grocery, you take time away from dating."

"So do you want groceries or not?" I asked.

Jia walked into my room, eyes wide and mouth agape. No surprise that she'd heard my parents on speakerphone through the thin walls and that they were rehashing the same topics from many times before. My parents offered Jia their own customized nagging, but with a "don't end up like your older sister" slant. These were the same people who drew a five-foot-eight-inch line on my closet door in middle school and told me that it was my target height.

I topped out at five-four in seventh grade. I'll never forget Umma's face when the doctor said I'd finally stopped growing.

The more they talked, the more apparent it became that all my message did was poke a sleeping bear.

I'd been gifted a Magic 8 Ball as a white elephant present at work and while they were complaining, I pulled it from the bankers box by the side table. Shaking it hard, a few questions came to mind.

Will Umma and Appa complain about how I didn't appreciate their sacrifices?
WITHOUT A DOUBT

Will they express disappointment about how their daughter turned out?
OUTLOOK GOOD

Will they mention for the thousandth time that I am husband-less, and childless, as if I didn't already know this fact?
SIGNS POINT TO YES

And as the Magic 8 Ball predicted, the nagging continued. For over three decades, I'd endured them. They thought I wasn't listening, but I was. In fact, all these years I'd internalized their words, pushed and punished myself because of my failures, developed self-sufficiency at an early age so I wouldn't need to rely on them for anything. Especially their so-called parental guidance.

I drew in slow, steady breaths. Maybe they would never change, but that didn't mean I couldn't change the way I interacted with them. It was time to stand up for myself. Let them know that I wouldn't tolerate their confidence-crushing words and that might mean they lose access to me. Maybe not permanently, but a long break would be justified until I could get my app into good shape for the competition, otherwise this relationship would distract me from my new goals in life.

"Umma, Appa, I need to say something." I took a deep breath and launched into it. "Sending that note to you was a mistake. Not because my feelings expressed in that message aren't valid, they are, but the timing was wrong. I meant to send that to you when I died."

I paused, offering an opening for them to ask about the death part, but they didn't say a word. It was just silence on the phone. But silence was better than ranting.

Clearing my throat, I explained, "It sounds morbid, but I was too scared to say these things to you because, well, look at what's happening right now. You're yelling. I'm practically shutting down. You're being defensive and not listening to my words and feelings. You weren't even concerned if I was actually dead."

My mom jumped in. "Yah! Jia would call us if you actually die."

Dad added, "No police come, no text from Jia. We know you are okay."

Was that the kind of relationship we had? "Well, you know what? Just pretend you never got the message. I might skip visiting you with groceries this month, I'm busy with a work project. But if you care to reach out anytime to express support or to see how I am, I'd be open to that. I'll reach out when I'm ready, when the time is right for me."

I'd finally said what needed to be said, and hanging up the phone came with mixed feelings. Empowerment, pride, and satisfaction, followed by fear, worry, and disappointment.

Moments later, something else hit me. A strong sense of loss.

It saddened me to think that if I had *actually* died, and the message I sent via my app was the last thing I said to my parents, that my mom and dad would have been dismissive. As if my feelings and opinions didn't matter. Maybe sending last words didn't end with many happy-ever-afters after all.

Jia sat on the bottom corner of my closet bed. She waited a few seconds before speaking. "That was brutal. You just broke up with Umma and Appa and said, 'It's not me, it's you.' What the heck happened?"

My sister's face contorted and scrunched when I explained how the app had fired off the messages with the latest software update.

I sighed. "Not the most ideal timing, but it was important for me to speak up and set boundaries with Mom and Dad. Loving someone doesn't mean enduring harmful consequences of traumatic stress. I needed to protect my inner peace. Especially now."

She nodded. "I'm with you. So all of the messages were sent? Even the lusty one to Harry, your high school crush?"

Lusty? Jia and I had written that one together. Drunk. There had been a lot of giggling, and squealing, and yanking the keyboard from each other's hands—

In a panic, I pulled my laptop onto the bed and logged in. But before I could read my lusty letter to Harry, a blinking icon in the upper right-hand corner of my screen stole my full attention.

A new alert: YOU HAVE THREE NEW MESSAGES. In the latest software update, Casey must have enabled the reply functionality.

I prayed it was some kind of inbox admin message, like "Welcome to Upon My Death, take a tour of the latest features!" but Casey wouldn't have programmed something like that without my approval, so it could mean only one thing.

Responses.

I clicked and braced myself.

A message that you sent could not be delivered to one or more of its recipients. This is a permanent error. The following address(es) failed:

Bruce@colorwheelcommunications.com

Oh thank God—I'd spelled Bryce's name wrong. Off by one letter. And to my knowledge, there was no Bruce at my old company. The thudding of my heart faded and my shoulders relaxed. I'd been so wound up since Casey had broken the news.

I clicked on the next unread message.

A reply from Marcia@colorwheelcommunications.com. "Hi, Sara, I received this message but I think it was meant for Marcus. It happens all the time—I think people hit the wrong keys on the QWERTY keyboard, the I-A letters are pretty close to U-S. Anyway, let me know if you want me to forward it on to him, I'd be happy to—I couldn't help but skim your message (sorry), and I agree with your assessment of the company's lack of prioritization. And he can be a real asshole. Good luck in your new venture. Godspeed, M."

Well, that could have been much worse.

The third message was from my landlord. I'd expressed my disappointment in him in my original message, specifically his inflexibility regarding ending the lease: "I'd been making an honest living, making ends meet, even at times of economic distress and lack of a safety net. You should appreciate that in my four years living in your unit, I always delivered rent on time every month. I was a good tenant and dependable. And at this time of financial downward mobility, all I wanted was a bit of grace here, and the courtesy of a shorter notice period and returning of my security deposit . . ."

His reply surprised me. "Sara, first of all, are you really dead? This message is very confusing. Second, I was wondering if we could come to an agreement. Would you be willing to end the lease a few weeks early and let me show the apartment to my niece? She wants to move into my building instead of returning to the dorms at UCLA and yours is the only apartment possibly available. I'd be willing to return your last month's rent and half of the security deposit."

I'd moved in with Jia so I wouldn't also have to pay for utilities and cable on top of rent. Plus the AC was an old large window unit and cost an arm and leg each time it was turned on. Another reason to move out early.

I unexpectedly found myself now in a back-and-forth discussion with him, resulting in getting my full security deposit plus last month's rent. A far better financial outcome than not having said anything to him at all. Even on the smallest scale, I'd learned that it didn't hurt to ask and request what I wanted. As small as this win was, it meant more money in my pocket and made me even more comfortable with negotiations involving finances.

Then with one double-click, my elation turned to mortification as I opened a new message arrival from my high school crush, Harry Shim.

"Hi, Sara, what an unexpected surprise! It would have been a pleasant one, but I really hope you're NOT dead. In case this is some weird hacker situation and you get this response, can you call my office to confirm you are actually not deceased, because I'd love to reconnect. If you are dead, apologies for making such a selfish request and I hope you rest in peace. My number is below. —H"

For years I'd harbored the thought that if Harry and I would cross paths again, I'd feel all sorts of things: sparks, electricity, rippling heat coursing through my body. But no, not even a single tingle anywhere. Instead, my whole body went numb.

I couldn't believe it. The guy I'd professed my lust to in my last dying words—my unrequited crush in high school—had replied without an inkling of acknowledgment of what I'd written, and what those words meant to me.

But maybe this was his way of saving my dignity.

Squeezing my eyes shut, I muttered, "Jia, please tell me this is all just a bad dream. Maybe even a nightmare, but one I can wake from. Something that makes me think a grown-ass woman is not going to need to confront a high school crush because she mistakenly sent him a note saying she wanted to bang him in high school."

Searing pain shot down my arm.

"Owwww!" I yelped.

My eyes flew open and Jia was squeezing my upper arm flesh and fat between her index finger and thumb. "It was a light pinch, geez you're weak. And no, you're not dreaming." She cracked a smile. "Also, you're lucky your sister saved your ass. I remember editing your note when you passed out and made it less horny and more . . . mysterious. Come hither and get me now, Harry."

She leaned over my laptop and pointed at my outbox. "It's a masterpiece."

All I saw were song lyrics to Taylor Swift's classic "You Belong with Me." A literal cut-and-paste of the entire song off the internet, with another mortifying canned sign-off: Forever Yours, Sara.

"What the hell is this?"

She laughed. "Look at Wikipedia about the song. 'You Belong with Me' was inspired by an argument between a male friend of hers and his girlfriend over the phone. It's about an insecure protagonist's unrequited love for an out-of-reach love interest. That's totally you two!"

I squawked, "And expressing this through the words of Taylor Swift is better . . . how?"

"It's direct and subtle at the same time; she's a genius with lyrics." She shrugged. "It's like your brain and Taylor's are like this." She crossed her fingers tight and waved her hand in my face like a little parade flag. "At best, he's a Swiftie too and can read between the lines. Or maybe he'll read the actual lines of the song, they're pretty clear, even for someone clueless. At worst, you play it off like you accidentally sent him random lyrics to a song, and he'll just think you're a freak. Trust me, Taylor's later romantic songs are much more depressing and angsty, so you should be happy I didn't dig into her more recent albums."

I had to admit, at least Jia's revised message came with an escape hatch: I could see myself backpedaling and saying I cut and pasted the song lyrics meant for something else. But now that Harry had written back, it seemed only reasonable to respond in a timely manner, especially if he thought I was possibly dead.

The last time I saw him was at our ten-year high school reunion; he'd just gotten his MBA from Stanford Graduate School of Business and was living in the Bay Area. I played it coy that night, so coy in fact that I basically ignored him. He hadn't come in with anyone, and when we did finally hug and catch up, there was no mention of a girlfriend, wife, or anything like that. Harry had dated his hot high school sweetheart, Claudia, throughout college, and I assumed they'd be married by then, but there was no ring on that finger. I thought I had a chance, a slim one, and right when I was going to ask about his relationship status, our mutual friend Kal came and clinked glasses with him.

"Heyyyyy Sara! Lookin' good!" He turned to Harry. "No Claudia tonight? Your bombshell girlfriend ditched you for someone better?"

Harry laughed. "I thought she'd want to see her high school friends, but nope. I came here alone."

Lots of questions ran through my head, but none of them seemed appropriate to say out loud while intoxicated. Harry and I had lost touch after high school. I had dated off and on since then and honest to God, forgot about him for months at a time. But then, every so often, usually while drunk, I'd think about him. His smile. The way he would run his fingers through his hair. His lively laugh, which made me believe I was the funniest person on the planet . . .

Jia snapped her fingers in front of my eyes. "Hello? Earth to Sara! I asked you what you're going to do. Call him now? Or wait? If I were you, I'd just bite the bullet and get it over with, then move on." Jia was totally the type to do this. Brazen, direct, and determined—all attributes I didn't possess.

I, on the other hand, was a complete coward. And I was bound to overthink my response and worry the longer I waited. "You're right. I'll call him in five minutes. Let me figure out what to say to him."

She closed the closet door most of the way but left a small crack, probably so I wouldn't suffocate. Pulling out a legal pad from a stack of office supplies, I drew out a conversation flowchart, because that was the only way I could keep cool when chatting with Harry. I would have rather texted about it—with a quick *LOL so sorry I sent that, won't happen again*. But he'd asked for a call to his office, and it was the least I could do given the circumstances.

The basic conversation diagram made me feel more at ease. And if I got nervous, I'd just look down at my pad of paper. After a little chitchat I would explain how this was all just a mistake and he could go back to his life and I could go back to mine.

I mapped decision points branching into several likely directions:

- So you're still happily partnered with Claudia? Great to hear! Nice chatting with you, bye!
- I'm doing great! Starting my own business soon. So busy. Great chatting with you, bye!
- Have you heard from anyone else in our class? Is that so? Well, hope to see you at the next reunion. A pleasure chatting with you. Bye!
- And so on.

Once I'd done this prep work, my clattering nerves calmer, it was time to speak with Harry.

The receptionist answered on the second ring. "Fireflame Capital, an Ultralight Ventures company, how may I direct your call?"

I hung up. Because (1.) I was a cowardly lion, and (2.) nowhere on my flowchart was a scenario of finding out Fireflame Capital was part of Ultralight Venture Partners, where my mentor Stan Mc-Guinness worked.

I dialed again on speakerphone, determined to speak actual words this time. The phone was picked up on the third ring. A different woman's voice this time. "Harry Shim's office."

"Oh, hello! May I speak with Harry?"

"We just got back from a team lunch and he's on the way to his office. He took the stairs while everyone else took the elevator. I'll put you on hold until he arrives, which will be momentarily."

Did Harry really work at Fireflame? And was Fireflame really connected to Ultralight? While I waited, I fired up my browser on my laptop: LinkedIn showed that Harry had bounced around the fintech space, which was where he'd been for over five years. Fireflame's website was no help. The "about us" section highlighted the founders' backgrounds but didn't mention Harry, or even Stan. Maybe they knew each other. Maybe this was nothing and the company names happened to be similar, like how some traditional banks, ad agencies, and law firms all sounded the same. Maybe this was just me, overthinking things as usual.

I opened the closet door and paced around Jia's apartment. Why didn't Harry just give me his cell number like a normal human? Was he worried about giving it to me? If this had been a direct interaction, it wouldn't have required a middleman (or middlewoman) who put me on hold with God-awful phone system music. *"Careless Whisper" saxophone solo, really?*

"Harry's back, I'll put you through!" his admin chirped. "Who may I say is calling?"

I gulped. "Sara. Sara Chae. He might be expecting my call today actually. But if he's busy—"

She insisted, "No, he cleared his calendar this afternoon so he could focus on work. Which he's never done in all the time he's been here, maybe six months? I figured he was super busy or . . . had *reasons* for blocking his time. Maybe he was expecting a call." The "wink wink" resonated in her voice. "Please hold."

Each ring felt like an eternity. Three rings. Three eternities.

"Hello? Harry Shim speaking," he barked, his voice cool and neutral.

"Oh, hi. Hey. It's Sara Chae." *Oh my God, I rhymed. "Hey hey! Ho ho! Sara Chae has got to go!"*

And this is why I needed a conversation flowchart.

"Hold on, let me take you off speaker." His voice softened. "Can you hear me?"

"Yes. I hope you're not busy."

"Not too busy to chat with you. Damn, Sara, it's so good to hear your voice. I'm guessing you're alive? Or are you calling me from the underworld?" His words had thawed, radiating vibrancy and warmth.

"Underworld? Don't you mean afterlife? Underworld is where villains go, right?"

He laughed, and the tightness in my chest eased. Here we were, kidding around like old times. "Right. I doubt that's where you'd be, but who knows? It's been a long time and apparently you're in the business of faking your death." He paused. "You're doing well though? This wasn't a cry for help?"

My lips curled into a smile. "It wasn't. I promise. But is anyone truly doing well?" I paused. "Sorry. That sounded more grim than expected." *Stick to the flowchart, Sara.* "I'm trying my hand at entrepreneurship with app messaging development, and failing apparently, hence this conversation to clarify that I am very much alive, and doing great."

I left out the part about living in Jia's closet. Being jobless. And needing to carry around an instructional conversation diagram in order to chat with a former crush.

Harry said, "Well, I have a few questions for you, so-called Sara Chae, to confirm you're who you say you are. Like security questions from your bank, but more fun. What was our school mascot?"

"The Burros. But you and I wanted to petition to change it to jackasses."

He laughed. "Correct! Okay, just two more. What were our high school superlatives?"

Easy. "I was Most Likely to Graduate College Early, basically the nerdiest human in our class. You were Most Well-Rounded."

"That's right. We were both robbed, we both should have gotten Most Likely to Succeed too."

I remember thinking that they'd made a mistake back then; the class had voted for Harry's best friend and . . . Claudia, of course. Looking at me in my current state, they had been right to vote the way they did. *Most Likely to Live in a Clothes Cubbyhole in Her Thirties.*

"Okay, okay last one. Who did you go to prom with senior year?" he asked.

My throat constricted. Panic rose in my chest, but I answered as calmly as possible, "I didn't go. I visited the colleges that accepted me instead of going to prom." A montage of memories flashed in my head. Me agonizing over whether to ask Harry to prom when he briefly broke up with Claudia, with Naomi egging me on, but me resisting. Him getting back together with his ex the same day I planned to finally ask him to the dance. All my friends one by one getting picked off by dates, except for me. Then me throwing together a last-minute college tour to save face.

"Oh! I thought you eventually went with Paul Griffin. He said he was going to ask you . . . I—I didn't know." He quickly recovered. "Well, that's all behind us."

Yes, it was in the past, but it was the kind of past that shaped the future. That was the start of what my therapist called my "avoidant attachment style"—essentially me finding ways to be self-sufficient at all times and not leave myself emotionally vulnerable. I replied to Harry with a fake laugh. "Thank goodness it is."

"You've passed my test. Congratulations! You're definitely Sara Chae, and not a bot. And I'm thrilled to make your reacquaintance. My primary email account that I've had forever was hacked a few months ago and since then I've been wary of all unusual emails and texts. I have to say, your message was definitely unusual, but in case it was real, I wanted to connect. I figured a bot or hacker wouldn't call my office. There's no way it would get past my intimidating admin."

Eager to change the subject, I looked at my conversation notes. "Speaking of offices, I can't believe you're at Fireflame. Congratulations!"

"Thank you. I'm mostly focusing on acquisitions, where it's all numbers and analytics. But so far so good, no complaints. The timing of your message is good though—I was wondering if you could catch up in person. I fly into LA later this week for work and would love to meet up. Are you still living there? Would you have dinner with me?"

He knew I was in LA? "Dinner with you?" is all I managed to squeak out.

"You do eat dinner, right?" He laughed. "Or have you taken a ghost form postmortal life and are unable to consume food? Has the spirit of Sara been messing with me this whole time?"

We both chuckled.

He continued. "I also have a lot of questions about, you know . . .

Taylor Swift. I've always wanted to chat about new Taylor versus vintage Taylor, and I think you're just the person for this conversation."

Relieved that he didn't question why I'd sent him those lyrics out of the blue, my face broke into a wide grin. "Yes, I'm sure I can answer your questions. Though I'll admit, I'm partial to the Swiftie songs I can listen to at the gym rather than the slower ballads." And . . . why did I say this? The last time I'd been to the gym was with one of Jia's guest passes, and I'd gone only because my building shut off the water and I needed to take a shower. I did walk to the gym then, which was twenty minutes round-trip, but still. Partial to baked goods, frozen entrees, and solving tough work challenges, yes. But partial to anything remotely gym-related? Hell no.

Jia walked into the kitchen, looking like she was pouring a glass of water, but she was clearly eavesdropping. How much of this had she heard? Damn it, I should have remembered that speakerphone was a bad idea with a nosy little sister.

Jia took her sweet time refilling the pitcher while Harry rattled off details about his hotel location and some ideas for restaurants, asking if I had any preference for any type of cuisine and whether six P.M. was too early for me, because he might need to hop on a red-eye later that night.

Jia waved her hand to get my attention. She mouthed, "You're having dinner with *him*?" Aggressively pointing at her left ring finger, she signaled for me to figure out the one important question.

"This all sounds great, Harry. Will it just be you joining, or your family?" When he didn't answer right away, I sabotaged my own question. "Or colleagues?"

He coughed. "Just me. Unless you want my mom to come. Possibly my boss, since it's a business trip. That's also why I want to meet up. You may know my manager, Stan McGuinness?"

My stomach dropped to the floor. My throat closed and my vocal cords froze. Stan? McGuinness? My VC mentor?

"Don't worry, I was just kidding, he's not coming. He'll be way too busy schmoozing around town. But surprise! He assigned me to co-mentor this year, and I just found out during our team lunch that I was going to be working with a Sara Chae from LA. Of course, I couldn't believe it was you, *my* Sara Chae from *my* Bedford High School, so I googled to see if it really could be you . . . and did you know a Sara Chae just died this weekend? It was in the *Korea Tribune*! What are the odds?"

I grimaced. "Yeah, about that." Taking a deep breath, I explained how deceased Sara Chae had unexpectedly played a big role in our reacquaintance. That her obituary triggered a batch of messages to be sent. How my app was still in development, had known bugs we needed to fix, and could really use a good mentor. I left things vague.

He blew out a large puff of air, slowly and steadily, like a balloon with a small pinhole leak. "So were you testing your messaging platform with me because you knew I'd be working with you? Or was it a bug or . . . you know, now this has me thinking, maybe meeting in person to discuss your app might be the best thing because we have a lot of work to do, on the business side and on the technical one. So dinner? Yes?"

I switched off speakerphone and held the device to my ear. "That sounds good. We do have a lot to discuss." Carefully, I sidestepped his questions.

Jia fanned herself, then pretended to swoon-faint. I turned my back to her so I couldn't see her "oooh kissy kissy" antics in my peripheral vision.

I cleared my throat and managed to find words. "So dinner?"

"Yes! I can't wait."

My full-body numbness disappeared and adrenaline kicked in instead. My heart beat double time as I clutched the conversation diagram on my lap. Staring hard, I searched for a way to politely end this call.

He could be MARRIED. With CHILDREN. And he was my mentor now. So many reasons to keep him at a distance. Taking a deep breath, I abandoned my conversation flowchart and tried to wing the rest of the conversation. "At dinner I can't wait to discuss the mentorship and catch up—it's been a while. It'll be way more fun to chat across a table over an expensed three-course meal." I gasped, appalled by what had come out of my own mouth. "Wait, I'm not looking to freeload, it was a joke. A bad one."

I could hear a smile in his tone. "I know, don't worry! You've always had that sense of humor. I'll have my admin assistant share reservation details with you. Honestly, I'm really looking forward to this mentorship, it'll be nice to work with you on something challenging. By the way, I'll be in LA for work a lot over the next few weeks, so we can meet in person throughout the next three or so months, if you'd be open to that. You don't have to decide now. You can let me know after we meet in person, so you can gauge if that's too much interaction."

Was too much interaction with Harry Shim even possible? Immediately, my mind wandered to other types of desirable interaction with Harry beyond phone calls and dinners. *Focus, Sara!*

An alarm chimed in the background, fortunately disrupting my train of thoughts.

He groaned. "That's my reminder to get back to working on a valuation due in an hour. My admin will be in touch about the place and time. See you soon!"

"Really looking forward to it." I gave him my number before we hung up so he could send me the details.

Jia rushed over and squealed. "Okay, what was that all about? Sara Chae, you sneaky fox. I had no idea you knew how to flirt!"

I raised an eyebrow. "Are you serious? He thinks I sent him Taylor Swift lyrics as a TEST message. And it's a work dinner. That's hardly setting us up for a flirt-fest."

She rolled her eyes. "You're having dinner with him! So maybe it's not a flirt-fest *now*, but it could be a THIRST-fest *later*. And he totally didn't divulge his marital status for a reason. Guys I work with always drop hints of having a girlfriend or wife if they're not interested. I listened to every word on your end, and part of his. Trust me, there are some sparks hidden in that tough, rubbery outer shell of yours. And he was definitely excited to reconnect. I predict at dinner you'll both have downed-power-line, immediate-electrocution energy."

"No way." I shook my head. "He's my mentor for God's sake, I'm not sure if you caught that when you were spying on me. Neither of us is stupid enough to make any moves. And this mentorship is all I have." I sighed. "He probably has the best life: a coveted trophy wife, three angelic kids, a newly remodeled house, and a fleet of high-end electric cars. The new American dream. Also, he mentioned I have a sense of humor."

Jia tipped her head. "You do though. And it's nice of him to say!"

I sighed. "That's what people like Harry say if he sees you as a *fellow dude*, not as a . . . you know . . . object of desire."

"Well, I heard flickers of interest even if you didn't. And I'll pretend you didn't just say *object of desire*. Can we change subjects for a second? Umma and Appa just called me right before you hopped on the call with hot Harry, who will be forever known to me as scintillating Electro-Spark Guy. Or Sparky."

I narrowed my eyes.

"Sir Sparks-a-lot?"

A groan escaped me.

"Talk-Sparky-to-Me?"

"Stop. Please stop," I begged.

"Fine. Anyway, our parents ambushed me after they hung up with you. Asking me all about that message you sent them, why you did it, and asked if you were ignoring them."

"And what did you say?"

She shrugged. "You know they don't listen. So I let them vent a little and told them I had to go to a meeting."

"Well, you didn't exactly try to make things any better by doing and saying nothing to help," I said flatly. "Did you at least tell them we *coauthored* that message to them? I noticed some edits in the final version."

She snorted. "Of course not. No need for both of us to be disowned. Anyway, they're really angry. Maybe you should apologize, just to keep peace in the family."

At first, my instinct was to say I was sorry and not mean it. If I did, then I could reach some level of harmony with my parents, restoring our relationship.

But there was something that bugged me. Was it that they still hadn't even acknowledged any wrongdoing or never asked me why I felt this way or wondered why I carried all this with me till my alleged death at age thirty-four?

No dialogue. No discourse. For the first time, I'd offered my true feelings toward them, using carefully worded constructive feedback, and they couldn't handle it.

No, I would not be taking back what I said to them. These deeply rooted emotions and heartaches had weighed me down my entire life. For the first time, I had been able to tell them my side and while it was scary and nerve-wracking, it was also liberating.

But what was my goal now? This was uncharted territory.

I leaned forward, crossed my arms, and put my head down on my kitchen table. I'd opened Pandora's box and now I couldn't stuff everything back in and pretend it didn't happen. Was Jia right? Should I apologize, reconcile, and reestablish connections with my parents and other message recipients? And what would that mean for the future of each of those relationships? Come to think of it, it wasn't just one Pandora's box I'd unleashed. My parents, with no hesitation, became reinvested in my life. Harry, my forever crush, was fully in my orbit now too. And Naomi, my former best friend . . . well, she was someone whom I had actually thought it might be nice to see or talk with again, but maybe that wasn't a relationship that could be resurrected.

At my request, Casey sent out a short "Oops, sorry about that last email, Sara isn't dead, please disregard" follow-up message to everyone. My parents and Harry had opened the email, and Naomi hadn't. She'd never opened the original one either. Even that random Marcia person and my landlord had viewed it. Naomi had either blocked me on email or just didn't care about me. This left me hollow inside.

I missed her.

I lifted my head slowly. "I can't deal with Mom and Dad right now. If they call you again, just stall or something. I need some time to think about what I want. They've been helicopter- and tiger-parenting my whole life. Yours too. I'm older though, so I've had eight more years of their nagging, snooping, and unwanted opinions. It really wears you down. The last thing I need is any parental intervention from them right now, but I also don't think I should apologize for speaking my truth, especially when I tried to explain why I said what I said."

Jia rubbed her temples. "I can bide some time. I'll say you're working hard to find a new career, and extremely busy, and not on drugs."

I laughed. "Thank you. Tell them I'm broke, so I can't even afford drugs."

She countered, "If I tell Umma and Appa you're broke, they'll get all in your business about being financially independent and saving money. You don't want that."

"Good point," I said, tapping my temple with my index finger. "You're always using your brain."

My phone buzzed with a notification. A message from Harry, letting me know that the press release for the mentorship was officially out in the world. He'd cut and pasted it into the text:

This year's VC Pitch Warriors competition and mentorship program started with over seven hundred applicants. Qualified entrants participated in a virtual venture review session, where one hundred teams and individuals provided a short presentation with pitch deck, a short statement about their business idea, and a Q&A with a panel of judges. Ten entrants were accepted as finalists into the competition, and ten were admitted into the mentoring program.

. . . In the next three months, the ten teams who will receive mentorship by a trusted advisor will be offered a stipend and a VC online or in-house residency. After completion of the mentorship program, a new set of judges will select a grand prizewinner to receive up to $250K in venture capital funding at the end of the year. The judges will review the teams' business plans and presentations, and consider the entire business concept, looking at overall feasibility, viability, attractiveness to investors and possibilities for growth. The participants are listed on our website.

My name was farther down in the press release, listed under Fireflame Capital, along with advisors Stan McGuinness and (gulp!) Harry Shim. My company, One Last Word, was in print! And the press release had me listed as the sole proprietor. Sara Chae, founder and CEO.

Founder!

CEO!

Everything about this would be perfect if it weren't for one thing.

Harry was my advisor. Once upon a time in high school, he had been my peer. And my unrequited crush.

But maybe this was good. Harry was smart. Ambitious. Well-connected. Maybe having him as a mentor was a blessing in a six-foot, athletic, strapping, muscular disguise.

Focus, Sara.

Stay focused.

Chapter Six

I didn't expect my mentorship to kick off with a four-page, single-spaced document from Harry questioning my product viability. And I especially didn't expect it to come from him at six A.M. West Coast time the day after our phone conversation, no less. He didn't even wait for us to meet.

"Some considerations. —HS"

That's all the email said.

I skimmed the attached document and closed my laptop. It was like he had taken my business plan and drawn a giant red X on all the text and diagrams. Wrong, wrong, wrong. I needed to redo the entire goddamn thing.

I fell back into my chair and squeezed my eyes shut.

The only person helping me with my app was Casey, and development for it was only in his spare time on evenings and weekends. He enjoyed it though and had offered his services free of charge, because he loved the freedom of working on a product from start to finish, and in his own words, because it didn't come with "any fucking corporate bullshit." He was super technical, not the numbers or strategy brains behind the operation, so he couldn't help me with most of Harry's concerns. It would take weeks to address and incorporate Harry's thoughts and assumptions.

Jia breezed through the living room and grabbed her keys in the foyer. "I'm going to work early. Don't let me find you curled up in fetal position on the couch, feeling sorry for yourself. Get your shit done so we can go suit shopping this evening. Or we can style you with some of my work clothes. You're going to need to look hot when you see Harry at dinner."

I cocked an eyebrow. "What? Harry's off-limits. He's my mentor!"

"Yes, I know that. That doesn't mean you can't have him wonder what he missed out on while he was dating that Claudia chick." She cocked her head as she studied me. "You want to look professional, with a tiny hint of hussy."

Tiny? Hint? Of hussy? "Did you really just say that?"

She smirked. "I can say much worse. Trust me. Oh! One more thing, I have a present for you."

Jia walked over to her front door and opened it. After stepping all the way outside, she wheeled in a well-worn two-sided green chalkboard, pushing it through the foyer to the living area. "They were throwing it out at the elementary school down the street this morning and I washed it. Good as new!"

It had to be at least thirty years old. "And what am I supposed to do with a chalkboard exactly? Times tables? Long division?"

She rolled her eyes and grabbed a box of sidewalk chalk from her messenger bag. "It's for brainstorming. No one throws out whiteboards these days, but I figured this would do the job." Pulling out a dusty yellow stick, she wrote "Hot outfit ideas" and "New app features" in two columns, then underlined her words.

"Anyway, you get the idea. I need to run. Ahnyung!"

The front door slammed behind her, sending a drafty airflow down the hallway. The papers on the coffee table rustled from the gust of wind.

Seeing "Hot outfit ideas" in scrawled print made me jump to my feet and riffle through my suitcases, trying to find something I could wear. Did I really need to get hussied up? Was that even a real word? Every photo I'd seen of Harry from the last ten years during my borderline-stalker Google searching suggested he was a button-down oxford, rolled-up sleeves, slim-fit tailored pants, medium-length-lush-thick-hair kind of guy. Harry had always been that effortlessly put-together type, all throughout high school even. And I was very much the type of person who was attracted to this sort of guy.

Aspirationally speaking, as an up-and-coming businesswoman, he and I could be a perfect pairing, but my wardrobe suggested otherwise. Lots of jogger pants and loose tank tops. And exercise bras in every color of the rainbow. It was as if there were a global shortage of loungewear and I'd hoarded everything I could possibly get my hands on, ugly or not.

After years of working virtually and then being employed at a company that touted a very casual work environment, I didn't have appropriate clothes to wear to a business meeting, or even any public place other than a gym. The only skirt I owned was a casual khaki one, and my one good pair of flats were scuffed. How did people fix scuffed shoes? Shoe polish? Who the hell had shoe polish? I contemplated using a black Sharpie but decided against it.

Jia was right. Not about needing more hussy energy, which was *not* something I wanted to entertain, but that I didn't have anything to wear that screamed, "GIVE ME YOUR VC MONEY."

I messaged her to request access to her wardrobe, aka my closet bedroom decor, and she responded with a thumbs-up emoji. After I scanned my blouse, skirt, dress, and shoe options, the bulk of my attire concerns were addressed and I could focus on my business again. In painstaking detail, I combed through page one of Harry's extensive notes, leaving comments and caveats as responses within the shared document. Before I knew it, I had worked through lunchtime. When I looked at the clock again, it was already three P.M.

To my surprise, I received an email from Harry. "Need me to clarify anything? Make sense? —HS"

Yes, I needed to clarify why you were already emailing about the never-ending notes and stressing me out already. "It's a slog, working through all these calculations with new assumptions. Any chance you could loan me all your personnel? Sincerely, Sara"

I hit send.

Ding! "How many people are we talking?"

Well, shit. Was he serious? "Forty? A hundred? Actually, I just need a numbers whiz."

"Done."

Done? What did that even mean?

My question was answered within a minute. When I refreshed my email, a new message from Harry appeared with the subject line "Intro."

"Sara, meet JC Salcedo. He's a business school intern here at Fireflame and he's perfect for your project. A quant whiz, thorough, and whip smart with macros. You can borrow him for the duration of the mentorship."

Was it really that simple? Ask and ye shall receive? Fireflame had plenty of resources and sparing an intern was hardly something that would cause a fiscal or personnel crisis. I was grateful for the help, and the timing was perfect. With some new forecast models built by JC, I would not only be prepared when I met Harry, but I would also knock this shit out of the park.

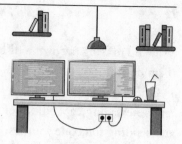

Chapter Seven

*E*nabling contact from my parents was like opening a portal to another dimension in a scary sci-fi movie: Umma and Appa continuously initiated unprovoked and unwelcome communication, and I couldn't seal them off. Sometimes they used my sister as their messenger: TELL YOUR SISTER TO CALL US. Some contact was direct and sent to voice mail: YOU NEVER CALL US, WE ARE WORRIED. On occasion, they'd email me through the app messaging interface, responding to my original message, knowing I would look: HELLO??? YOU IGNORE? WRITE BACK. Then, they texted photos of my favorite Korean dishes that Umma had made: tender galbi jjim, thick jjajangmyeon noodles, and haemul pajeon savory pancakes with shrimp and calamari, offering them to me contingent upon my agreement to see them in person. Good old-fashioned bribery.

As an Asian woman in her thirties, with no boyfriend or husband, no kids, no house, no job, and, worst of all, living in the closet of my younger sister, I was a hot mess one-stop shop and a nagging field day for them. But even so, I didn't need my mom and dad's persistent parenting counsel. I needed less of it. Letting them know that it was a busy and stressful time wasn't easy, and after I was honest with them, the sinking feeling in my stomach remained.

Why did making my own well-being a priority feel like I was letting them down?

One of the critical changes I needed to make was disabling the reply messaging capabilities of the app. After all, saying goodbye and sending someone your last words was not supposed to invite a rebuttal. That was the last thing you should need for an eternal resting soul.

Harry had mentioned in his product notes that we might consider adding in an option to forward messages to next of kin, like a beneficiary for an insurance policy or bank account. But given the priority levels of everything he'd sent me, that would need to happen much later, version 20.0.

My parents called multiple times while I was in my rideshare car on the way to dinner with Harry, and I debated whether to answer. Dad had just texted Important message! You and then not sent anything else. Of course I took his call when my phone rang soon thereafter.

"Hello?" I asked, putting in my Bluetooth earbuds so the driver couldn't eavesdrop.

"Oh, now you pick up phone, when you think it is emergency?" my mom cawed into the phone. "When I was your age I was so busy, I had two kid and still working full-time. But I still pick up phone when family call. Why you can't answer?"

Already anxious from running late to my dinner, it wasn't the right time to play this "I was better than you at any age, let me prove it" one-upmanship game with her. My therapist had said it was possibly a way she was trying to relate to me, but for me, all it did was provoke distress.

Life today was nothing like how it was when my parents were raising us—with single-digit admission rates to colleges and grad schools, evolving societal pressures, diminishing job security, skyrocketing housing costs, and increasingly violent anti-Asian sentiment—and somehow, they couldn't see things had changed. Or maybe they didn't want to see it.

I sighed. "I have a lot going on right now workwise. Is everything okay?"

"Your umma, she is going to ultrasound."

Ultrasound? I rarely went to the doctor, and all I knew about ultrasounds was that it was for potentially pregnant ladies. But for people in their sixties? "Is she okay?"

Mom chimed in on speakerphone. "I'm fine. Doctor is just checking liver after they take my blood last week and some of the number was strange."

My stomach sank. "Is the doctor worried or is it normal for someone your age?"

"I'm sure it not problem. It is probably from my allergy."

For whatever reason, Umma always thought any issue with her health was allergy-related. Fatigue? It was allergies. Headache? Allergies. Irritability? Allergies. And now added to the list: liver blood panel irregularities.

I hesitated with my next words. While my mom did dismiss many health concerns by attributing them to pollen and seasonal allergens, she could also be a drama queen when the pendulum swung the other way, usually when she felt any pain. Suffering quietly was not her style. She let the whole world know about her latest colonoscopy, her shingles scare, and her worsening IBS. It was hard to tell if this liver issue was a mild thing or not. But it was better to err on the side of caution given her age.

"Let me know how the tests go. Or you can tell Jia and she can let me know, since we're roommates now."

I winced. My parents didn't know I was living with Jia. The last thing I needed was Mom and Dad complaining about that too. Not only would they harangue me about my financial circumstances, but they'd worry that by living with Jia and hanging out with her, I was also preventing her from finding a husband. They thought spinsterhood was contagious.

"I'm living with Jia now to save money. I have a business idea that's looking promising, and it would allow me to be a company founder and leader, not just a worker."

Dad asked, "Like Jeff Bezos?"

Mom added, "Maybe you can be famous!"

Fame wasn't something top of mind for me. Rich? Well, yes. But famous? That seemed to be something my mom and dad would want for me. Not something I'd want for myself.

"I'm on my way to an important work meeting with a former high school classmate. If it goes well, I'll share more details. I'm hoping he can help me win a competition with a big cash prize."

Umma said, "Waaaaa, okay. Don't forget about Appa's hwangap party. We expecting lot of people to celebrate! And if you want to bring a special date we can make room."

My mom had texted me no fewer than ten times to remind me about Dad's sixtieth birthday milestone, for which I'd helped book the hotel venue and Korean catering, so it would be impossible to forget the date. Once the pandemic hit, we postponed his big party several years in a row, and this was the first year we could safely gather a bunch of geriatric Koreans together for a special night of celebration in a hotel ballroom. The last text I'd received from her a couple of days earlier was about whether my old friend Naomi would be interested in playing her cello for the event. A weird coincidence considering I'd sent Naomi two messages that she hadn't even bothered to open.

"Well, if I happen to find a date in the next few weeks, I'll bring him so you won't be ashamed about your daughter not being married yet," I said with an acerbic bite.

She replied, "That's good. Better than coming alone."

Shaking my head, I thought about all the unsavory types of men I could bring to the party who would cause a scene, in a not good way. Though it was fun to entertain in my mind, I knew this milestone birthday meant a lot to my parents, and since it had been postponed a few years already, I would try to make it a wonderful, peaceful night.

My car pulled up to the Beaumont Bistro, and I stepped out of the back seat. Smoothing out the A-line dress my sister loaned me, I walked through the open double doors and met the hostess.

My phone rang as I tried to stuff it into my micro-purse.

It was Casey.

"Hey, I can't talk right now. Meeting Harry for dinner," I whispered.

He screeched into my Bluetooth earbuds, "Seriously? I'm programming all night and you're being wined and dined?"

"It's a business dinner, I have to go!" I checked my bag for my wireless headphones storage case and couldn't find it. *Shit, I just had it!*

"Your party just arrived, follow me." The hostess led me to the seating area with a hillside view, where a man with black wavy hair was seated next to the window, his head turned slightly away so I could see only his profile. No doubt, this was Harry. Not exactly the Harry I remembered from the last high school reunion, but a more mature and handsome version. As I walked around the table, I could see him studying the menu, brows furrowed, lips pressed flat. Turning his head toward us as we approached, he smiled wide, putting me immediately at ease.

Harry stood up while I took my seat across from him. "Hi! So glad you could make it. I ordered a petit bottle of the recommended wine, I hope you don't mind red," he said as he sat again, pulling apart the silverware napkin burrito and placing the white linen square in his lap.

I said, "I love red but I might start with water," at the same time he blurted, "I normally drink whiskey neat."

Talking over each other was new for me. It signaled we were both nervous, yet also in sync. Maybe I needed wine to take the edge off.

A voice rang in my ears. "Water's a good idea. You also get Asian flush, so watch your alcohol intake. But let him drink as much as he wants if he's paying!"

My heart nearly stopped. I hadn't ended the call with Casey and he was still on the line, talking to me. Or rather, squealing to me.

"Cut it out," I whisper-hissed.

Harry asked, "Pardon? So no red wine?"

Casey guffawed. "This is so fun to be your third wheel! It's a threesome! A LOVE TRIANGLE!"

I pulled my earbuds out and shoved them into my tiny bag, sans case. "I'm sorry, Harry. I was just trying to be funny." Grabbing the water glass, I chugged nearly the whole thing. Why was it so hot in here?

He grinned. "Oh! Well, it was pretty funny."

He offered me a sympathetic look as I unrolled the silverware and almost knocked over my empty wineglass. Nerves a clattering mess, my heart rate began to speed up and my body temperature rose. I felt like an imposter wearing this designer dress and carrying a Prada mini clutch. All I wanted to do was to peel off my fake exterior and relax into my true self, the Sara who wore pajama sets from Old Navy while working from home.

But back to Harry. The years had been kind to an already blessed human. He must be one of the few men in the world who had a nightly skincare routine, because his face had a brightness that naturally highlighted his high cheekbones and sharp jaw. As for his physique, he either fit perfectly in off-the-rack designer clothes or he had them tailored to his specific body. Whichever the case, his black sweater, gray blazer, and designer jeans hugged his athletic build like they were custom fit. This charming man wasn't just hot, he was radiant.

The menu was printed on a sheet of coarse paper affixed to a polished wooden slab. I tried to control my facial contortions as I skimmed the prices. This was a four-dollar-sign restaurant and the cheapest thing on the menu was a bruschetta, which was the price of a medium pepperoni pizza at a two-dollar-sign authentic Italian joint. It seemed unlikely I'd be able to have only a piece of bruschetta and a water for this business dinner, so I eyed the second-least-expensive thing on the menu. A tomato bisque for twenty-one dollars.

He cleared his throat. "These aren't Agnes's Diner prices, are they?"

Agnes's Diner was walking distance from our high school and it was where all the kids in different cliques would hang out after school on certain days of the week. He was a Monday afternoon guy, with his group of sporty and popular friends. I was a Thursday girl, who rolled with the high-achieving brainiacs. Harry was popular AND brainy, but when it came to choosing a community, his social leanings were clear.

Agnes's was a cash-only dive. The Beaumont Bistro had a footnote at the bottom of the menu underneath the dessert listing, letting patrons know they proudly accepted the American Express Centurion Card.

"I loved Agnes's!" we both joked at the same time.

My face flushed. Teasingly, I said, "You're doing the verbal equivalent of stepping on the heel of my shoe as I'm walking in front of you."

He laughed and folded his hands on the table. "I'm sorry. It's nerves. I haven't seen you in so long and I'm excited. And honestly, a little uncomfortable with this place. My assistant picked it, and it's not exactly my scene. Full transparency, this meal is fully expensed, so order whatever you'd like. But I might only get the bruschetta."

Relief flooded over me. "I was eyeing the same thing! They're nineteen dollars for a pair. Should we split it?"

Harry coughed out a laugh into his fist.

After skimming the menu one last time and placing it on the table, I glanced up at him and noticed Harry's fixed gaze on me. How long had he been staring? Instead of looking away, embarrassed that he'd been caught, he smirked and took a sip of wine. A current rippled down my neck to the bottom of my spine and at that very moment, something shifted between us. It was like he saw past my pretend clothes and awkward conversation and we were back to how things were between us in high school, when we were familiar friends. His shoulders relaxed and he eased back into his chair.

Harry muttered, "Would it be terrible if we went somewhere else? I'll let you choose the location."

Raising an eyebrow, I asked, "Well, you're paying, so I'd think you'd want a say in where we go. Because I was thinking pizza, but that doesn't seem very businesslike."

"Pizza? Seriously? Are you kidding me?" Before I could backtrack and say *Just kidding, I meant lobster*, he raised his finger to signal to the waiter for the check. "I *love* pizza, and there's a place I'm obsessed with that's not too far from here, it's the wood oven kind. Chewy, crispy perfection."

The waiter came with a bill for our wine, and within a minute, we were heading out the door to our next food destination.

Harry booked a rideshare car, because it became clear after a few steps toward the door that I was not going to make it to the destination walking in two-and-a-half-inch heels. As Harry tapped information into the app, it gave me a chance to sneak a look or two over at him.

Hmmm, athletic, but not beefy. Not too veiny either, which sounded weird but some guys had veins running down their arms and neck the width of licorice twists and it wasn't my thing. Pretty tall. Taller than I remembered. Even with the added height from Jia's heels, I only came up to his shoulder. That made him what, six feet? Maybe more?

"Do I have something on my face?" he asked, wiping his cheeks and the sides of his mouth.

Dear God. I must have been staring at him without realizing it. My throat tightened and rather than fess up, I said what I thought was best.

"Yeah, looks like you got it."

He nodded. "I had a granola bar before I arrived and I was seated early so they brought out breadsticks and I ate all of them. I was a little worried about the food options when I looked at the menu online this afternoon, so I pre-ate. Sorry about that. I didn't want to stress you out by changing the venue so last minute, especially after not having seen you in so long." He tucked his chin down and his eyes searched mine. "I'll make it up to you though. This pizza place is the absolute best, and I'm including New York and Italy in the data set."

Under the heat lamp at the valet station, his eyes reflected the bright flame, shimmering and dancing as we chatted about mutual friends, people we both knew fairly well once upon a time but had lost touch with because our careers got in the way. Even though the heater was doing its job, it felt like something was off with the controls, where my front side was toasty, borderline burning, and my backside was freezing cold. I turned myself slowly, like a rotisserie chicken rotating on a metal skewer.

"Are you hot or cold?" he asked.

"Sort of both? I'll be okay."

He eased out of his charcoal gray coat and placed it on my shoulders. Smiling, he said, "A weird memory just popped into my head. Remember in PE when I threw a basketball to you and you caught it the wrong way, then claimed you were fine, and it turned out you broke your middle finger in two places?"

His cashmere-wool-blend coat smelled like him. Woodsy and clean. Like a forest after a long rain.

I wrinkled my nose and grimaced. "I remember that. The only upside was that it helped me sit out of PE for a couple of weeks. The biggest downside was having to go to homecoming with a finger splint, and that I couldn't give anyone the middle finger for a while."

He laughed and straightened his coat, which had started to slip, on me. My entire body tingled as he pulled, smoothed, and patted my shoulders. My hair brushed against the fabric, causing it to get staticky. To my surprise, he moved his hand toward my face, then swept a few flailing strands of hair off my cheeks.

My breath tightened as I tried to think of something to say to get my mind off his fingers gently brushing my skin. "Did you ever think you were going to end up in VC? I thought you'd be, like, president one day. Or maybe some kind of professional athlete." Harry was one of those guys who played varsity everything, in addition to doing student government and getting good grades to boot. He was voted Most Well-Rounded after all.

He scoffed. "Me, in politics? No way. I thought I had athletic prowess until I got to college, when I was lapped in every long course swim meet. I quit freshman year. When I went to Stanford for business school I was amazed how many of my classmates had gone to the Olympics. Nothing like playing a few soccer matches for charity against other business schools only to find out that you had two international medalists in your starting team lineup. Honestly, it was kind of unfair for everyone we competed against."

My eyes rounded. "That must've been a surreal experience."

He nodded, then showed me the pizza menu on his phone. "I'm so excited to go here. It's been ages and I can't get that crust out of my head. When I move to LA I can eat here all the time."

My stomach flipped. "You're going to live here?"

He laughed. "Sorry, I thought I mentioned that. We have a new SoCal office that we're opening soon and they put me in charge of it. I've been commuting back and forth a lot over the last six months and decided to buy a place since I'll be running the new office for at least a couple of years. I'm in escrow on a bachelor pad in a new development not too far from here in Culver City."

This was good news for me. At least I hoped it was. But he said bachelor pad . . . did that mean he was uncoupled? "Well, welcome to LA!"

I glanced at his left hand. No ring.

The dinner plan change had reenergized him, to the point where he almost seemed like an entirely different entity from his "Harry Shim, Venture Capital" persona. This was excitable Harry. Gung-ho Harry. Hotter Harry.

He groaned as the car pulled up. "Damn, I'm starving. I might eat a whole pie by myself."

Same Harry from high school: charming, decisive, and . . . hungry.

When Harry's phone buzzed as soon as we hopped into the back seat, he pulled it out of his pocket and frowned. "Oh, I forgot . . . you need to sign something. Check your email."

In my inbox were a few DocuSign forms from Stan needing my

signature. A mentorship contract, an NDA, and the company's code of conduct policy.

Harry scratched his chin. "Stan wanted me to tell you that since you're getting a stipend for your mentorship, we need you to sign to make everything official."

The mentorship agreement and NDA were fairly short and standard, but signing a company's code of conduct policy was new for me. There were two sections of note: One about how conflicts of interest can arise when personal relationships or financial interests overlap with our responsibilities at work. The second about having a safe workplace that inspires trust, and how discrimination, harassment, and unsafe working conditions can diminish what we can achieve together.

In short, Harry and I could be workmates. Friends.

The stipend was enough to pay for my groceries and a professional laptop with a long-lasting battery, so that was good news. And signing a code of conduct was standard these days—it served as a formal reminder that nothing at all could happen between Harry and me while we were working together. And to be honest, that took the pressure off. By focusing on bringing my app to market, there would be no sparks. No flirt-fest. And NO thirst-fest.

E-signing the forms took only a few taps on my screen. It was officially in writing that I would stay laser-focused on the job and would not put myself or the company at risk. I hereby declared I would not let past feelings for Harry get in the way.

After navigating through the crowded parking lot, the driver whisked us away to our destination. Quite literally—he drove fast and took hard right turns as if he'd mistaken the gas pedal for the brake. I tipped to my right, pressing into Harry so hard it was like I was trying to stamp myself onto his body. Trying to put any distance between us was useless: any attempt at pulling away resulted in another full-body press with the driver's wild turns. Were there really that many rights and lefts on the way to this pizza place? It was like we were in a live-action *Mario Kart* simulation.

Harry whispered, "Don't fight it."

It? Did "it" mean gravity? Or—

To my surprise, Harry stretched out his arm and placed it on the top of the seat just behind my shoulder. This meant the next body fling would be into his chest, not his arm.

The driver turned on the radio and the speakers in the back blared Taylor Swift's latest breakup song. Harry tapped me on the shoulder with his draped hand.

"Oh! I'd been meaning to ask about your Taylor Swift lyrics message. Was that like *lorem ipsum* placeholder copy? Just wanted to make sure because—"

We flew over a speed bump and landed so hard my teeth clicked.

"You okay?" Harry asked. "I might have to give this guy one star. I didn't sign up for a DeLorean experience."

I nodded and acquiesced to the jostling of the ride while Harry asked the driver to slow down. Over and over, I pressed hard into Harry's chest, and his strong arm resting on my shoulders helped stabilize me. It was like he'd either seen this exact thing happen before and knew how to handle it, or he was a supersmart back-seat body engineer troubleshooting on the fly and getting it right every time I jostled and launched from my seat.

At a red light, he asked, "Remember how we were obsessed with obscure phobias in high school and used to pass notes to each other about them?"

I squealed. "Yes! Your favorite one was ergophobia, the fear of working."

"And yours was doraphobia, which was the fear of . . . fur? I remember you wanted to petition the dictionary companies to add a second definition, the fear of Dora the Explorer."

I let out a belly laugh. I'd forgotten about that one. "It wasn't just her. The talking monkey sidekick and the creepy rolled map gave me nightmares. My days as a babysitter were short-lived because of them."

The driver whipped into the red zone in front of the restaurant, announcing that we should exit curbside, allowing one final smash into Harry's upper torso before idling the car.

Harry slid out the door and offered me his hand to pull me out of the bucket seat. My first inclination was to refuse his help, because it seemed silly to need assistance to get out of a car, but one look down at my wobbly heels made me cast aside my stubbornness and accept his offer.

With a firm but careful yank, upward velocity helped me pop out of the car seat and stumble forward a few steps. Harry held my hand as we walked, then slowly let go when I had my footing. I could still feel his hand imprinted on mine as we approached the restaurant.

Harry pointed both index fingers at the neon sign "Frankie's." It was packed, and there was a to-go window with some public benches outside, where a number of patrons were blissfully munching on their pizza slices in silence.

He put our names down for a table. It was a forty-five-minute minimum wait and the seating inside was scarce. Technically, this was supposed to be a business meeting and at the Beaumont Bistro we would have been eating bruschetta by now, but I wasn't complaining. It was great catching up with Harry, and I was relieved we were out of that pretentious, overpriced restaurant.

After finding an open bench, I saved the seat while Harry went to the window to order for us. He returned with a giant pizza hacked into bite-size pieces, carrying a brown bag under each arm. He took a seat. Handing me one of the sacks, I peeked inside. "Hard cider? Isn't that alcoholic?"

"Yes and yes. Just keep it in the bag and drink it, no laws broken if you hide it like that."

My eyes widened. "Did they sell it to you this way?"

"Ha! No. The pizzas were double-bagged and I used them to conceal the alcohol."

"Pizzas? There was more than one slice?"

His cheeks flushed. "There was one more, and I ate it while I waited for them to bring the cider to the window. Sorry."

"Don't be sorry, that's fascinating, actually. You ate a whole slice within a minute. And came up with a way to drink an alcoholic beverage outdoors without arousing suspicion." I pulled back the metal tab on my can top, and the cider hissed and bubbled up. "Cheers!"

He opened his drink. "To making your app a success!" he said with an exaggerated toast.

After taking a gulp of cider, I reached for a pizza bite on the plate he'd placed on the bench between us.

After chewing and swallowing, I proclaimed, "This is the best pizza, you're right!" The food was lukewarm but still retained the texture and consistency I loved in a pizza: chewy dough, a little crisp in the crust, and sauce that wasn't so watery that it made the tip floppy.

He beamed. "Better than anything else in LA. I'm trying to think of East Coast places that are as good but I've chugged half a can of cider already and it went straight to my head. Probably not the best idea after drinking only wine at the last restaurant."

It wasn't until he said it that it hit me too. I peeked at the can's alcohol content. Twelve percent! Holy shit.

I polished off one small doughy chunk after another, leaving only one piece on the plate. Harry and I grabbed it at the same time, and let go simultaneously.

"You take it," we both said.

"No you," he and I said synchronously.

We both sat in silence. Then I said, "It's yours," just as he said, "I had my share."

This weird jinxing thing we were doing was cute and funny at first, but as the night wore on, it was borderline frustrating. I asked, "Rock paper scissors?"

He pulled out his phone. "I built an app for situations like this." He tapped the screen and said, "It's yours."

I sipped my cider. "You created an app to help choose who gets the last piece of something?"

"Yes, it was a program I created in college and still use. My Asian friends would never take the last of anything, and this way it forced the situation so someone had to. You can spin a wheel, roll dice, or, in this case, flip a coin." He turned his phone so I could see. A big banner took up the entire screen. "YOU LOSE!" If that wasn't clear enough, the word "LOSER" flashed three times before vanishing.

He shrugged. "I suppose I could have made it more user friendly. Anyway, you get the final piece. It's only fair you take it. The app has spoken. Plus, this was just an appetizer, when we get seated we can have custom-made pizzas and other stuff off the menu. Courtesy of Fireflame Capital."

I honored the app's wishes and took the last portion. While I chewed, he said, "Speaking of apps, sorry we've gotten so sidetracked tonight. This was supposed to be a business meeting primarily, and I did want to offer some additional feedback on the design and programming of your app, if you're open to suggestions and changes."

I swallowed hard. He'd already sent me an email, and now he had even more suggestions and changes? He looked at his notes on his phone and rattled off a long-ass list of bugs and feature shortcomings, which took over five minutes. Some were critical, including the one I hoped he would forget about, the obituary trigger. My stomach clenched as I sank into the bench. By the time he finished, I had lost most of my appetite and had left a chunk of crust, arguably the best part of the pie, on the paper plate.

Tucking his phone into his front pocket, he said, "I'll add it to my notes document and send it tonight. Let's talk about Taylor Swift and your message. Wait—are you feeling okay? Did you not like the pizza?"

I straightened my saggy posture. "No. I mean yes, I liked the pizza. It's just . . ." My voice trailed off as I remembered that this was a business meeting first and foremost, so I course corrected. "It's just that I see I have a lot to do, so maybe I should head home and work—like always." Immediately, I regretted my words. I'd openly admitted to my high school crush, the guy I'd sometimes see in my most vivid and sensual dreams, that I had no social life. Sure, there were loads of people our age who rarely went out. Sometimes I would rise to the occasion and go meet someone for a happy hour drink and then be home by dinnertime, but this was clearly not one of those nights. In fact, I had been out only once in the last few weeks. With Jia. When she'd persuaded me to leave her apartment to celebrate my application submission for the mentorship program.

Good. Fucking. Grief.

I made things worse by speaking before thinking. "Actually, I need to go out for drinks after this. You know, for fun. Because I'm fun."

I could feel my insides self-imploding, like one of those planned building detonations where they set off dynamite and everything just crumbles and caves within.

His eyes twinkled. "Oh, am I keeping you from something? Or *someone*?"

Jia popped into my head first, but I couldn't use my own younger sister as part of a partygoing ruse, even if that really was her role in my life. She was a different generation than Harry and me, and to say I was going out with Jia and her entourage came off as desperate and sad.

Harry's phone chirped with a notification. He pulled it out of his shirt pocket and I saw an alert that he'd just matched with someone on the hot new Korean dating site, Keopi. A borrowed English word for "coffee." It was a site Jia had signed me up for months ago, but I'd deleted the app because of the annoying push notifications.

My brain fixated on the fact that Harry was matching with people on this dating site. And Carina looked like a model with a pinup girl vibe: voluptuous, pouty, and sexy. Did this mean he was single? Or cheating? Or in an open marriage?

He took a sip of cider and waited patiently for my answer. I blurted, "I'm seeing someone. A guy I used to work with . . . at work." *Worked with at work? Please stop talking.*

He flipped over his phone. "Oh! That's cool."

My throat constricted and I couldn't speak. But that was good. Any words I could dare say might lead to a bigger proverbial foot in my proverbial foot-size mouth.

Maybe this wasn't as bad as it seemed. If anything, it was fortifying the "code of conduct" wedge between us, making it even more unlikely to stray from our working relationship.

He scooted over, allowing a few more inches of distance between us. His rattling off all the problems with my app had already brought down the energy of the night, but this felt even worse knowing I'd lied to him.

Harry cleared his throat. "I hope you're happy. I'd love to meet him sometime."

Dread hit me like a massive tidal wave, making it hard to breathe.

Should I tell him it wasn't serious? Or say I was joking all along? *Ha ha Sara's hilarious fake-boyfriend gag, gotta love it.*

Before I could clear anything up, my phone, situated between us on the bench, buzzed loudly. A message from Casey via our app.

Then more notifications appeared on my locked screen. I tried to not fixate on my phone, but Casey continued sending messages. His contact name was listed as "Sexy AF Work Bae."

"It's work-related!"

"BISHHHH answer my texts!"

"Are you STILL out to dinner with Harry hot stuff?"

To my dismay, Harry was also glancing at my messages. How could you not, especially if the phone was buzzing like crazy, and someone mentioned you by name, along with a "hot stuff" descriptor?

Oh God, I wanted to die. Right there. *RIP Sara Chae, this can be your memorial bench.*

Then Harry did something I didn't expect. He laughed. Hard. To the point of crying.

"Shit, Sara. Is that your boyfriend? He's so fucking funny." He wiped away tears with both palms. "I haven't laughed that hard about anything in a long time, so please thank him for that. It's been so great hanging out with you. We didn't talk much at the reunion the last time we saw each other, and I wish we could have caught up back then. I was dealing with a lot with Claudia . . . then we became unhappily married right around that time. Anyway, please believe me that I'm glad we reconnected and I do consider you one of my favorite people from high school. You're one of my oldest pals, you know that?"

As soon as he said "oldest pals," my heart dropped to the ground. But what else was he supposed to say? It's not like all those years while he was married he'd been pining for me. Did I think that as soon as he found out I had a boyfriend, it would force his hand, making him profess his love so I wouldn't marry the other guy, code of conduct be damned? Well, that was ridiculous. Did that even happen in real life?

No need to make this work dinner any more awkward. Mentor and mentee, and that was it. Nothing more.

I stood from the bench and he followed my lead. "I'd better head out. It was great catching up, and I'd love to do this again sometime."

He moaned. "I feel bad . . . all we did was eat a slice of pizza. That's not much."

Technically, he'd had more, I had only seven-eighths of a slice, if even that.

The hostess popped her head out the door. "Shim, party of two!"

Harry offered me a puppy-dog look. "Any chance we can still have a quick dinner? It doesn't have to be here. There's a new Korean noodle place that opened up around the corner and I know the owner. It'll be quick and you can head out right after. They have really good seolleongtang if you want something warm. But they also have naengmyeon if you want cold instead. I know you love Korean food."

My stomach growled, betraying me. Korean food on the Westside was hard to come by, and aside from Shin Ramyun and soon tofu instant soup packets, if that even counted, I hadn't eaten it in weeks.

I considered things again. "Sure, let's do it." Even though the night hadn't gone as planned, Harry was still offering me a free meal and some one-on-one mentor time. This was a moment of good fortune, and I was not about to turn it down simply because I'd stupidly pretended I had better things to do that evening.

In the three minutes it took to walk to KUKSU, Harry had texted and arranged to have a table waiting for us when we arrived. He'd whetted my appetite mentioning the seolleongtang oxtail noodle soup, the restaurant's specialty, so we ordered two bowls plus a side order of bulgogi. Looking around at the clientele—mostly young, white, and affluent—I hoped that the food would be reasonably authentic. I set my expectations low, because we were miles away from K-town, where there were more Korean barbeque restaurants than days of the year.

Harry asked for extra radish kimchi as soon as the server arrived with our piping-hot bowls of soup and banchan. We added sea salt, black pepper, and diced scallions to our milky broth and waited for it to cool off. I lifted the steaming glass noodles with the metal chopsticks and blew on them saying, "Bon appétit!" as I wolfed down my first bite.

The texture of the noodles, the tenderness of the meat, plus the depth of the flavorful broth made me want to order another serving. By the time the server came back with our sizzling platter of bulgogi and Harry's kimchi, we had nearly finished all our soup and noodles.

The next hour flew by as we eased into chatting and joking like old times. Harry was like a crackling campfire, lighting me up and warming me thoroughly. I liked how I felt being with him.

He moaned. "I'm so out of touch. I used to ask Claudia about everyone; she was great at keeping up with everyone's whereabouts and into all the gossip, but now that we've split it's been hard to stay in touch with people." He sighed and took a sip of beer.

My body flushed with prickles of heat. He'd confirmed that he and Claudia were no longer together. I didn't want to presume earlier from his ringless fourth finger and what he'd said about his unhappy marriage or from his dating app notification, but I was glad he had clarified.

Harry asked, "Whatever happened to your friend from high school, Naomi?"

I froze. Mid-chew.

He studied my face. "So not friends anymore, I take it?"

I replied weakly, "We drifted."

His worried expression softened. "I definitely know how that goes. It happens."

I chewed the last piece of bulgogi and stared at my plate.

"Hey!" he said, grabbing my attention. Harry peered at me through his dark lashes. "Sometimes time flies by without your realizing it and by the time you reprioritize your life, opportunities are long gone."

I gulped so loudly it sounded like I'd swallowed a microphone. "I definitely have regrets, but with Naomi it's different. She ghosted me, and it really hurt my feelings." There, I'd said it out loud. My brain rewound time to the exact moment I'd realized she was out of my life: when she'd moved to Boston and didn't even tell me she'd left LA. I found out from an alumni newsletter.

"I'm sorry about that." Harry put both elbows on the table and propped up his chin with his two fists. "I can tell you have a million things going on in your head."

I nodded and shrugged. "Lots to think about tonight."

An assuring smile spread across his face. "I haven't talked like this with anyone in a long time. I feel like we could chat all night."

Staring into his deep brown eyes, I wondered how it was possible to feel so comfortable around him. There was a certain easiness and understanding we shared that couldn't be explained in words. Was it chemistry? Pheromones? Magnetism? Whatever it was, it didn't take long for us to hit a rhythm and then find harmony. It was as if no time had passed since high school, and we picked up where we left off nearly fifteen years ago.

Before we knew it, the server had placed our check on the table and the restaurant staff was bringing in heat lamps and removing tables around us so they could mop the floors. There was one other group of people eating at a booth nearby, but their matching black shirts embroidered with the restaurant logo suggested they were either workers there or an intramural team sponsored by the owner.

Once we settled the bill and walked outside, it became clear neither of us knew the proper way to end the night. For two people who were annoyingly in sync earlier in the evening, it was odd that we would now stand in deafening silence, perhaps hoping that the other person would say something to put both of us at ease.

After Harry requested a car service, he said sheepishly, "Sorry I kept you most of the evening . . . It was selfish of me, but I'm glad we had dinner. Would a hug be okay with you?" Harry's head bent down, his eyes meeting mine.

"A headbutt or handshake would kill the mood, I think," I joked.

He laughed and without hesitating, he opened his arms wide and brought me into a hug. My brain flashed memories of our high school graduation, the last time we'd embraced. We were about to go onstage and give our speeches. Me as salutatorian. Him as class president. He fixed my tassel on my cap and brushed away the white and gold fringes sticking to my makeup. After giving me a hug, he mumbled, "I'm going to miss you, Sara. More than you probably realize. I hope we stay in touch." After he pulled away, his eyes glistening, I couldn't tell if he was being sentimental or if he was high. Either way, I loved how it felt to be enveloped by him, and now, a decade and a half later, it was as if nothing had changed. His strong arms pulled me to his firm chest, holding me in a tight squeeze.

For a moment, I forgot about the rest of the world. It was only him and me.

Even though he was muscular, it was still comfortable to be enveloped by him, like he was a human-size memory-foam pillow, custom built for my body. I relaxed and hugged him back.

We stayed like that awhile. It wasn't the influence of booze, and it wasn't cold outside. We didn't hurry our goodbyes. Instead, we savored the moment.

But there would be many more Sara and Harry encounters in our future. Three months of mentoring was a long time.

My phone buzzed again. We loosened our hold as I pulled my cell out of my purse and sneaked a look. Casey again, asking me to call him using all shouty caps.

"I need to take this," I said.

Harry placed his hands on my shoulders. "I'll connect with you later. Have fun tonight. Your dream guy is waiting."

I sighed. Actually, my dream guy was right in front of me. And he was letting me go.

Harry helped me into the back seat of the rideshare car and as I drove away, a word I hadn't thought about since high school popped into my head.

Eremophobia. The dread of being alone.

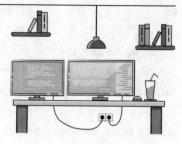

Chapter Eight

Casey barked, *"You told him you had a BOYFRIEND?"*

He didn't like the next part either.

"You want me to pretend I'm your BOYFRIEND? How exactly is that supposed to work?"

I had to pull my earbuds out of my ears because of Casey's shrill screaming.

He continued to chastise me, accentuating certain words while nearly blowing out the tiny ear speakers.

"NO WAY. Are you KIDDING ME? I can't EVEN—"

"You've actually LOST YOUR MIND! How could you—"

"Girl . . . I need a DRINK—"

"I swear. You OWE ME."

"Are you done?" I asked when silence finally fell between us.

He groaned. "Not even. Do you know how many people just stared at me in Gold's Gym? Dozens. That's a lot of potential dates I'll never have because you have me ranting like a maniac in this place with your terrible fake dating plan that will certainly implode because it's so poorly schemed." He huffed and snorted air from his nose. "Now I'm on my way to the smoothie place to get something with a destressing tonic boost just to calm me down."

"I apologize for my ruining your dating pool. But listen, this is *not* an active-duty fake-boyfriend situation. You're on standby mode. I'm hoping Harry forgets I mentioned I was seeing anyone and we just stick to talking about work and this whole dating nonsense doesn't even come up. But I *did* want to give you a heads-up in case I needed you to send me cute text messages when I'm out with him, so Harry thinks I have a doting boyfriend and a flourishing social life."

"Sara, I love you to death, you know that." I did know that, and that's why I wasn't going to act precious right now. This was Casey . . . blunt, honest, fiercely loyal Casey. So I knew what he was about to say next would be brutal and direct. "But this plan is total shit. You're a terrible actress." He snorted out his nose. "And I'm not getting involved in any kind of boyfriend scheme unless it's to find my OWN person."

This was very fair and it was something I could turn into a mutually beneficial situation. "How about this, you text me as my so-called boyfriend only if the situation calls for it. When the mentorship is over, I'll be your wingwoman at the Cabana." It was a gay nightclub Casey always kept trying to drag me out to, but I always used work as an excuse to not go with him.

"Tempting," he said, his voice shifting from grouchy to contemplative. "You also have to go to the gym with me on kettlebell day. A lot of people go to the gym in pairs and I want you to come."

I pursed my lips. *Me? Go to the gym? To do exercise?*

He added, "You can do it. Remember, your body is your temple."

"Yes, and as a reminder, my temple is run-down and beyond the state of restoration."

He let out a hot air snort from his nose, signaling I needed to concede.

"Fine, I'll go. And I'll swing one of those cannonball suitcases with you."

"And one more condition. I must be allowed to spruce you up so hunky-hunk Harry will be sad he's not your real boyfriend."

I scoffed. "Spruce me up? Like a tree?"

He fired back, "If you mean a Sara-shaped sad little sapling with no fashion sense? Then yes. Spruce."

I groaned. "Deal. But I do get to veto anything sequined, neon, glittery, or shimmery."

"Damn it, Sara, you're so boring. But fine."

"And no leather, lace, or dramatic cat eyes. It has to be work appropriate."

He sighed. "I'm not excited to play your pretend boy toy, but very eager for the opportunity to work on your facade. You know I'm not here to tear you down, but to build you up, buttercup. I want to bring out your gorgeous skin and your hourglass shape, and highlight your killer eyebrows."

This was the thing about Casey. If he was teasing, it was all in good fun. If he was criticizing, it was tough love and I needed to hear it. Deep down, he was a soft and huggable teddy bear. I knew it came from a good place. Far different from my parents. Even after all these years I still doubted they had my well-being in mind when unsympathetic words effortlessly tumbled out of their mouths.

Casey cleared his throat. "I need to go work out. Don't bother me for the next two hours while I get back in the good graces of my buff gym cohort. Bye."

It had taken some coercion, but at least Casey would play along if I needed him. My goal was to dodge any discussion of my dating life and avoid having Harry and Casey interact, because Casey had a big mouth and would for sure spill everything. Now all I could do was hope that Harry would drop the issue and never ask about my relationship status ever again.

* * *

"How's your boyfriend?"

It was the first thing Harry asked when we hopped on a video call. Not "Did you consider the changes I recommended?" or "Are you still on track to deliver?" or even "How has your week been so far?"

No. None of that.

I cleared my throat. "It's complicated." Technically, this was absolutely true. "And I'd rather not talk about it." Face flushed, I quickly changed the subject to something technical to bait Harry, a temporary distraction to get his mind off my fake beau. After a few minutes of going over the next round of features updates and next steps of research and development, he had to hop off to take an important call.

Jia came out of her bedroom as soon as the video call ended. It was her day to work from home. Luckily, we didn't have to be on-screen at the same time: there was only one spot in the common living area that had a suitable background. I was heading out to the coworking space anyway and therefore wouldn't interrupt her work-from-home Friday schedule.

"Why does Harry want to know so much about some so-called boyfriend?" Her eyes widened as she sipped her coffee. "Are you dating someone?"

I shut my laptop. "So you were eavesdropping, as usual."

She shrugged, still waiting for an answer.

"Well, somehow Harry has the idea that I'm dating someone, who in fact is not a real person."

She coughed. "And why would he think you're dating a fake person?"

Jia leaned on the bedroom doorframe, waiting for an answer to her very good question. It was funny, I couldn't think of a single time she'd had any kind of awkward dating dilemma. She had always been the kind of person to get what she wanted in a direct, no-nonsense way. Why were she and I so different? I'd heard that two sisters' DNA could be 50 percent the same, but our genetic code didn't appear to be that way—neither physically nor personality-wise—and it was hard to believe we were even related. Was her dating and relationship success from genes? Youth? Confidence? Or something else?

"Maybe because I told him I was dating someone so I wouldn't look like a loser?" I confessed.

She barked a laugh. "Are you serious? Why don't you just fess up?"

Why not admit to my crush that I made up a boyfriend? Well, because an embarrassment like this could alter his opinion of me forever? And telling Harry the truth would be so mortifying I might die? And hot women on dating apps were sliding into his DMs? I could think of a hundred more reasons, in fact.

Jia sighed. "Look, sis, I know what you're thinking. That I'm younger than you, and what do I know about dating and relationships."

Yes. I crossed my arms and waited for her truth bomb.

"I'm pretty sure I've had at least as many relationships as you have, and I continue to date, to play the numbers game. And you, the brainiac sister, should know that your number of prospects needs to be higher than zero for this dating thing to work out."

She was right. The math was mathing. Jia was more experienced, even though she was younger. And she was more likely to end up in a long-term relationship just by being open and available when it came to dating.

"And I know you think because I'm so many years younger than you that I shouldn't offer you my advice, but I'm a grown woman now, entering my upper twenties. I'm not a kid anymore. I have crow's-feet around my eyes and I need to do exercise daily to eat the way I do. And just this past weekend . . . I got *ma'amed*."

My brows furrowed. "You got what?"

"I got ma'amed. Someone carded me at a club, and for the first time I wasn't called *miss*. The bouncer called me ma'am. I admit, it stung a bit."

Transitioning from "miss" to "ma'am" was a milestone no one prepared you for, and I hadn't passed down any aging wisdom so she'd be mentally prepared for her first entry into older ladyhood.

"That's awful, ma'am." I offered her a caring smile. "Okay then, tell me your relationship advice, oh wise one."

"I should meet Harry and help with the boyfriend cover story," Jia said in such a definitive way you'd think it was a command.

"Well, that's definitely not going to happen," I scoffed. "The last thing I need is to add more random variables into this crazy mix. Casey messaging and calling me as my pseudo-boyfriend is enough to deal with right now."

She narrowed her eyes. "Still, I need to meet this perfect guy who got you to set ridiculously high boyfriend standards."

"What are you talking about?" I asked, slightly offended.

"What am I talking about? Are you kidding me, sis? Because of this Harry guy, you have this knight in shining armor mental model of what a guy needs to be. Smart, funny, handsome, and . . . unattainable. There's an image in your head of who the perfect guy for you is, and that flawless person doesn't exist. Or maybe he does, but in AI form. Not a real human, at least. Because of him, who is built up in your head and way too good to be true, you have unreasonably high standards, and I never see you putting yourself out there at all."

"Well, damn. That's pretty harsh. But you don't know what you're talking about. I've dated guys since high school."

She cocked her head. "Yeah? And how many of those had some

issue you couldn't get over? Like that guy Caleb, who you said wore pleated pants too often. Or Sam? The guy who was really into orchestra music and opera and you thought he was too pretentious because he didn't listen to any music from the twentieth and twenty-first century? Both of those guys were nice. With quirks that were *not* deal-breaker territory."

Jia acted like she knew everything about me and my past boyfriends, but these guys had really not been compatible with me.

"Look, Caleb's pleated pants weren't just ugly, his mom bought all his clothes. What thirty-year-old would allow that? And Sam only liked classics. Don't get me wrong, some modern art, plays, theater are a little out there for me, too. But I would at least try them out every few years just to make sure I wasn't missing out on something revolutionary. Sam refused, calling everything past 1900 'boring and pedestrian.'" I rolled my eyes. "When I joked I was born in that time frame, he shrugged, then lit up a cigarette. One of those weird clove kinds he'd seen people smoke in Europe."

Jia conceded. "Okay, but were those really deal-breakers? Couldn't you just buy the dude new pants? And couldn't you just compromise on music? Yeah, maybe they were duds, but you avoided conflict by breaking up with them and didn't date widely enough for comparison. Both of them were guys you worked with too, so you didn't really go on blind dates or anything like that. They were, as we say in the business world, low-hanging fruit."

More like bottom-of-the-barrel. Were guys I'd met through work really the only people I dated? I sighed. It's not like I had a long list of men I'd been with to mix up and confuse my brain. "I don't want to talk about this now. I had my reasons for breaking up with them and dating out of convenience isn't a crime."

She made a harrumph sound. "Yeah, reasons. That you wanted them to be exactly like Harry."

I stared at her. Unbelievable that she'd say this shit like she knew the first thing about why I'd had a crush on Harry throughout high school. It wasn't superficial. He and I used to sit together during study hall on Fridays to complete worksheets and problem sets so we would have a homework-free weekend. We'd study together sometimes during lunch and after school too. Passed notes in class. When I found out he was a fan of Stephen King, I read ten of his novels back-to-back to make sure we had stuff to talk about, and I had nightmares for years because of it. But it wasn't all disturbing and horror-filled: When he was sick with mono, I helped him catch up with schoolwork. When I got pneumonia, he came by my house and dropped off his notes and homework so I could study them. I returned to school a week and a half later, to find a "Welcome back!" sign on my locker in his handwriting.

Tell me that wasn't anything special.

I conceded. "You're right. Harry was . . . IS . . . the gold standard. But because he exists and I *know* him, I also know that finding an amazing guy is *possible*. Is it wrong to have standards? Even if they're high?"

Harry had been a good guy back then . . . well, mostly, when he wasn't caught up with his obnoxious friends and his gorgeous girlfriend. His *lucky* girlfriend, Claudia, whom he'd doted on with flowers, and chocolates, and grandiose prom-posals. Harry had been all about grand gestures, and I'd dreamed of having a boyfriend just like him.

Jia sighed through her nose. "Of course you should have standards. And it's okay to have them, as well as deal-breaker traits, which you figure out and adjust over time. But some traits or habits are NOT deal-breakers. Everyone has quirks and faults. Everyone struggles with something. Standards are great, but not if they're so high you're looking for something that isn't real." She added, "You know, I hate to say it, but your memory of him is probably a version of him that no longer exists. Fifteen years is a long time. People change."

To my surprise, she added, "By the way, I'm glad that message was sent to him. You were catapulted from your comfort zone and had to confront your crush beyond the mentorship, to see if he was as perfect as you remember. Maybe once you hang out with him more, you'll be able to see him for who he is and adjust your expectations about relationships and dating. You're an amazing person, I mean it, and any guy would be lucky to have you. I want to see you happy."

Was she right? Were my expectations too high? And if that was true, was my lack of relationship experience a reluctance to settle . . . or a fear of inferiority?

Before I could answer the question I'd posed to myself, my email notifications alerted me to a new message from One Last Word. *Weird, we don't have any tests scheduled today.* After opening the email and clicking on the URL, I saw it was a note from "BEST BOYFRIEND" called "Testing 1–2–3."

"Hello snookums. This is your boyfriend. I wanted to say hi and to let you know you're hot. Sincerely, Your sexy better half."

I fell back into my chair and grimaced. "What was I thinking? Casey's going to egregiously expose or weaponize this fake-boyfriend ruse somehow. I didn't even ask him to do anything, just be on *standby* in case there was a fake-boyfriend emergency. I better just face the music and tell Harry I lied. Let him know I made up my relationship because I didn't want to look like a loser who works all the time."

"But you *are* a loser who works all the time," Jia said, her lips turned up with a self-satisfied expression.

"First, ouch. Second, true. But Harry doesn't need to know that."
Who would be interested in someone with no social life? Not that
he was interested . . .

Ding! Another email. From BEST BOYFRIEND again.

"Babe, what's cookin' for dinner tonight? Your honey is hungry
after extra kettlebell strength training this week."

I groaned. "I have to stop Casey, he's turning into a messaging
monster."

Jia looked over my shoulder and laughed. "I mean, at least your
app is working, right?"

Another message came through. Just when I was going to call
Casey to tell him to knock it off. It was from "admin."

"Hey, it's Harry. I think these messages were meant for you. Btw
your bf does kettlebells? Only powerlifters, MMA fighters, and triath-
letes do that at my gym. Impressive! —H"

My chest tightened when I scrolled down. Casey had sent the
messages to the admin account, and I'd granted Harry full app
access a few days after we'd had dinner.

Casey texted me. Shit, I fucked up. I forgot Harry was admin too
and could see everything. I'm sorry please don't murder me.

I squeezed my eyes shut. *Why can't anything go smoothly?*

After sagging into the couch and taking a few deep breaths, I
replied, I can't murder you because I still need you to fix bugs. Now
you owe me big time.

He sent me back ILU! with a kissy face.

I let out another groan. Was it possible to dump a fake boyfriend?

Chapter Nine

*T*wo weeks after our business dinner, Harry asked me to meet him at his company's cafeteria.

"Good news, we did some UX testing for your app and we just got the research back. Lots of good insights." He handed me a spiral-bound report.

It was a purely business lunch meeting scheduled for thirty minutes. There was nothing social or romantic about daily sandwich and soup specials or rubbery pizza sitting under heat lamps. But having the opportunity to review research data with him, and to enjoy the visual of Harry Shim hunched over the report, elbows on the table, eager to dive into the numbers—it was one of the best experiences I'd ever had while eating a BLT with crinkle fries.

He took bites of his roast beef sub while leaning over his printed copy, reviewing aloud the number of participants, their demographics, and overall research findings with me. Seeing him geek out to numbers like this—it turned up my internal temperature a few degrees. When I glanced up, Harry rolled his shirtsleeves and placed his bare, muscular forearms on the tabletop. I continued to watch him as he shifted in his seat, rolling back his broad shoulders and straightening his neck to adjust his posture. Even though he'd grown taller and broader since high school, he still had the type of body I found most attractive. Athletic, muscular, and lean.

As he flipped to the appendix, my gaze traveled away from the data-filled pages to his boyish face, then to his chest, and then back to his well-developed, tan arms again. His strong hands gave me the impression he was still into sports or spent some time doing construction or something mechanical. Hard and rough, but not too calloused. My mind flashed back to our dinner, imagining his hands on my shoulders again . . . running down the sides of my body this time. I shifted in my chair, staring hard at my copy of the report.

I caught his eye when I looked up at him again. My face flushed as he spoke. "It looks like many of the challenges they found are ones I already shared with you. It means we were on the right track," he said with a reassuring smile.

Yes, we were on the right track, but it would be so much work to fix everything. Harry would need to help me prioritize, which was exactly why I had wanted to be in the mentorship program, so that someone with many years of expertise could help guide me. Why couldn't I have just created a simple app that let parents upload their bento box fails? I could have called it Bent-NO box. Easy. Relevant. And it had viral potential. Ads could be targeted to parents for the main source of revenue. Maybe it wasn't too late to go back to that.

Harry took the last few bites of his sandwich, the corners of his mouth still upturned as he chewed. Sitting across from him brought me back to high school when we studied together. He had the same furrowed brow, slightly cocked head, and studious face that relaxed after he solved an equation or problem. In this case, he'd collected data, confirmed important findings, and provided metrics suggesting that with a ton of work, One Last Word was an idea that could take off. Harry was offering me something I didn't have before and couldn't have gotten without his mentorship. Validation with reliable data.

He closed the cover of the research study. Beaming at me, he asked, "Any questions? I don't think anything we discovered, uncovered, or validated today will derail your release date. If anything, you have all the confirmation you need to push forward. This is so exciting! I'd love to be in your shoes right now, rolling out a product with solid data on your side."

I scratched the transparent cover of my report with my fingernails. "Was this really expensive to conduct? Should I pay you back with any future cash flow?"

He shook his head. "Oh, definitely not. This is all part of the idea incubator process. We have resources that you don't, and we also do so many studies like these, domestically and globally, that we get a volume discount. I don't want to say this is a drop in the bucket, but since we had interns working on this, and an audience panel ready to go from a product research study we paid for already and canceled, it was like it was written in the stars for us to do this. I also may have called in a few favors, but they were small ones."

I tilted my head. "How small, like firstborn child small?"

He lifted his shoulders. "More like letting a research vendor friend bring his buddies to our corporate suite at the next Dodgers game. I also promised a few people first access to One Last Word when it's ready. They were more interested in that than the baseball suite, to be honest. And we always have a hot dog and baked potato bar."

I shrugged. "I guess a lot of people want their one last word."

Harry nodded and leaned in closer. "I mean, who wouldn't? I can think of so many instances I wanted to admit something to someone and didn't have the guts to say anything."

The way he looked at me made my heart race. A light flow of electricity rippled across my skin and I felt a rush of coldness, then prickling heat.

He pointed at my lunch tray. "You done?"

I nodded and Harry stacked our dirty dishes. "Sorry that this lunch was here in our cafeteria. It's been a busy month getting people moved into our new office, and I haven't explored the area as much as I would have liked."

He took the stacked trays loaded with dishes and silverware to the conveyor belt. While he was up, his phone on the table buzzed several times in a row, then someone started calling. Claudia's face popped up on the screen, and after a few rings, the call went straight to voice mail.

Harry returned to the table with a huge grin on his face. "I just realized we never talked about Taylor Swift!"

My voice broke. "Taylor?"

"Yeah, those lyrics you sent me. I assumed you were a huge fan."

I'd honestly forgotten about that. My face flushed and I scrambled for words. "It's true, I'm a fan, but it wasn't exactly a test. It was my sister who dropped the lyrics into the message."

Before I could elaborate any further, Harry picked up his phone to read a flurry of texts. His smile faded. "Oh no," he said, glancing up.

Harry plopped down into his chair. "Any chance I could get a huge favor from you?"

Whatever he needed, it didn't seem good.

His down-turned lips and furrowed brow were concerning. I raised an eyebrow. "Look, I don't blindly agree to favors. It's something you learn with having a sister." *Can you do me a favor? Can you tell Mom and Dad I was with you when I was supposed to be touring colleges? Can I borrow two hundred dollars? Will you let me crash with you while I'm in town? Oh by the way, my boyfriend and his best friend are with me.*

"I need a preview."

"I'd say that's fair." Scratching his temple, he explained, "My ex, Claudia, you know her from high school, right? She's the chair for the Wildlife Wonders nonprofit's LA gala this year, and I bought VIP tickets for Ultralight Ventures a few months ago. I forgot all about it, and she needs me to send in names to the event coordinator for place cards and name badges. Stan can't go and I was wondering if you'd like to come. It's in two weeks. It's short notice, I know."

My mouth fell open. Before I could even process what he was asking, what this could mean for me . . . for us . . . he quickly clarified, "If we had three tickets I'd invite your boyfriend, but maybe he'll be okay with letting us go together. Most of the guests are tech or VC people with cash to burn and you'd benefit because it's a great networking opportunity. There's an open bar too."

"You should have just led with *open bar*," I joked. "Count me in!"

"Great! And um, if Claudia came around and you happened to pretend for a few hours that you were my . . . *date* . . . so my ex would see that I've moved on, I wouldn't be opposed. And I'd owe you the world."

I had no idea what my face looked like, but I could feel it contort, twist, and pull, like one of those movies where someone is put under a spell and it either doesn't work as planned or starts to wear off too early.

"I'm so sorry, I should have clarified that attending the gala is not part of the mentorship program and you're not obligated to go. In two weeks, you and I will be done with my onboarding phase and I'll pass you back over to Stan for the remainder of the mentoring." His face reddened and he ran a hand through his hair. "I thought it would be fun to go to the gala with you. As friends."

And there it was. The F word. Well, the other F word. Typically, a good thing in most circumstances, but for someone who'd had a forever secret crush on a guy that was never reciprocated, it was devastating to be friend zoned officially, even after all these years of knowing deep down in my heart that was the kind of relationship we had.

Still, I wasn't sure I could pull it all off. Going to the gala as his plus-one, while pretending to be his date if his ex-wife came around. That seemed like I was setting myself up for some kind of sitcom disaster. Like Cinderella at a ball, but the plan for the entire night all goes to shit and I run crying home at midnight.

It was too chaotic.

Too dangerous.

Too sad.

His doe-like brown eyes rounded as he offered a hopeful smile that melted my insides. "It's just that I really missed talking with you. And the thought of hanging out the entire night of the gala, well, for the first time, it made me look forward to it."

My pulse raced. "I mean, if you put it that way . . ." I sat up straighter. "Fine, I'll go. And you promise to introduce me to anyone there you know whom it might be good to meet for networking purposes?"

"Yes! I should give you a heads-up though, there are a lot of guys in VC and tech whom I *won't* introduce you to because, well, they're assholes. Chauvinistic, sexist racists who are walking human dumpsters of hazardous waste. So trust me with that part, okay? I've seen firsthand how some of these guys treat others like trash and I'd rather not expose you to that using my own connections. There are plenty of good people in the industry, and those are the folks I'll focus on for you."

You're doing a favor for a friend, that's all. Just like Casey is doing a favor for you by programming in his spare time.

But then I thought of one more thing. "One more condition. Or depending on how you look at it, a reciprocal favor. I need a date to an event too. Could you pretend you're my boyfriend at my dad's birthday party?"

He asked, "What about your actual boyfriend?"

I blushed. "They um . . . don't know about him, so he's not invited. It's a long story." I'd created a Jenga tower of lies because *he didn't exist*. And the only truth to it was that it was truly a long story. I added, "My dad has his hwangap birthday gala in a couple of weeks, which you know is a big deal in Korean families, and I'd love to show up with someone who would make people stop asking when I was getting married."

His eyebrows jumped. "That's it? That's all you want? Well, that's totally doable! And how is your dad only sixty? My parents' sixtieth hwangap celebrations were a long time ago."

"My mom had me in her mid-twenties, and my sister was born way after that. People always talk about youngest kids being an accident, but in my mom and dad's case I think the accident was me. Then, with the pandemic, we had to postpone the party twice, and now we're finally having it after a couple of reschedulings. Better three years late than never!"

He nodded. "Definitely worth celebrating. Are they retiring soon?"

"Thanks to some early strategic real estate investments in high growth areas, their retirement is still on track, just a couple more years, I think."

"Wow, I hope I can retire by the time I'm in my sixties," he remarked. "Maybe when I have my hwangap I'll be done with work. It must be nice to not be so stressed about money."

"Well, yes and no. Now they have all this free time to nag me about my life." I rolled my eyes for dramatic effect. "And they've been frugal for decades and now it's all working out. They plan to live a long time, which means they will nag me until the end of eternity."

"Ha! I know how that is. Ever since Claudia and I split, my mom calls nearly every day, accusing me of not eating right and asking me to take herbal tonics and supplements. It's funny, because neither

Claudia nor I cooked, so it's not like I was eating much differently then."

"So Claudia and you . . . I'm assuming you two are amicable if you're going to her gala?" Prying and pressing for answers wasn't my forte, but I really wanted to know why they broke up.

"It's both simple and complicated. We were always a good team, you know? But when we seriously started to plan for the future, like buying a house and taking demanding jobs to support our lifestyle, around five years ago, we started to argue more. Then, that was all we did. We disagreed about everything, especially about finances and the volume of social appearances. She was always looking to do the next big showy thing, and I wanted to relax more and enjoy what we already had. I used work as an excuse to avoid going home—taking lots of business trips and working late—and I put work first above all else. Turns out even marriage counseling is hard to commit to if you're working nonstop." He took a deep breath in and out. "Claudia leaned on one of her client friends during this rocky time, someone who matched her needs to a tee. Professionally, emotionally . . . and physically. They got together on business trips and she denied the affair at first, but I had a few friends confirm my suspicions. I couldn't really be with her after that. They seem happy, they're still a couple, but I admit it still hurts a bit when I see them together."

I barely had experience breaking up with someone, and that was nothing like leaving your spouse who was your high school sweetheart and watching her fall in love with someone else. "I can't even imagine. I'm sorry," I whispered.

He gave me a weak smile. "But hey, that's all in the past. As for your favor, my answer is absolutely yes. I'd love to be your faux date at the hwangap."

To make this as platonic as possible, I held out my hand. "Deal."

Harry reached out and clasped my fingers. Trying to ignore the blast of tingles running from my hand and up my arm, I wiggled my hand out of his grasp and offered a heartfelt grin.

"Be sure to let your boyfriend know I'm stealing you away from him for a night, and I appreciate it," he teased.

I tried to keep my cool. "Knowing him, he'll be more than fine with it. And he'll want everything to work out for both of us."

Chapter Ten

"When was the last time you showered?"

I raised my arms above my head and sniffed.

Jia shouted, "Don't smell your armpits, and don't lift your shirt to get a whiff of your chest! If you can't remember your last bathing experience, I'm here to tell you that it's time for a shower. Not just a quick hosing off and trickling some water on your head either. You need suds. Lather. Rinse. Repeat."

I let out a guttural moan. "I only have a few more lines of code to review. It's still not working right."

She sighed. "Isn't that Casey's job? And the sacrificial intern that Harry offered you to help during the mentorship? You have him for another few weeks, right?"

It was the intern's job, yes, but it was also easier if I did it myself.

Jia approached me and put her hand in front of the laptop screen. "You've been working nonstop. Do you even know what day it is?"

"Saturday," I said confidently.

"It's Sunday." She pushed aside some take-out containers on the coffee table. Pulling my computer off my lap ever so carefully, she placed it on a cleared area on the wooden surface in front of me and sat down on the couch. "After you shower, you need to eat and call Mom. She's been calling me twice as often thanks to you, because you never pick up. Umma's worried, can you just call her back to tell her everything's okay? I'm pretty sick of being your handler these days."

"I guess a short break wouldn't kill me," I said, standing up and stretching. Jia winced, making me wonder how badly I needed that shower. But she was looking at my screen, where my mom was popping up in my messages, asking me to call her.

Letting out an exasperated sigh, I grabbed my phone and walked to the bathroom. My mom had tried to reach me three times, all within the last hour. No wonder little sis was on my case, Mom was asking Jia to pass along a message to me to return her calls.

Umma picked up after two rings. "Hi, Sara, is that you? Let me get Appa."

"It's me, I was just working. Anything wrong? You called and messaged a LOT."

My dad chimed in. "Hi! It's Appa!"

I laughed. "Hi, Appa."

My mom cleared her throat. "Sara, my daughter, how was your day?"

I looked at the phone screen. Did she just ask me how I was?

"Gooooood," I replied, suspicion residing in my voice. "Just busy. Is everything okay?"

My dad said, "Everything fine. Everything good. Umma ultrasound good. She healthy. I'm healthy."

"Do you want me to . . . bake something and give to you?" Mom asked in a stilted way.

This was too much. Why were my parents acting like this? "Seriously, are you two okay? Why are you suddenly being so nice to me? It's weird and making me uncomfortable."

My dad whimpered, "We just trying to be nice."

My mom stated, "I take some note from *Dr. Phil* rerun show.

He has some good idea about how to parent difficult child. Maybe you should go to bootcamp. Dr. Phil usually solve kid problem with that."

"Umma, bootcamp is for teenagers and young adults entering the military, not for grown Korean women in their thirties." My lack of sleep and hangry-ness put me on a short fuse. "I'm glad that we're talking, and I'm happy to hear you're healthy, but I really don't need any parental advice at the moment. I have critical career stuff happening and don't need any additional stress in my life. Especially you trying to send me to bootcamp because of a talk show."

My mom's voice sharpened. "Aigooooo! I just call to ask how is my oldest daughter! I not trying to cause trouble."

A slamming noise blasted through the speaker, like the phone had hit a hard surface.

Dad came on the line. "Umma left house. Her feeling is hurt. After you sending that message she trying to be nicer. Maybe more like your American friend parent."

I was pretty sure my friends' parents were not watching *Dr. Phil* for parenting tips about unruly offspring. Through all my irritability and snappiness, I could still recognize something significant about what he'd said. She was trying. Which meant I'd been wrong all along. She was capable of change.

If they could make an effort, I could too.

"Dad, can you get Umma back on the phone? Can you tell her I'm sorry and want to know how her day is too?"

A muffled, swishing sound echoed on the speaker, along with the sporadic shouting of "Yeobo?" and "Sara want to talk to you!"

"I found her. She is in the garden!" He let her know I was asking how she was.

She grumbled into the phone, "You not even notice I not asking you on purpose about whether you making any money yet, or if you dating anyone."

I sighed. Because she wasn't nagging me and I hadn't noticed right away, she was now nagging me about that. Incredible.

She added, "I have some more liver blood testing because I am still tired sometimes. But doctor think I'm just old and it's not the allergy."

My stomach twisted into a knot. "Dad said the ultrasound came in and it was good."

"The test say I have low iron. I have to take supplement now. We also moving, did Appa tell you?"

I covered the phone and shouted, "Jia! Did you know Mom and Dad are moving?"

She walked over to me. "No, they never told me!"

I shrugged and put my parents on speakerphone so Jia could hear. "Mom, Dad, when are you moving? And why?"

Dad said, "Our house is too big. We need condo, one floor only. Time to downside."

"You mean downsize," Jia corrected.

"That's what I say," he said.

Jia shot me a look, and I shook my head. Not the hill to die on today. Not after they were letting us know they're moving out of our childhood home and moving into a smaller place seemingly out of the blue. Throughout college and during my early twenties, I'd always referred to their quaint two-story house in Orange County as "home," but over the last decade I'd visited less frequently, old neighbors had relocated, and my childhood friends had left the area. LA was my home now. My heart squeezed tight, knowing that when my parents moved out of their house, a little part of me would be left behind.

In fairness to them, they were at the right time in their lives to find a smaller place to live. Both were in good health, presumably, assuming nothing else was wrong. They were mobile and financially stable. On a hunch, I asked, "Umma, are you doing okay? Is it just low iron?"

"I am fine. No big problem. But . . . I find out I have type two diabetes. I take a pill every morning this week, Mrs. Lee and Mrs. Kang have same thing. Lucky we catch."

"Yes." I sighed with relief. Discovering she had type 2 diabetes wasn't exactly good news, but I was glad it was something manageable with medication.

"We going to clean out your room. So tell us what you want to keep," Umma said.

I replied, "I'm glad we had a chance to talk about it, thanks for letting us know before you toss everything."

Logically I knew my parents were aging, but I hadn't thought through how getting older would affect them physically. It wasn't something Jia and I talked about much, because my mom and dad skillfully skirted around topics involving money and health. Financially, I knew they'd be okay in their retirement years because there was one thing our entire family had going for them: self-sufficiency. My mom has a life mantra: "Life isn't joke. Don't depend on anyone else. You only depend on yourself. Work harder. Money isn't free."

It was a lesson I took to heart. Admittedly, to an extreme.

"Is there anything Jia and I can do to help you move?" I asked. The thought of doing physical labor made me want to die, but I knew my parents would try to skimp out on hiring proper movers and try to do a lot of it themselves to save money.

My parents declined any assistance after they hemmed and hawed. But I thought I'd try a little harder to meet them halfway. "If you need anything, anything at all, night or day, rain or shine . . . Jia can help you."

My sister smacked my arm.

I laughed and rubbed the spot on my biceps where she'd slugged me. "I can too. Geez."

My dad said, "We just downsiding right now. If we have anything you should keep we let you know."

"Sounds good," I said, shrugging at Jia.

"Oh, don't forget about the hwangap party. Now we have all reservations, so many people coming for Appa." Umma continued, "You know what? Dr. Phil is pretty smart guy. See, we talking and not yelling."

Jia and I laughed. *Thank you, Dr. Phil, for helping out the Chae family.*

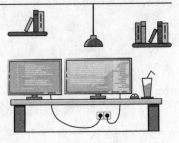

Chapter Eleven

"Can you zip me up?" Sucking in my breath, I closed my eyes and prayed that Jia would be able to work fast.

Yank.

Zip.

"Damn it."

Yank.

Zip.

"Fuck!"

Ziiiiip.

"Holy shit! You're in!"

I exhaled.

She spun me around. "For the record, the zipper was stiff and stuck, it wasn't your back fat."

"Thanks, sis, way to boost my self-esteem," I deadpanned.

She propped her hands on her hips. "Hey, I said it *wasn't* your back fat. And you look hot. There's no way Harry's going to be able to take his eyes off you. Casey did a good job with that eye-makeup tutorial."

Casey had sent me a step-by-step guide on how to use primer, liner, shadow, and highlighter, applying it on his own face first to show me how to pull it all together. His smoky-eye technique was on point.

Just as I pulled out my phone to thank Casey for investing so much time in helping me look my best, he texted me. You better bag him tonight! Xoxo, Bae

Before I could text back, Harry sent a message. I'm here! In the black Cadillac Escalade. No rush, I'm early

I stood in front of the full-length mirror on the door of Jia's walk-in closet. When was the last time I'd gotten fully dressed up like this? A wedding? A company holiday party ages ago? I couldn't even remember.

Jia rested her chin on my shoulder. In the reflection were two sisters who shared a percentage of their DNA but couldn't look more different. My monolid eyes were smaller than Jia's, who was born with an eyelid crease, giving her an eye shape I could get only with cosmetic surgery. Her lips were fuller and naturally darker pink; mine were shaped into a daintier Cupid's bow that older Korean people thought was darling. I'd inherited my mom's small button nose, whereas Jia's was longer and narrower, all from Appa's side. To sum it up, Jia was naturally pretty and effortlessly elegant, and I was maybe kind of cute . . . at best.

And wearing this designer dress, with a blowout and impeccable full makeup coverage, I was truly at my best.

"You look gorgeous," Jia remarked, with an absence of sarcasm or sass in her voice.

"Thanks, J."

"Your carriage awaits downstairs." She held up a pair of sparkly shoes to pair with the gown. "Try to take it slow so you don't fall, but don't walk so cautiously that you look like a baby giraffe in a safari park."

I snorted and put on the heels. The lift helped me gain over two inches in height.

At the door, she handed me my shimmery clutch and cashmere cape. "Have fun. Make some good connections. If you decide to have an after-party in your pants, do it at his place, not mine. I need a good night's sleep."

With a smirk, I said, "Joke's on you, I'm not wearing pants."

"Touché. But seriously, I'm home all night working on a project due tomorrow, and if you bring the dude back here, I'm kicking you both to the curb, pants or no pants. I love you, sis, have fun!" She waved and closed the door softly behind me. Jia wasn't being a jerk. She was just busy and needed me out of her space, and had no problem being direct about stuff like that, which I respected.

Outside the apartment building, Harry's Escalade was waiting in the red zone with hazard lights flashing. The back door opened, and Harry's handsome face became visible. "You look stunning."

I bit back the self-deprecating words forming on the tip of my tongue. "Thank you," I managed to say as I slid into the back seat next to him. But of course, I couldn't just accept the compliment and leave it at that. It wasn't my style.

"I picked this dress because it has pockets," I revealed.

He raised his eyebrows. To prove I wasn't lying, I tilted my hips up and showed him the sewn pouches cleverly hidden on the sides.

Harry nodded. "So it does. Stunning *and* practical. Like you."

Instead of deflecting with another weird outburst, my face flushed as I said softly, "Thanks . . . again."

Stop. Talking. Sara.

He grinned, and I blushed some more.

The driver hardly picked up any speed as we rolled down the street, passing the new Ethiopian and Vietnamese vegan restaurants a few blocks down from Jia's apartment. Crowds spilled onto the sidewalks in front of these new eateries thanks to their being featured in a recent *Los Angeles* magazine article, "Hot Westside Restaurants." People walking around in the neighborhood diverted into the edges of the streets to avoid the masses, making it harder for cars to stay in their lanes.

It was a much more pleasant ride than the previous fast and furious experience I'd had with Harry in the wild car ride we had a few weeks ago. When I looked at him, a coy smirk tugged his lips.

"What?" I asked, suddenly self-conscious about whatever he could be staring at . . . was it smeared eyeliner? A dribble stain on my chest? Birds liked to poop on me—was it that?

His gaze diverted to something out the window. "It's nothing. I was just thinking that it looks like we are going to prom."

I let out a relieved laugh. "Didn't all the guys rent their suits from Frank's Formalwear? Is that where you got your tux?"

Brushing his index finger on his lapel, he examined his collar and replied, "I'm pretty sure this is Armani. It's the tux my in-laws bought me for my wedding." He cleared his throat. A few seconds passed. "Sorry I made it weird."

"Are we close to the gala?" I practically shouted to counteract the awkwardness, but in doing so the outburst was forced and abrupt. "Playing dress-up has put me way out of my comfort zone, apologies for filling the silence with something worse than silence."

"Hey," he said, his eyes locking on mine. Leaning into me, a faint whisper escaped his lips. "Sedatephobia."

"Sedatephobia?" Confusion clouded my brain as I tried to process and comprehend.

"The fear of silence," he crowed, grinning his face off. "It's a good one, right?"

I spat out a laugh. "Have you been holding on to that one for, like, fifteen years? I don't think I've ever heard that one before."

"No comment. Let's just say I only have a few more obscure ones in my arsenal, and I plan to work them all into conversation with you. But to answer your question, we're thirty minutes away."

For the life of me I couldn't figure out if he'd planned to make things awkward on purpose to force one of his obscure vocabulary words into the conversation, or if he'd accidentally made things so awkward that he needed to figure out how to add levity, dropping the word "sedatephobia" into the dialogue like it was nothing. In either case, he impressed me by warming up my geeky heart and making me laugh. Being funny was one of the sexiest attributes anyone could have.

His shoulder continued to press into mine as he showed me the guest list for the event on his phone and photos of all the high-level donors.

"Have you seen this app before?" He tapped on a black-and-white spiral icon. "It's called Blindr, and there's a post about tonight's event." He handed over his phone and let me scroll. Lots of VCs, start-up founders, and angel investors would be among those attending the gala, mostly men in their thirties and forties, many with dates, but some without.

Blindr wasn't just news about who's who in the world of tech and VC, it was also filled with gossip, like TMZ for nerds. For someone trying to break into the industry, I could see how it would be invaluable. I downloaded it myself and set up alerts and notifications for "Pitch Warriors," "Fireflame Capital," and "Harry Shim." Before putting my phone away, I added "Sara Chae" and "One Last Word" too.

When we arrived, I was even more nervous, because Blindr confirmed that so many of the Silicon Beach elite would be there. We walked up the stairs and strolled into the main entrance of the

Natural History Museum, walking between two banners that read "Welcome to the Annual" and "SoCal Wildlife Wonders Gala."

The volunteer at the welcome table checked off our names. "After you take photos at the step and repeat, you can come back here to get your name tags," she chirped.

I whispered so only Harry could hear. "What is she talking about? I don't know what a 'step and repeat' is."

He cocked an eyebrow. "Really? I get to teach Sara Chae something she doesn't already know?"

My cheeks flushed. "There's plenty I don't know, especially about your elusive VC ecosystem."

Holding out his arm, Harry said, "Getting your foot in the door is the hard part. And keeping the door from automatically shutting on your foot while you try to get through."

"And making sure the door doesn't cut off any body parts," I added.

He chuckled. "That too. Anyway, let me introduce you to the fun world of getting your photo taken and hoping you don't blink or have a double chin in them like I always do."

I linked my arm in his as he guided us to a large backdrop with the Wildlife Wonders' logo plastered all over it. "This is the step and repeat. When it's our turn we'll have our pictures taken, and then we can go inside."

Three couples went before us, and when we were next up, Harry asked, "Do you have a side you like better?"

I did actually. "My right one, thank you for asking." We rearranged ourselves, and with a slight chin tilt upward, Harry and I grinned while flashbulbs popped. After about ten seconds, I wondered, *But where do my hands go?* and then became obsessed with shifting them from my hips to my front, fingers intertwined.

Harry glanced at me, then placed his hand on the small of my back, distracting me from my thoughts. *Holy electricity bolts.*

"One, two, three, smile!"

While Harry had found a place for at least one of his hands, mine were still midair when the last photo was taken. Harry asked, "Would it be okay with you if we held hands?"

Would it be okay? I wanted to cry with relief and kiss him for saving me from all this torture. "Yes, please, I'm terrible at this!" I managed to blurt out.

"Could we get one more?" he asked the photographer directly in front of us.

We situated ourselves again, this time with our fingers locked together. "Adorable!" a second photographer yelled. More flashes bursting from not just the photographer, but also from bystanders directly in front of me and in my peripheral view. After our session, Harry led us back to the check-in table.

Harry chatted with the person manning the welcome desk while I pulled a handkerchief from my purse and blotted my forehead. I wasn't cut out for all this fancy fanfare. We were handed name tags: Harry's read "Harry Shim, Fireflame Capital" and mine, "Sara Chae, Fireflame Capital Affiliate."

The volunteer explained that most of the museum had been roped off, but we would still have a nice experience in the North American Mammal Hall, the largest of all the museum's galleries. We followed our escort and when a server walked by with a drink tray, I grabbed the remaining two champagne glasses. Handing Harry the drink in my left hand, I lifted my bubbling flute and said, "Bottoms up!"

"Thirsty?" he asked as I took a few large gulps, almost emptying the glass. Once he had a few small sips, Harry followed my lead by chugging the rest.

Letting out a satisfied sigh, he said, "That was a great idea, it really took the edge off. I'm feeling warm and fuzzy now. Let's hope the rest of the evening is just as pleasant." He held out the crook of his elbow in my direction, and I locked my arm into his as we walked through the grand double doors leading us to the hall's immersive rustic plains of Wyoming experience like two royals making a grand entrance at a coronation ceremony.

A giggle formed in the back of my throat, and I took a last swig of champagne to suppress my urge to laugh. Each diorama encased different scenes of an America from long ago. A herd of bison drinking from a pond near the mountains. An ominous lone wolf hiding in the brush, scoping out its next kill. It was the perfect backdrop for the Wildlife Wonders fundraising gala, but it had to be acknowledged that the taxidermy mammal scenery made a strange backdrop for a quasi-date.

While our eyes adjusted to the dark setting, Harry became more in focus. His knitted brow. Pressed lips and agitated rocking of his heels. Why was he so down on this gala? We were saving furry woodland creatures! Preventing wildlife-critical deforestation! Even networking with the brightest tech minds in the region. How was all of this making him turn into Mr. Grumpy Penguin Pants? The only thing I could think of was Claudia. She was hosting the event, but it wasn't like he would be forced to dance with her all night. He might not even have the opportunity to chat with her at all depending on how busy she was throughout the evening.

We walked into an adjacent room to check out the silent auction items displayed on the banquet tables in the rotunda; at first glance it was mostly ski trips, med spa treatments, and obscure Hollywood memorabilia. As more attendees arrived, we took advantage of our proximity to the catering staff, who continuously walked by us with full trays of hors d'oeuvres.

I tugged on Harry's tux sleeve and pointed at the last item with no bids. "So how do you feel about us adopting a beaver?"

His eyebrows shot up. "You know that's a rodent, right?"

"Yes. And this one lives in Missouri, by a pond. Like Thoreau," I quipped. "And didn't you have a pet rodent in high school? A guinea pig?"

He laughed. "How did you remember Tutu? I haven't thought about her in years." He held out his elbow for me to lock arms with him again. "I'll think about the beaver sponsorship, another drink might sway me in favor of it. And I call dibs on naming it if we outbid everyone."

We returned to the main hall and wandered over to the rectangular charcuterie tabletop in the middle of the dining area. Imported cheeses, cured meats, milk and dark chocolates, nuts, olives, seasonal berries, and an assortment of crackers took up every inch of space on the flat wooden surface. The three-tier shrimp cocktail centerpiece caught my eye, triggering my stomach to growl. Most impressive though were the intricately crafted marzipan animals sprinkled throughout the food displays. Wrapping a few in my napkin to save for Jia and Casey was high on my priority list for the evening.

Harry popped a baby rabbit into his mouth.

I cried out, "Hey! You can't do that!"

His eyes widened as he chewed. *Gulp.* "I just did. Are they not edible? It tasted fine to me."

"I mean, I'm guessing it's consumable, I'm just saying that it seems, I don't know, disrespectful here. You know, to eat an animal . . . at a Wildlife Wonders gala."

He pouted. "But why are they here then? They're delicious. Plus, this place is a carnivore's dream: they're serving steak for dinner and this charcuterie is loaded with cured meat." Picking up a fox and studying it, he asked, "Split one?"

I gasped and Harry laughed. "Fine, I'll save it for the ride home." He scowled playfully and put it in a napkin, which he stuffed into his pocket.

We filled our appetizer plates and found our nameplates at table twelve. Not the best location in terms of viewability of the stage, but maybe not the worst considering it was positioned in the back by the restrooms and open bar.

Harry picked at his food with his small fork, while I cleared my entire plate. I eyed his uneaten wontons and asked, "Anything wrong? You seem kind of bummed out. And it's not just because I wouldn't let you eat that baby fox."

He smiled faintly. "If I'm ruining the mood, I'm sorry about that. This place, this gala, it's all a little much. And not because of all the fanciness and all that . . . it's because it reminds me of my wedding. Claudia is the chair for the gala this year, and she was the one who planned our entire wedding reception. Two hundred guests. It looks like she used similar vendors, because I'm getting real déjà vu with the decor and charcuterie spread, although we didn't have edible woodland creatures or flora and fauna backdrops. It's the first time the organization's held a gala in LA, and Claudia's got her eye on the deep pockets of Silicon Beach." His mouth turned downward. "When I moved down to LA I thought it would help me get a fresh start . . . but I'm wondering if it might have been a mistake to come tonight."

This event did seem very wedding-like. There was even a multi-tiered cake with a brown-and-green forest theme. All that was missing was a bride and groom cake topper.

Without thinking, I grabbed his hand. "Well, one thing that's different is *me*." With the champagne hitting me hard, thoughts barely formed in my head before spilling out of my mouth. "I'm here with you, and I'm in your corner tonight. Let's do what we set out to do, try to have some fun and network too. We can ditch early if there's any kind of SOS situation."

He squeezed my fingers. "You're right. So smart, it's what I love about you, Sara." Lifting his fork again, he consumed his entire appetizer assortment in a few bites. "My appetite's back. I might grab some shrimp."

My stomach fluttered from his compliment. He'd said my name and the word "love" in the same sentence. But . . . he'd also said *grab some shrimp*. There was nothing sexy about that any which way you looked at it.

A dropkick back to the friend-zone.

Before he could make his way to the seafood tower, the emcee for the event walked onto the stage. "Welcome to the gala! It's time for everyone to head to their tables for dinner. We have the Museum Maestros string quartet here to entertain us all while we eat. And soon we will have a few words from our gala chair. Thank you all for being here. Enjoy your meal!" Two violinists, a cellist, and a bassist began playing a familiar Beethoven piece from the opposite side of the room, in front of the large bobcat family display.

We took our seats. The waitstaff placed salads in front of us as the spotlight high above us aimed a beam of light to the side of the room where my high school classmate Claudia stood. She smiled and waved at the audience as she walked to the podium in her three-inch-high sparkly heels that matched her gorgeous, flowy silver gown.

Claudia Lee-Shim. Enchanting. Charismatic. Influential.

Sara Chae. Jealous. Awkward. Fragrant with squeezed lemon and cocktail sauce.

When she took center stage, my gaze averted to Harry, fully expecting to see him either enthralled by his ex's presence or oozing animosity from his pores.

But he was staring at me.

Not Claudia.

Me.

My eyes locked with his. He smirked and looked down at his mixed green salad. Lifting his fork, he stabbed some mixed greens and shoved them in his mouth while still wearing a smile.

I felt around the plate for my utensils, but there was no silverware around my place setting. The server who'd picked up our appetizer plates must've taken everything with him.

"You can have my fork," a voice boomed to my left. A handsome man pulled out the chair next to me and sat down. "I'm David Webb, nice to make your acquaintance." He lifted his fork placed above his salad plate and handed it to me.

"Are you sure you don't need this?" I hesitated to use it, in case he was just trying to be chivalrous and not eat while I greedily stuffed my face with fresh spinach, cubed beets, and aged Gorgonzola.

He insisted, "Nah, I'm not a salad person. I don't really eat green things. Well, with the exception of green peanut M&M's. But that really is all."

I laughed at David's anti-green manifesto and looked over at Harry. He was not as amused. In fact, he was glaring at my new friend while gnawing on a bread roll. Clearly Harry was back to being in a foul mood, so I turned to David and asked, "Out of curiosity, what is your opinion of great green macaws?"

He raised an eyebrow. "As a representative of birds in the animal kingdom, or as a main course? I need more information before I can make a sweeping general statement about something I know nothing about." David winked at Harry. "Isn't that what we do at work all day, Harry? He and I were at the same VC firm just out of business school. Harry was always a numbers guy—"

Harry chimed in. "And David liked to talk out of his ass," he grumbled.

David cackled. "I never quite understood where that term came from. Just as I don't understand why great green macaws would come up in any dinner discussion."

I opened my clutch and pulled out a napkin. "You mentioned all the green things you'd eat, and it was a pretty short list. Was just wondering if you'd eat a green *marzipan* bird."

He held out his palm and I placed it in his hand. "Oh God no. It's so awful. And hideous. This looks like a plastic toy you'd see at a preschool." To my horror, he squeezed his palm tightly and released the crushed bird wad onto his bed of mixed greens. The bird's head rolled off and hit a large glob of cheese.

What the . . . why would he do that? I thought it was cute! And he'd just wasted a perfectly good bird I was planning to eat later.

No longer smiling, I carefully tucked away the napkin hiding the other animals I'd stolen in my purse for safekeeping—my baby grizzly, arctic fox, and snowy owl would need to survive this event. Those were Jia's. Casey would get the North American prairie dog, because I knew he'd get a kick out of it.

Harry blurted out, "Hold on a sec." From his suit pocket, he pulled out a napkin wad and loosened it. Inside was an identical green bird to mine—well, before David smashed and beheaded it. Harry placed it by my handbag and whispered, "You can have mine. Sorry he was being an asshole. He's one of many here tonight."

My face flushed with happiness. Claudia started her speech and was at the part where she thanked all the donors in attendance. While the waitstaff took our salads away, I whispered to Harry, "Thank you. Your friend David seemed okay at first, but wow, he's a real jerk."

Harry placed his hand on my wrist, sending a shockwave from my fingers down to my spine. "Well, I never said he was my friend, he's more a frenemy at best. He was an asshole back when I knew him and looks like he still is now. He was dating one of Claudia's bridesmaids a long time ago, which is how he ended up at my wedding. He's one of the losers I *don't* want you to chat with tonight."

"Ah, gotcha." I tried to pay attention to Claudia reading the mission statement from the teleprompter, but I couldn't focus, not with Harry's fingers where they were. His light-as-a-feather touch pricked my skin, making it hard to concentrate on anything else and nearly impossible to breathe. It wasn't until she ended her speech that he removed his hand to offer a round of applause. It was then that I was able to inhale sharp breaths to calm myself.

David leaned behind me and said to Harry, "Claudia's such a superstar. I heard you two split. I'm guessing you're at least on speaking terms if you're here." He shifted back to his seat. "Must be weird being at a function when your ex is the hostess for the evening. I mean, especially since half of the room was probably at your wedding."

Harry turned a deep shade of crimson as he gulped his water. He set down the empty glass with a thud. "If I recall correctly, you got wasted and asked Claudia if she had a twin sister you could take up to your room."

"No disrespect, man. It was a joke." David excused himself and left his napkin on his chair. I hoped he wouldn't return, for Harry's sake and mine.

Attentive servers witnessed David's departure and swooped in to remove all the remaining bread and salad plates. They plunked down knives while simultaneously placing our entrees in front of us. At our table, it was filets mignons all around. Once our table had received our main course, my fellow delighted carnivores picked up forks and knives and cut into the tender meat. The quartet began playing a few contemporary songs as we took our first bites.

"How's everything?" I asked Harry, not sure what else to say with all the clinking and clattering around us. The meat, mashed potatoes, and sauteed carrots were cooked to perfection, so it would be surprising to discover if he wasn't satisfied with the meal.

"Good, I guess," he replied. The way his shoulders slouched and he barely touched his food, he seemed far from good.

Harry wiped his mouth with his white cloth napkin. "Sorry, it's just bringing back weird memories again. I had this exact meal at my wedding . . . even the same baby carrots with the little green parts sprouting at the end. I barely ate anything that night either." He pulled another roll from the breadbasket and tore it in half. "Being here makes me feel like I'm reliving my wedding, as morbid and sad as that is." He looked around to see if anyone else was listening, but between the quartet and the one-on-one discussions at our table, it was clear no one was within earshot to hear his grievances. "I couldn't hold my marriage together, and tonight I'm reminded of that." He swiped a chunk of butter on his bread and stuffed the half roll into his mouth. He chewed only a few times before he swallowed the chunk of dinner roll like a boa constrictor gulping down its prey. "Maybe I'm not cut out for marriage, like my parents. This gala is a nice reminder that I don't want to relive this all again and set myself up for another doomed relationship."

All those giddy, warm feelings toward Harry from before? Poof, into thin air. What was he even saying?

My seat neighbor came back at the worst time with a scotch in his hand. David dove into his filet and with a mouthful of food, reminded Harry again about his wedding day. "You two were babies when you got married, I remember that day well. I was so hungover! And speak of the devil, hi Claudia!"

My head snapped up as Harry's ex approached our table, stepping between Harry and me to greet everyone seated around us.

I couldn't read Harry's body language because Claudia was literally blocking my view of him, but when she shuffled a couple of steps back, I could read hers. Arms crossed. Double line crevices in between her eyebrows, one brow arched high as she glared at her ex.

She let out an exasperated sigh. "I thought you were bringing your boss, Stan," she complained. "I requested that they put you at a table with other industry types so you could talk business. I wasn't expecting you to bring . . . someone else."

Looking at all the other place settings with names and companies listed on the placards, I realized it wasn't just any men at the table, it was specifically men who worked in banking, tech, and VC. Men with high net worth. Clout. Connections. All dudes. Plus me.

Attempting to be civil and cordial, I held out my hand. "Claudia, I don't know if you remember me from high school. I'm Sara Chae. We were in the same graduating class."

She tilted her head and returned the handshake. "Sara. That rings a bell, and I thought you looked familiar. Were you in any sports?"

"Definitely not." I grimaced.

She twisted her mouth in thought. "Not a cheerleader, I'd have remembered my own squad. Did you do student government? Theater? Band?"

Claudia was running down the social pecking order, and I had been involved in none of those things.

"I had my own tutoring business, which took up most of my time outside of school. And I volunteered for an elementary school literary program."

Biting her lip, she asked, "Where'd you go to college again?"

"Caltech undergrad. Go Beavers!"

She nodded slowly. "Ah, now I remember you. I was wait-listed there. I didn't get in because they only usually accepted one person per high school back then."

That one person that year was me. I didn't know Claudia applied to Caltech. "This gala is lovely, everything about it is wonderful."

Harry said, "You've outdone yourself, Claudia. Stan sends his regards, he couldn't make it, so there was an extra ticket. And since our firm is a generous donor, I figured it made sense to bring someone from our Pitch Warriors mentorship program rather than have an empty chair."

He could have said I was a colleague or a friend, but he didn't. To him, I was simply "Sara Chae, marginally better than an empty chair."

Claudia ran her hand along his right shoulder. "Well, we do appreciate your contributions each year, Harry." Her voice brightened, noticing there were people around us watching her. "Have a wonderful time, both of you."

The table had gone quiet at the exact moment the quartet was taking a short recess, which allowed our tablemates to overhear part of our conversation. A few of them congratulated me for being accepted into the Pitch Warriors program and wished me luck on winning the grand prize. Others wanted to talk about business after dinner. A few of them immediately went into flirting mode as soon as their drinks kicked in, including my annoying neighbor, David.

It didn't feel right at first, chatting with everyone around me, like I was betraying Harry somehow. Shaking those thoughts out of my head, I reminded myself that this gala didn't count as a date, that I should absolutely spend every moment taking advantage of this promising networking opportunity—wasn't that the deal we made? When would I ever be in a room with so many Silicon Beach powerhouses again? There was that saying about shooting fish in a barrel . . . and in this expensive barrel there sure were a lot of big, fancy fish.

When I excused myself to check out the open bar, others from the table joined me. After ordering my drink, I turned around and took in the lavish setting while waiting for my top-shelf vodka martini.

I couldn't believe it. Here I was, at a gala wearing a fancy gown, the belle of the ball, with a number of handsome and rich men surrounding me. A true Cinderella moment.

"Well, well, well. I remember *you*." I turned around to see Tom, one of the panelists who had interviewed me for the mentorship contest. The asshole who'd offended me. "Congratulations are in order," he slurred. "Stan convinced us that you were the real deal during the mentorship selection process. You made it, I hear. You're officially a Pitch Warrior."

The fragrant tequila in his half-full glass wafted in the air between us. He took a few steps closer. Too close. I could smell the liquor on his wet breath.

"I'd love to take you to dinner sometime, to discuss whatever topic you'd like." He grinned and then took a slurp of his drink. "Or later tonight, I have a room at the hotel across the street. With an extra keycard."

I looked down at his wedding ring.

He responded, "Don't mind that. I can take it off if it bothers you."

I looked over my left and right shoulders for a route to escape. With so many bodies around me, I was trapped. The downside of being a fish in a barrel.

Harry appeared by my side and placed his empty wineglass on the bar. "I hope I'm not interrupting. Would you like to dance, Sara?"

I nodded and turned to Tom. "I'm passing on your offer. Which was disgusting, just so you're aware." To Harry, I said so everyone could hear me, "Thank you for rescuing me from that scumbag!"

Harry held out his hand and I grasped his fingers. We made our way to the laminated floor and joined the drunk, older couples who had flocked to the dance area when the quartet switched to upbeat country.

"I would have asked you to dance anyway, but the timing seemed right to butt in if Tom was there." He groaned. "I'm so sorry you had to deal with that pervert; I wanted to give you some space to network on your own and then I saw the VC vultures swoop in. I wish we would have agreed on a signal, like a nose scratch would mean to steer clear, and an ear tug would mean 'Go get 'em tiger.'"

I laughed and pressed my cheek against his chest. "Maybe we need that for the future. He wasn't just obnoxious, he's also married and was trying to get me to go with him to his hotel room! Can you believe his nerve?"

"I do believe his nerve, he's awful." Harry fell silent and we swayed to the music. I continued to rest my head against his shoulder and squeezed my eyes shut, hoping to push aside my memories of Tom and his foul breath. After a few minutes, the adrenaline spike from my earlier encounter had subsided. My heart beat more steadily. I could focus on taking in the moment and enjoying this closeness with Harry.

He pulled back to look at me. "Are you having an okay time? Well, aside from being seated next to your horrible neighbor David, my ex coming over to our table and making things awkward, and gross, slobbery Tom trying to pick you up?" Smirking, he added, "And the fact that I can't stop stepping on your toes even though I took ballroom lessons in high school?"

Yes. There had been multiple unpleasant moments throughout the night, one of the worst being Harry revealing he was not interested in getting married anytime soon, if at all. I shoved them to the back of my mind and tried to enjoy what was happening in the present. Harry. Me. Dancing. This evening could end on a high note.

High school Sara would be dying right now. A dance with Harry!

I'd dreamed about this moment, and not just in an aspirational sense. I'd danced with him so many times, in my wistful daydreams, and in my visions during sleep at night. Every time, it was magical.

He was right though, he was treading all over my feet, not like the debonair dancing Harry I'd imagined in my mind.

Instead of focusing on all the toe trampling, I concentrated on the strong pair of hands situated on the small of my back and the gorgeous eyes peering down at me through long dark lashes. This was a fairy-tale moment. Everything was perfect.

And then the music changed.

Normally a crowd-pleasing Adele song wouldn't get a visceral reaction from anyone at a formal event, but as soon as the violin's melancholy melody and the cello's deep somber tones filled the room, the energy on the dance floor became less frenetic. Harry stopped moving altogether, which was both good and bad. Good because he was no longer smashing my toes. But bad because something stopped him completely, and for the life of me I couldn't figure out what or why.

"You okay?" I asked softly.

His gaze shifted back to me. "I'm so sorry, I haven't heard this song in a long time, since my wedding. It was Claudia's favorite and just a little weird it's playing now. Like I said before, just being here in my old tux and dancing to this song again—"

My hands dropped from his shoulders to my sides. "This was the song you chose for your couple's dance?" Surely this was just a coincidence and not some weird game his ex was playing with him. With us. Even for me, the similarities to Harry's wedding were getting to be too much.

He smiled weakly and shrugged. "It's not a big deal, it was so long ago and I'm not that rattled, it just took me by surprise is all." Harry's hands rested on my back again, this time positioned a little lower, sending a surge of heat from the base of my spine down past my thighs. Leaning into his chest, we swayed.

"See, I'm already over it," he whispered. "But this definitely isn't something I'll be doing again."

Confused, I murmured, "You mean dancing with me? Or coming to galas? Or . . . getting married again?"

Why did I ask that? I didn't want to know the answers to those questions, so why did those words escape my mouth without any filter?

To my surprise, he chuckled.

He looked straight into my eyes. "Dancing with you has been one of the best things to happen to me in a long time." He cracked a smile. "And going to a gala with you as my pseudo-date is so much better than going stag. Stan would've made a terrible slow dance partner. I used to dread going to all of these social events with Claudia . . . the nonstop introductions, the small talk, the schmoozing. Hey, want to head back to the table to get dessert and I can introduce you to the other investors at the table?"

"Harry, would you ever get married again?" I asked sheepishly.

He sighed. "I'm not sure if I'm at a place in my life where I see myself being serious with anyone right now. And given my parents' divorce, maybe it's in my genes or something. It finally hit me recently that I hadn't dated anyone other than Claudia, so I'm not exactly sure how to move on except to date a lot and try brand-new things. For example, right now I'm learning how to slow dance without putting scuff marks on my partner's beautiful shoes." We both looked down at the thin black streaks he'd left on my shiny footwear.

The quartet behind us transitioned smoothly to an upbeat tempo, getting the crowd to clap along to a One Direction cheesy cover. Like everyone around me, I bopped along to the tune, trying my best to not think about Harry revealing that he wasn't looking for anything special. Not now. And maybe not ever.

"I need a drink," I remarked. *The stiffer the better.*

Leaving Harry to fend for himself on the dance floor, I ordered another martini at the bar and took a long sip when it arrived. The cellist played a lyrical and deeply emotional solo, which received such a warm reception that the audience erupted into applause, offering a rare standing ovation from those seated at the tables. Other members of the quartet moved their music stands and pushed their seats back so they could give the talented instrumentalist a moment to shine.

That's when I realized that the cellist with the surprising "it factor" was Naomi Matsumoto, my former best friend. I shattered my fancy glass as it dropped out of my hand and hit the laminate floor.

The entire room looked in my direction, including the musicians. Naomi, who had jammed out during her solo just moments earlier, stared back at me through her jet black curtain bangs like she'd seen a ghost.

David walked over to me and drunkenly snapped his finger in the air. "Cleanup on aisle one!" Then he yelled, "Well shit! With all this glass on the floor, I can't breakdance!"

Seeing him fall to the floor and do the worm and/or windmill would have been one of the highlights of the evening, but no way was I sticking around any longer. It was pretty clear that Naomi was not happy to see me. She hadn't even bothered to respond, reply, or reach out because of my messages, and that alone was enough to know that our friendship was completely over.

Then, the unimaginable happened. People around me pulled out their phones and studied their screens. Harry yanked his own iPhone from his inner blazer pocket and glanced down like everyone else.

Then he looked at me from the dance floor, head shaking and eyes wide.

I pushed through the crowd to retrieve my phone at the banquet table. Notifications filled my screen from the Blindr app. Text messages rolled in from my old friends in tech. And Casey had called five times in a row. An anonymous Blindr member had posted a photo of Harry and me at the gala. It had been taken at the step and repeat, and we were laughing and holding hands; it was a surprisingly flattering photo given the angle. The caption and the rest of the post were not nearly as complimentary, making my stomach sour and clench at the same time.

"Harry Shim, VC Superman, Fireflame Capital . . . with his Lois Lane? Harry and gala hostess Claudia Lee-Shim have been splitsville for a while, so we're not surprised to see Harry in attendance at the Wildlife Wonders gala, dressed to the nines, wearing Giorgio Armani and draping a lovely date on his arm. Sources say she is former high school classmate Sara Chae, who is one of the participants in the prestigious Pitch Warriors competition. Are they colleagues? Friends? JUST mentor and mentee? Hmmm, take a look at the chemistry in this photo and you be the judge."

There was an underlying implication that the relationship between Harry and me was inappropriate, and it didn't sit well with me, especially with the call to action at the end, asking members to offer their judgmental opinions. Which they did.

Claudia vs. the off-rack version of Claudia, no contest. Who is this sidechick?

He went on a date with my friend, I guess he's single and ready to mingle!

Yeah we know how she got *that* mentorship . . .

I could see Harry trying to make his way over to me as I held back tears, but the last thing I wanted to do was be seen with him. In true

Cinderella fashion, I grabbed my personal belongings from my seat and left the museum in a hurry before the clock struck midnight. I ran down the marble steps and pulled tissues from my pocket to wipe my tears, unwrapping and unleashing woodland marzipan creatures onto the ground, leaving a fairy-tale-turned-shit-show trail of small decapitated animals in my wake.

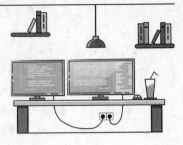

Chapter Twelve

I knew I might find you here. Is this seat taken?"

After avoiding him for an entire week, Harry found me on a weekend evening, working by myself in a neighborhood café. There were only three places around Jia's neighborhood that offered free Wi-Fi and a five-dollar order minimum to sit there indefinitely, and Gray Pup Coffee was one of them. I wasn't exactly tucked away from view, sitting at a glass-top iron bistro table next to the giant windows looking onto the street. All he had to do was look up from the sidewalk to see me. I was too careless.

Immersing myself in work had been a good way to distract myself from the horrible night at the gala, but my days of hiding from Harry had come to an end.

"Have a seat," I yelled above the noise of the grinding of coffee beans.

He slid into the metal chair and pushed aside my cherry danish to give himself more room to place his elbows on the table. "You hardly replied to my texts. I need some answers . . . When you left the gala that night in such a hurry, I looked everywhere for you. I bumped into one of the investors I wanted to introduce you to, but you had taken off."

I dropped my chin and stared hard at my laptop keyboard.

His face fell. "Was it because of the stupid Blindr app post? I'm mentioned all the time on there, don't let it bother you. It's already mostly blown over too. We're old news."

It was probably easy for someone like Harry to dismiss the Blindr post, but it wasn't for me. That was the first "Sara Chae" entry. Acid bubbled up from my stomach as I thought back to the insinuation that I had some "mentor with benefits" arrangement. Was that how men in VC saw women? As opportunists who would do anything for a leg up? How abhorrent and demoralizing.

He continued, "Of all people, Claudia said in an exclusive Blindr interview that if you and I were in fact a real couple, that she would be happy for us. She mentioned that we had adopted a beaver together from the silent auction and that was what mattered the most, the wildlife animals. She shared the QR code for donations and beat her annual fundraising goal. Amazing how she turned this bullshit into a lucrative opportunity. But that was always her strength." He sighed wistfully. "And her weakness."

My shoulders relaxed. "And we saved the beaver?"

The concern on his face shifted to amusement. "Yes."

I checked the Blindr app, and while the post was still on the gossip feature page, it was far down. There was breaking news of hirings and firings and messy divorces that had far more views and comments. Harry was right, we were old news.

"I got dibs on naming him, so he's Brandon the Beaver. I'll send you photos of him tonight. By the way, you missed the breakdancing," Harry added.

I cleared a few more business books off the table so he had more room. "I apologize for going MIA that night. It wasn't my best moment."

After taking a sip of my drink, I asked, "Was David's breakdancing any good?"

He showed me a video taken from his phone. David had managed to find a clear area on the dance floor and was doing the worm, with the entire crowd going crazy. He transitioned to the windmill with ease, and the audience freaked out. A few people threw dollar bills at him, which he proudly stuffed down his tuxedo pants.

Hilarious as it was, my attention was drawn to the background of the video, where Naomi was chatting with Claudia. I had no idea they even knew each other. I mean, we all went to the same high school, but I didn't know they were friendly. In fact, in high school, Naomi knew I had the biggest crush on Harry, and therefore hated Claudia. Those were the rules of best friends back then. I didn't write them.

The one person who would know if Naomi and Claudia were chummy was sitting right across from me, breaking off a piece of my pastry and shoving it in his mouth.

I asked, "Did you see Claudia chatting with Naomi in the background? Are they friends or something?"

"That's Naomi?" Replaying the video, his eyes rounded when Claudia and Naomi laughed while David pop and locked. "Oh right, the string quartet. Claudia mentioned she'd heard them play a long time ago at an outdoor concert during the pandemic and probably reached out when she became part of the gala committee."

My stomach twisted into a pretzel knot. The last time I'd seen Naomi perform was a few years after college. She'd invited me to several gigs after we graduated, but they were always at some weird time or hard-to-get-to location. Still, it jabbed me in the heart knowing Claudia was more in tune with Naomi's music career than I was. It was expected that friends drift apart with marriages, parenting, and physical distance. It seemed that in your thirties, you were primarily left with people who were either convenient to hang out with due to similar life circumstances OR they were the ones you cared about the most. How did Naomi and I become estranged? She should have fit reasonably well into both of those categories.

Harry remarked, "Such a gifted cellist. I'm glad Naomi's doing something that brings joy to people's lives." Clearing his throat, he added, "Not that building apps and websites isn't joyful. So why are you avoiding me? Why'd you leave the gala so abruptly? Why didn't you at least say goodbye to me? I left with pockets of stolen marzipan animals and no one to give them to; I had to eat them all myself."

I envisioned him eating one after another, like movie-theater popcorn. "I'm sorry I left you there; it wasn't only the Blindr breaking-news alert about us. I should've said something, but I freaked out and my body went into fight-or-flight mode, and you can see how well that turned out."

Lowering my gaze to the floor, I continued. "Seeing Naomi there was the first thing that threw me into a tailspin. We had a falling-out a long time ago, and when she didn't open or reply to my initial 'I'm dead' message, it hurt. What was sent to Naomi wasn't nearly as bad or as weird as the others. It was more heartfelt. More concerned about reconciliation given our history and not wanting to live, or die, with regret. I looked at my sent mail and it showed that my messages to her were opened over a week ago, and even then she didn't check on my well-being. She could have sent me double middle finger emojis, and it would have been jarring, but at least it would have been something. Instead, nothing. And all I can gather from her response, or rather lack of one, is that we're better off not being in the same room together."

I bit my lip and looked down. "And then the Blindr post had all those people staring at me, and it seemed like running over to you could feed the rumors. So I fled the scene. I'm not good at apologizing, or confrontation, especially when I'm overwhelmed by so many emotions, and I feel terrible about all of it."

"Hey," he said softly. I glanced up, my gaze meeting his warm, dark brown eyes. "Everyone's entitled to have adult freak-out moments. I was sweating bullets nonstop when Claudia came over to our table. I had no idea how she'd react at my being there with you. But then it worked out."

"You don't sweat anymore?" I joked.

He laughed. "I wish I could control that. You have a way of calming my perspiration glands, which I appreciate. When I'm around you, I feel comfortable in my own skin, more like the person I'm supposed to be. Maybe over time you'll be able to be in Naomi's presence without the flight reflex."

"This whole time I've been pretending that conflict avoidance was a 'them, not me' problem, but I really hate having difficult conversations."

Harry scooted his seat toward the table. "Whether people respond the way you want or not, one thing I've learned over the years is that communicating that someone's hurt you can be better than letting it fester deep inside. It might be uncomfortable and really awkward, like this conversation we're having at this very moment, but talking things through feels right for us. I'd rather discuss what's upsetting us so we can set ourselves up for a stronger future. It's one of the things I learned about myself after Claudia and I went our separate ways."

I nodded. "Honestly, the more time that went by after the gala, the more vulnerable I felt and it became harder to bring all of this up with you. Thank you for tracking me down and saying something. You've given me a lot to think through—not just about us, but also Naomi, my parents, and my app design. I promise I'll do better next time, especially if we create another scandal at a gala in the future."

"Well, I'm happy to support you any way I can, although I'm no adulting expert. Especially in the marriage department."

And there it was again.

Not thrilled to be back on that conversation topic, I felt it was time to shift the discussion. "Want to see One Last Word's glitch-free, seamless message sending?" I pulled a chair from a neighboring table and invited him to sit next to me. "I know you're technically not my mentor anymore, but can I get your input as a prospective user before I show Stan?"

His face lit up like a Christmas tree. "I'd be honored!"

Before we could look at the updates and added features, the barista called out "Large latte, coconut milk, extra espresso shot, one raw sugar, with caramel drizzle!"

Harry jumped out of his seat. "That's my order, finally!"

When he returned, I teased, "Could your drink order be any more complicated?"

"Don't knock it till you try it." He offered me a sip, which I gladly took, expecting to hate it and tease him more afterward. But it was good. Amazing, in fact. I took a second swig before handing it back to him.

"It's great," I conceded.

"Fireflame has coffee carts that go to every floor on Fridays, and this is a variation of one of their signature drinks. Next time you're in the office on a Friday, you can get a free one."

While I sneaked sips of his coffee, Harry created a fake user account, wrote a short profile, and crafted a message. Five minutes passed and he still wasn't finished. Not a lot of time was needed for a user test: as long as there was a working email, the message could be gobbledygook and it could still be used for testing. Harry could write "I like pee pee, poo poo, and big farts" and it would go through. It wasn't rocket science.

I checked my watch. "Is something wrong?" I asked, leaning over to see the screen.

A few beads of sweat visibly formed on his forehead as he typed. "Almost . . . done." He sat back in his chair as my email notification dinged. I clicked on "A message from Sir Harry Jin-Yeong Shim has arrived. Please read!"

Clearly I needed to work on the subject line template. It was clunky and spammy. Another thing to add to Casey's queue of improvements to work on next.

"You're not even going to open the message?" Harry asked, hurt emanating from his voice. I couldn't tell if he was joking or not.

I shot him a questioning look and double-clicked.

It read: "Could fate have brought you back into my life? You make me happy . . . too bad I'm unalive now and didn't tell you earlier. Sorry about that."

I reread it twice before speaking. "That was nice. Do you really believe in fate?"

He leaned toward me. "Do you?"

My heartbeat thumped. "I sometimes think certain things turn out the way they do for a reason." Swallowing hard, I added, "And if something is meant to be, the universe finds a way to make it happen. Like me quitting my thankless job and starting my own company. Me reconnecting with you, albeit under weird circumstances. And then us working together."

He smiled and cocked his head. "It does seem like this means something, us crossing paths again. Whatever it is. Fate. Destiny. Miracles." He placed his hand on mine and squeezed, triggering an eruption of warmth that traveled from my fingers, up my arm, and throughout my entire body. It was impossible not to notice how this heat traveled from my entire upper body to pulsing below my waist, intensifying the longer his hand touched mine.

I tried to not let anticipation ruin the moment. My heart pounded as I leaned forward, my lips meeting his. Grazing lightly at first, Harry pressed his mouth on mine a second time, firmer and more intense, like a final kiss in a movie. My body lurched with excitement because it was exhilarating.

Sensual.

Perfect.

My eyelashes fluttered as I waited patiently for more, but there was nothing. Instead, Harry groaned. "Oh shit, Sara. I got so caught up in this . . . in you . . . in us . . . that I didn't even think about you having a boyfriend. I'm so sorry. I mean him, and you, no disrespect. My emotions got in the way."

I swallowed hard and pulled away. I'd forgotten too. Was this the time to confess? Heaving a sigh, I said, "Right. About that—"

Before I could admit to him that I'd avoided confrontation and dragged out my false dating narrative because of pride, stubbornness, and to protect my heart, Harry blurted, "I don't want to blur the lines of our working relationship. Let's keep it professional."

To my horror, Harry stuck out his hand for a handshake. The same hand that had just sent a quiver through me with a single touch. With his one squeeze, he had sent warmth throughout my body, and we shared an unspoken promise of more to come.

What. The. Hell.

While I tried to figure out how to respond, his phone dinged twice in a row. Luckily, he put down his hand so he could check his messages.

Witnessing his face fall, I asked, "Is it an emergency? Do you need to go?"

He shook his head. "I didn't turn off notifications for this new dating app I signed up for and I need to do that. It's really annoying. Maybe you can integrate your messaging app with some of these relationship sites—a few people I've had dates with need *one last word* from me. I can see why sending someone a final message might be a better alternative than ghosting or stringing people along. There's definitely a broader market for the capabilities you offer, beyond your standalone platform."

The soft, warm kiss from moments ago had made me forget that Harry wasn't looking for a long-term relationship, and here he was admitting to me in such a nonchalant way that he was going on dates with other women and goodbyes were more his thing. If he was playing the field and wasn't interested in anything serious, why should I even bother wasting any more time thinking about him?

His entire face lit up. "Maybe anti-ghosting could be our platform. Is 'Ghostbusters' trademarked? We should look into that."

Biting back my bottled feelings, I faked a smile to hide my misery. *There goes my opportunity to engage in a difficult conversation about my dating life.* "Well, we can talk about expansion of the product another time, because I'm just about done here. Did you want to stay or are you leaving too?" To make it all more believable, I stood up from my chair, shoved my books into my bag, and powered down my computer.

He stared at me. "You're leaving? Before you go, are we . . . okay? I overstepped and I can't apologize enough."

Don't cry, don't cry, don't cry. "We're fine." I thought about saying more, but my throat tightened and no more words could pass through. I slung my large tote over my shoulder and scooted my seat back.

He followed me outside and watched me intently as I zipped up my jacket. The hesitant look on his face suggested that he wanted to say something more. His mouth finally parted and unexpected words poured out. "You are the most amazing woman I know."

As he stoked my inner fire again, he added, "And I'm ready for round two of fake dating at your dad's birthday party this weekend, as promised. I'm so glad we're chingoos." He grinned.

Chingoos.

Friends.

Out went the flame. Poof, just like that.

Chapter Thirteen

A life-size cutout of my dad in sunglasses, holding a sign that read "Sang-Joon Chae, Hottest SEX-agenarian" at the ballroom entrance, wasn't the warm welcome I expected at my dad's birthday bash.

Jia squealed, "Don't you love it? I've been working on this for a few weeks!" In charge of what she called "the fun stuff," she'd also arranged the elaborate pearl white and shimmery silver balloon arch positioned over my parents' table, a lei necklace station, and a three-tier chocolate fondue fountain with cascading dark, milk, and white flavor options. An enormous multitiered cake sat on its own table near the buffet line, and I prayed that Jia didn't have someone inside it who would jump out. The last thing we needed was a jump scare at a birthday party for seniors.

Jia and I came to the venue an hour early to ensure that the decor was set up and the food had arrived. The last head count my parents' had sent us was eighty people attending, including our family, down from a hundred. Some of their older friends had canceled due to last-minute health issues and illnesses. We were a little bummed out, but pleased with their consideration for others, especially given the demographic of those attending the party being more at risk.

My mom wore a light pink and ruby red traditional hanbok, with a white bow embroidered with intricate flowers, a perfect dress to match her pale hue and rosy cheeks. She flitted around the food stations, admiring the breadth of dinner and dessert choices.

"Waaaa everything look good!" When she got to the final table, she paused. "Why this is *no sugar* and *low carb*? It say 'For the health-conscious.' What that mean?"

I shrugged. "I added a caterer who specializes in dietary restrictions. Because of your diabetes, I wanted to make sure you had something to eat. And that your friends Mrs. Lee and Mrs. Kang could eat too."

At first, she didn't say anything. I waited for her to tell me the chicken skewers looked too dry or the salad needed Thousand Island dressing (it was balsamic). Or that she had already eaten and I was wasting money by spending a premium on the healthy table.

But she said none of those things. Her face crumpled. "I don't need any special food, this is Appa's big day. Not mine. Don't worry about me. I can eat trail mix." Sure enough, she pulled a little bag of nuts and dried fruit from a pocket of her dress and shook it, as if to prove there was something inside the packet.

I scrunched my face. "Mom, you need to eat more than that rabbit food. It's going to be a long day. Plus, I found someone who makes tasty diabetes-friendly Korean food. You deserve to be happy tonight too. Dad and you both have lived a long time and we're grateful for that. We want you to be healthy so we can celebrate your seventieth and eightieth birthdays too. Your chilsun and palsun celebrations will be just as spectacular." My parents showed their love by feeding us, and I was hoping I could do the same for them. To express love in a way they could understand. Copious amounts of delicious food.

Dad entered the room wearing a light gray suit and shiny pink tie that perfectly matched Umma's dress. He surveyed his potential dinner options, exclaiming, "All the food look good! That healthy table going to be popular!" The dessert cart had just arrived, and he scampered over to see what was on those trays.

"Your appa seem happy," Umma conceded. After a long pause, she added, "Thank you." She reached out her hand and patted my forearm. A sign that she was truly grateful as well.

While the DJ set up his station in the corner, guests began to trickle into the ballroom. Neither Jia nor I were interested in making a fuss over speeches or family-related entertainment, so she instructed the DJ to also be our emcee for the evening. The itinerary was simple: my dad would give a speech with a toast, then we would all eat dinner, take pictures, and open up the floor for dancing.

The only customary old-school tradition we upheld because my dad wanted it (and Jia obliged because it would make good photo ops) was a table in the front of the room topped with special ceremonial foods. Chewy, colorful rice cakes, fresh fruit, and various types of cookies were stacked to represent the many achievements of my dad's life. My sister added a few of her own touches, including a macaron tree and a Belgian chocolate pyramid.

I brought over two glasses full of red wine to my table setting and placed them next to my name placard. My mom asked, "Why you drink so much? Too much stress?"

I grimaced. "It's not just for me."

She looked over at Jia, who was sipping a glass of rosé. "She is drinking pink wine." Then she laughed. "You bringing handsome date you not telling us about?"

But just as she concluded her giggling fit, Harry walked through the doors. He scanned the room while straightening his Armani tux.

"Who is that?" she asked, pointing at my fake beau. "He is good-looking waiter!" She waved at him and yelled, "White wine please!"

I gasped. "He's not a waiter! That's my—" My voice hitched. I couldn't say "boyfriend." Even "date" sounded wrong, since I'd coerced him into coming in exchange for my gala appearance. And if the words "just a friend" came from my own mouth, it might officially quash all hope of anything more than friendship blossoming between Harry and me, even though he had confirmed that we were platonic buddies when we last spoke, and my own fears of putting my feelings out there and being vulnerable had gotten in the way.

Elderly Korean heads turned from all over the ballroom. Harry commanded a presence. I'd seen even Prince Harry walk into a coffee shop in Silver Lake and everyone ignored him. This was different though. In their eyes, I'd snagged the grandest of all prizes, the coveted eligible Korean bachelor.

Harry, broad-shouldered in perfectly fitted formalwear, walked toward my mom and me with a winning smile on his face. I thought having him here would quell any gossip about the lone, unmarried thirty-something-year-old daughter in the room, but all it did was fan the flames.

Whispering. Unsubtle pointing. Photo taking. These geriatric Koreans were relentless. Worse than the Blindr gossip app.

Hopefully Harry knew that in a crowd of Korean gossipmongers, it was good to keep some physical distance between us. When he approached me, he looked like he was coming in for a hug. Closer . . . closer. I flinched and took a step back. I signaled to him "Whoaaa there, okay, that's good!"

He took the hint and shoved his hands into his pockets. "Mrs. Chae, what a wonderful birthday event. So happy to be a part of this big celebration." Harry then extended his hand, which my mom cautiously shook while eyeing him with suspicion.

"Thank you for coming." She looked at me, then at him. "Who are you?"

My mom's bluntness caught me off guard. I let out a nervous laugh and explained, "This is Harry Shim, from my high school. He lives in LA now and he's . . ." I swallowed hard as I tried to muster the right words. "He's my plus-one."

Her face shifted from wide-eyed bewilderment to narrow-eyed suspicion. "I see." Her gaze moved to his left hand. She was no doubt looking for a wedding ring and had no concerns of being subtle about it. But there was no ring, or even a ring tan line.

"You have job? What about any kid?" Mom demanded.

"M-m-me?" Harry stammered, and I'd never seen him so flustered. He was a heavy-hitting VC guy. In high school he'd won all the debate awards and had given tons of school-wide speeches. But he could barely hold it together during my mom's interrogation. "I-I've been working in Silicon Valley for a number of years, but I'm now opening up an office in Silicon Beach, near Playa Vista." His voice cracked as he continued. "No children. At least none known to me." As soon as he said it, he groaned and so did I. "That was a terrible joke. Definitely *no* kids. But I love kids. Don't think I hate kids, because I don't."

To my surprise, my mom cracked up at his agitated state. "You're funny and nervous. No one else tell good joke but Sara Appa." She looked over at Dad, who was walking around the room, mingling with guests. Appa was charming, that was for sure. And so was Harry. And I could see from how my mom relaxed her shoulders while offering a hint of a smile that she thought so too.

"I go help Appa get something to eat. Nice to meet you." She scampered away, and Harry sighed in relief when she was out of earshot.

He pulled a tissue from his pocket and dabbed his forehead. "That was more intense than any savage business meeting I've attended, and I've been involved in a few hostile takeovers. How'd I do?"

I leaned into his biceps and gently nudged him with my elbow.

Even doing something as simple as that sent a wave of tingles down my arm. "You did great."

"Hey, you two fake lovebirds." Jia wedged herself between us and laughed. Her slight stumble suggested she'd already had one drink too many.

"Harry, this is my little sister, Jia."

"Nice to meet you," he said, reaching out his hand.

She didn't return the handshake, and instead wagged her finger in his face. "I drank a bunch to get the courage to say one thing. You better not break her heart." Jia waved her hand above her head like she was practicing lassoing. "Even if your relationship is a ruse." Then she shoved her index finger into his chest. "Trust me, you don't want to be on my bad side."

His dark brown eyes danced. "I definitely do *not* want that. And you don't need to worry about me. I have no intention of hurting Sara."

Fiery heat flushed my face. It was good to know that Jia had my back, but this came at the cost of my dignity. With much restraint, I chose to not make it a big deal since the night needed to be drama-free, for everyone's sake. I replied so only Jia could hear, "Thanks for looking out for me, Sis."

As the night wore on, shyness wore off of everyone at the party: ahjummas and ahjusshis danced and sang along to the music, pulling me aside to ask me if I was married yet or planned to have kids. Some people recognized Harry from when he lived in the same neighborhood: his striking face was memorable, as was his reputation. The conversations quickly turned from being focused solely on me to talking only about him.

"He graduated top of class of Stanford business school and I hear he make good money now!"

"I heard he has a Lotus car. That's nicer than Tesla. Lotus is like Air Force One, Tesla is like propeller plane."

"Sara! If he stops dating you, can you tell him I have a daughter who is younger than you who needs boyfriend?"

I reconvened with Harry at the buffet line. "Well, the last hour has been pretty brutal. How're you holding up?"

He laughed as he filled his plate with kalbi and pajeon pancakes. "Okay, I guess. Are you getting unsolicited marriage proposals on behalf of people you've never met too? Apparently someone has twin nieces living in Chicago and they both need a husband, and Mrs. Hong said I should call one of them if we ever break up. And if it doesn't work out, I need to call the other one."

"No marriage proposals for me. Mrs. Hong and Mrs. Jo, two of my mom's oldest and nosiest friends, trapped me in the bathroom to interrogate me about my job and marital status. It did not go well. Even when I informed them I'd brought a date to the event, they berated me for not settling down already, saying the next big party they want to go to is my wedding or my baby shower." I sighed. "I think unsolicited offers of marriage only happen to wealthy un-married Korean men, the unicorns of our community. Unmarried Korean women in their thirties are pretty much the opposite of that. We're like the unicorn's droppings. The human equivalent of a uni-corn's toilet."

He shrugged. "Some toilets in Korea are fancy though. They have buttons that warm you, and spray water, plus play music!"

"Hey, I can do all those things!" I said cheerily.

"And I'm sure you're amazing at them too," he said, laughing.

We walked to our table with full plates, and while we enjoyed the Korean food, the DJ announced that my dad, the guest of honor, would be saying a few words.

He handed the mic over to my appa, who had a small pocket-size spiral notebook in his hand, the kind you see news journalists and TV reporters use in movies. Dad cleared his throat and said in Korean and English, "Thank you all for coming tonight. I appreciate." The crowd clapped politely and quieted down so he could have the floor.

He said, "Thank you everybody," then paused. Everyone clapped again, more vigorously this time. Then he handed the mic back to the DJ without saying anything else. Muzak-type music kicked on quickly to fill the silence. The murmuring swelled, as people complained that they had expected more.

Harry leaned over and said in a loud whisper, "At my parents' hwangap, I had to bow. Made a big show out of my mom and dad reaching this milestone."

Jia, sitting on my other side, pulled out her phone. "Shit. He's right. We're supposed to bow to the floor in front of Umma and Appa to show respect."

I asked, "Isn't that supposed to be a little kid thing? Even people our ages need to bow?" Jia and I had wanted this celebration to be more progressive and conventional, like a big birthday bash with decorations, presents, and gift bags. Less ceremonial and more fun for everyone. But something was missing, a speech, or dance, or presentation. Unfortunately, Dad hadn't delivered any of those.

Jia took a swig of wine and continued scrolling. "If we want to go old school, it's in birth order, from the oldest to the youngest, so you'd be first. Four bows." She looked down at her lap. "My dress is not forgiving, there's no way I can crouch on the ground and not flash this geriatric crowd." She muttered after pulling down her dress hem, "Yeah, this isn't going to happen. I'm wearing a standing dress, which is not designed for being down on all fours. I can barely sit in it, it's so stiff."

"Please excuse me." Harry abruptly stood up and ran out of the ballroom without any sort of explanation. Jia looked at his empty seat and shrugged. "Well, that seemed like an emergency. Maybe it was the cheese station that Dad requested. We should have had Lactaid pills available. Or a Pepcid AC dispenser to help with Asian flush so fewer people turned bright red while drinking wine."

Did Jia and I really have to bow and speak in front of everyone? Blood pounded as it rushed to my head, making it harder to think with the pulsing and thumping in my temples. Adrenaline kicked in too, causing my breathing to quicken.

My date charged back into the room just as quickly as he'd left. But this time he was carrying large items of clothing draped on each of his arms.

He panted and said, "I tipped the coat check guy to let me borrow two coats from the wedding next door. They should be longer in length than your dresses. I tried them on to make sure of that."

The first coat he held up was a charcoal gray trench with fur trim. I grabbed that one from his hands before Jia could. It was a little big and had shoulder pads, but it would do.

That left my sister with the other one. Harry peeled it off his left forearm and shook it out with his right hand. Navy blue cashmere blend, and up close you could see it was accented with ebony zebra stripes. The interior was lined in white and black zebra-striped silk. "Fuck me." Jia moaned as she took it from him. "And thank you."

Harry was resourceful, I had to hand that to him. I opened my mouth to offer thanks, but before I could form the words, he placed his arm around my shoulder, then leaned in to say, "You should get up there before everyone finishes eating. If it's anything like my parents' party, people come for the free food and then ditch the rest of it."

Ignoring the rush of electricity flowing from his touch, I nodded and approached the stage. The DJ saw me coming and prepared the mic, doing a quick sound check and a couple of "testing testing one two three"s.

I took the mic with my right hand and flapped my left one toward me, gesturing for Jia to join me up front. She put on her coat and came forward while I welcomed everyone, just as my dad had done a few minutes before.

"We want to wish Appa a happy birthday! Saeng-shin chook-ha-deu-ryeo-yo!"

"Saeng-shin chook-ha-deu-ryeo-yo!" Jia echoed into the mic.

I looked at the DJ and asked him to play "Happy Birthday," which he already had cued because it played immediately. Lifting our hands like philharmonic conductors, Jia and I instructed the audience to sing along. The room swelled with music and laughter.

I whispered to Jia, "Okay, I'm bowing now, but if I can't get up, you have to help me."

She laughed. "Same."

Handing back the mic, Jia and I approached our parents, and taking turns, we bowed four times. On the fourth child's pose–like bend, a seam ripped on my new dress . . . exactly in the worst place imaginable.

The audience erupted in applause, covering up the sound of the continuous ripping of stitches from the seat of my dress as I struggled to transition from being on my knees to an upright position. Jia pulled me up with a powerful yank and checked my ass. "Okay, that tore your seam, but it wasn't the coat. I could have sworn that would be me, thank God it wasn't," she joked.

I mouthed "thank you" to Harry. He grinned and pointed to his phone.

My phone buzzed. I pulled it from the coat. That dress was no good anyway. No pockets.

I laughed and nodded at him.

"Thank goodness Harry was here. I like him a lot, and I hope things work out the way you want," Jia confessed.

My date wore a lopsided grin while clapping for me, and my parents had giant smiles on their faces as they applauded too.

Yes, thank goodness for Harry. I needed him tonight, and he delivered.

Chapter Fourteen

Are you sitting down? I have good news and bad news." My mentor, Stan McGuinness, Harry's boss, called me at 6:30 A.M. with an update the morning after the big birthday bash. I figured it had to be important to call me so early. Now that we'd entered the third month of the mentorship, the top three finalists for both the mentor program and pitch competition were being announced soon. But even if I made it to the finals of the mentorship program, where I would have had a shot at a large sum of money, why would he have good AND bad news?

Stan said, "I'll start with the bad news first. You weren't one of the top three finalists for the Pitch Warriors mentorship program; you came in fourth. The other three mentees were farther along and sadly, that helped give them an edge when it came to looking at business plans and market readiness."

I swallowed hard and closed my eyes, trying to stabilize my vocal cords. I needed to thank him for the mentorship, and I couldn't bear to do that with a shaky voice.

He continued. "Now for the good news. The founder of Deliverobot came down with chickenpox."

I managed to speak. "I-I'm sorry to hear that. And how is that good news, just so I'm clear?" I didn't know what else to say, Deliverobot sounded familiar, but what did it have to do with me?

He chuckled. "Oh, yes. I should have clarified. Damon Manning, who created Deliverobot, was chosen as one of the finalists for the pitch competition. When we notified him yesterday morning that he was the winner of the prize money, he was ecstatic but informed us he would not be able to participate on *The Bullpen* due to his illness. Apparently he's covered in papules, vesicles, and scabbed lesions, and although he's recovering, he won't be camera-ready for quite a while. All of this is to say that there's a last-minute opening on *The Bullpen*. None of the other remaining candidates who were selected for the pitch competition are as prepared and polished as you, and the producers weren't thrilled with the products and services of the Pitch Warriors semifinalists. They said, in their words not mine, that your app was the *sexiest* option for camera, and asked that we make an exception by letting a mentee into the Pitch Competition finals. I was wondering if you'd be interested in participating in pitching One Last Word on the show's livestream in two weeks. Of course, it's short notice, but Harry has been singing your praises and he thinks you're not only ready, but also that you have a good shot at getting funding because of your pitch."

"Yes!" I screamed, my vocal cords fully functional again. "I'm in!" Maybe I was a little too enthusiastic with my reply, considering it wasn't even seven A.M. A neighbor's dog barked in response through the wall.

Sorry, Fido.

My heart soared. "I really want to do this, it really is a dream come true. Thank you for considering me."

"Love the enthusiasm, let's use that energy for the competition! But maybe with less screaming." He chuckled again. "You'll need to submit some of your latest financial projections, plus a few slides that summarize your business that our judges can read ahead of time. ASAP. And of course, you'll need a camera-ready, succinct pitch for *The Bullpen*."

Holy. Shit. I would be broadcast live in a couple of weeks. And there would be a total of a million viewers of the show across the globe. My stomach churned thinking about all of this. Was it too unoriginal to use the chickenpox excuse if I chickened out, pun intended? How would I even prepare for all of this on such short notice?

But . . . I *had* to do this. I needed to be fierce. Determined. Strong. Channel the same strength I'd put into squeezing out the last bit of toothpaste from Jia's Colgate tube.

Stan added, "You'll need to do a thirty-second promo video, basically like a short commercial. Do you think you could do that by tomorrow end of day? It's not mandatory to have a promo piece but it will really help you stand out and they can use it to promote your upcoming episode so the other contestants won't have an advantage over you. Isn't this all so exciting?"

So exciting. I gulped. "I . . . I can do it. No problemo. I'll figure out a way."

"If you need any lighting or editing software, we could lend you one of our interns or someone on our creative services team. It's a tight turnaround, but we can help with the technical parts."

The technical aspect was easy. It was the actual presentation I was worried about: the enthusiasm, camera-readiness, and creativity were the challenging parts. There was also the lack of "it factor," but that wasn't something that could be fixed in a day. Or at all. But I sure as hell would try my best.

"Well, it's done. I just submitted you to the show as Deliverobot's replacement. It's official now," Stan announced. "Remember, if you need bodies to help you, I have a couple I can spare this week. I think Harry's tied up in a deal, so it might be someone else."

I gulped. The idea of moving forward in the competition without Harry left me with a sense of dread. Regardless, I offered false cheeriness in my voice with my reply. "That sounds great. Thank you."

We hung up and I turned on the overhead light. Staring at my reflection in Jia's closet-door mirror, all I could see was matted bird's-nest hair, lackluster skin, and eyebags with shadows that gave me a smoky under-eye look. How was I supposed to transform all of that into an on-air personality? If I couldn't look good naturally or with makeup, hopefully with Jia's wardrobe assistance and with Casey as my trusted stylist, I could figure out a workaround solution. Because I would need to work around this hot mess from the neck up and the shoulders down.

Just then, I was at my physical all-time low, my calendar notification buzzed, a reminder that I needed to be at the gym in half an hour. I'd promised Casey I'd go and he wouldn't let me flake out.

A flurry of text messages came through.

Almost time to swing!

And squat!

Can I call you Kettle-Belle?

I replied, What if I kettle-bomb?

I won't let you! I swear. See you soon!

Casey, being a man of his word, wouldn't let me down. Putting on a clean high-impact sports bra, gym-appropriate clothes, and the only sneakers I owned—my black Chuck Taylor high-tops—I dressed like a middle school kid going to gym class.

But I intended to keep my promise. It was time to go to kettle-hell.

* * *

Eight kilograms was the lightest kettlebell at the gym. Eighteen goddamn pounds. The weight of two large newborn babies.

"You want me to do a two-handed swing?" I cried.

"*Swings.* Plural. Watch me." The kettlebell swung like a pendulum between his legs, making Casey look like one of those Viking ship rides at an amusement park. He huffed and blew out his cheeks as he completed multiple reps. "Your turn."

"Am I supposed to be barefoot too?" He'd taken off his shoes before his demonstration.

"Chucks are fine. They're flat, which is perfect for this. I forgot to wear my Vans, which also work well."

I completed five swings. Instead of huffing and puffing like he had, I groaned. Loudly.

He offered consolation. "Squats are next and then you're done. I'm letting you off easy."

As he showed me how to maneuver, I asked, "Why did you ever get into kettlebells?" I looked around at other people who were also swinging and squatting. Lots of lean bodies with muscle definition.

"Strength development. Endurance. During the pandemic I bought a set of kettlebells to use at home because the gym was closed. I felt bad for the delivery guy." He blew out his cheeks. "There's a group kettlebell class here that's really popular. The instructor is a former Navy SEAL."

I squatted. *Only nine more to go.*

"There are a lot of single guys in the class." He waggled his eyebrows.

Eight. Seven. Six more to go.

Casey continued. "I can ask around if you want. A bunch of them go to happy hour at the pub across the street."

"No thanks," I wheezed. "Maybe after the show." *Five. Four.*

"Suit yourself. Just know the kettlebell world is your oyster."

I giggled mid-squat and almost lost my balance.

"That was my fault. I should let you focus. After you're done here, we'll do a cool-down walk on the treadmill."

Three.

Two.

One.

Done.

Plunking the kettlebell on the floor, I lifted my arms above my head in triumph.

"How do you feel?" he asked.

A grin spread across my face. "Relieved. Proud. Like I can do anything."

He agreed. "You're unstoppable, Sara. Promise me you won't limit yourself."

I gave him a sweaty hug. "Thank you for pushing me, Case. And yes, I promise."

Chapter Fifteen

I fluffed my hair and tipped my chin. Taking in a deep breath and slowly exhaling, I tapped the record button.

Take number seventeen.

"My name is Sara Chae and I can't wait to tell you about my new service available for download today, One Last Word."

The teleprompter app Casey had added to my phone was scrolling words too fast; it was hard to catch up. "One Last Word . . . is-a-groundbreaking-new-technology-that-gives-you-the-ability-to-have-the-last-word. A-mic-drop. A-final-farewell. Here's-how-it-works—"

"Cut!" Casey cried out. "Please, for the love of God. Cut!"

I ended the recording and sighed. "The speed is set too fast, and picking up the pace made me sound like Alvin of the beloved Chipmunks."

Jia came out of her bedroom. "Sis, I can hear panic in your voice from the other room. You need to chill out, or you'll sound weird and desperate on camera."

"I am weird. And desperate. I need funding. And I look like an ass making this video."

Casey straightened my blazer. The blouse neckline had gone askew too, and he fixed that as well. "You do *not* look like an ass.

I know this for a fact because of the filter plug-in I put on your phone. You look glamorous with a healthy glow and even complexion."

That part was true. I did look good. A tiny bit too airbrushed for my personal liking, but that was okay given I needed to look professional. The VC world was notorious for being more critical of women, both intellectually and physically judgmental. I couldn't leave myself open to scrutiny, which was why I needed to nail this soon so I could focus on preparing everything else for the show. "You didn't have a lot to work with, Case. I appreciate you making me look polished."

"Hot, Sara. You look hot. In a non-slutty, boardroom baddie way."

I coughed. "Please never say boardroom baddie ever again, especially while describing me."

Casey touched up my makeup one last time before he had to run to the gym. "You're having a great hair day too, very sexy," he said, ignoring my comment.

Jia nodded. "What's got you rattled? Why are you messing up?"

I showed her the script. "I memorized this but I can't do it. And the words are just not coming out of my mouth fast enough."

She took a pen and marked up the page. "You have a few clunky sentences and a bunch of trippy tongue twisters. Like this monstrosity: 'When One Last Word rolled out recently.' I fixed it."

I read my new lines and didn't stumble a single time. "You're brilliant, sis." I updated the teleprompter script with her changes.

She curtsied. "And now that it's fixed, I know you'll nail the recording in one go."

Jia was wrong. It took two. But the second one was flawless. A ten out of ten, no notes.

An hour later, the door buzzer blasted a few times in a row. Probably an aggressive delivery person, I thought to myself.

Half undressed, I kept my blazer and blouse on and threw on pajama pants. "Coming!" I yelled.

I flung open the door to find my parents standing in the hallway holding two bankers boxes. My dad was also carrying two clear shopping bags full of Korean apple pears, one on each arm, just below the elbow.

Their jaws, and mine, hung open as we stared at one another. For once, my mom and dad were speechless.

Jia came up behind me. "Umma? Appa? Why are you here?"

Mom thrust her box forward. "This is yours. Appa has other one for Sara, we hoping you could give to her. She told us not to bother because of work. We are cleaning and throwing out for moving and this is all for you. High school award, some toys, and photo albums. And more junk." She looked at me. "I keep all of your report card, even ones with Bs." She shot a glance at Jia. "You take dance class but never win real prize, so I throw away all participation medal and ribbon."

They both pushed past us and set down the boxes and fruit in Jia's hallway. "Why you have all the lights?" my dad asked, pointing to the video setup in the living room.

"I had to record a promotional ad for work." I ran over to Jia's bedroom to shut the door.

Umma narrowed her eyes. "Why you do that . . . too messy in there? You girls always messy. Maybe you hide something."

Dad suggested, "Or you hide a boyfriend?"

Before Jia and I could properly block them, my mom made a break for it. Wiggling the bedroom door handle, she went inside.

She screamed, "Aigoooo!"

Dad joined her and chimed in with a howl. "Aigoo! You going to give us heart attack!"

They were standing inside Jia's closet. Aka my bedroom. It was hard to miss that I'd been sleeping there.

"Who is living here?" My mom folded her arms. "Jia, are you hiding boy?"

"Technically, it would be a man, if that were true. I'm not a child abductor." Jia's sarcastic comment went over my parents' heads. She cringed when it became clear it was not a situation she could joke out of.

"Who you hiding?" demanded Dad.

Jia shot me a look. She was sinking and I needed to throw her a life-saving device. This was not her fight. It was 100 percent mine.

"It's me," I blurted. "I'm living here until I can get my company funded."

"You?" my dad asked. "I thought you stay over with her only few days."

Then Mom. "Thirty-four-year-old sleeping here? You . . . live here? In Jia closet?"

"Yes," I admitted while bracing myself for more questions.

"But . . . this is a closet," my dad observed. "It big, but this not . . . big enough for somebody like you."

There were a lot of ways to interpret his statement, but I chose to go with the version where he was a concerned parent and worried about the square footage of livable space and lack of a window.

"This walk-in is pretty quiet and spacious." I pushed some of Jia's winter coats aside. "I might put in a small fridge. Add some plants and a rug to make it more homey."

A heavy sigh came out of my mom's mouth, signaling that a string of critiques would soon follow. *You're getting old. You need more stability. Maybe you should have stayed in your old job. Are you getting married anytime soon? What about grandchildren?*

I knew how this was going to go, I'd heard it hundreds of times. Preempting it all, I said, "I think it might be time for you to go."

Jia nodded. "Thanks for stopping by, but I was on my way out. I can walk you to your car. Definitely call next time and we can plan lunch or dinner."

If they lived far away I would feel terrible, but they were in Santa Ana, and we were in Venice. An hour drive. Still, a pang of guilt flooded my body that they'd come all this way to drop off our things. When the competition was over and I had a good grasp of what I needed to get my business off the ground, I would find time to hang out with them. By then, I'd be more sure-footed financially. Hopefully.

"When are you moving?" I asked.

Dad said, "We moving to condo in Fullerton soon. But we need to sell our house. That's why we bring junk box."

Jia looked at me and laughed. "Sara's box is trash. Mine is all treasure."

A snort blasted from Umma's nose. "Sara have no place to put her box, she doesn't own condo or have a good place to stay—"

Jia walked to the front door and unlocked it. "I *asked* Sara to stay here, she's been a wonderful roommate. She's just trying to save money. Surely you both understand that." Pulling the door open, she said, "I'll walk out with you, Sara needs to stay here, she's still working."

As my parents shuffled toward the exit, my mom directed one last thing to me. "Try to save more money so you move out faster."

I locked the door behind them and rested my head on the wood. I'd thought my biggest regret was sending the last word message to Harry, but having my parents reinserting themselves into my adult life stressed me out even more. They'd always been tough on me, and their meddling now seemed as bad as it was when I was younger and living under their roof. This accidental message sending was turning out to be one of the worst things to happen to me in my thirties.

Just as I thought, *What else could go wrong?* a notification buzzed on my phone, alerting me there was a new message in the One Last Word app. It wasn't from Casey or Harry.

It was Naomi.

"Let's talk. —N"

I reread those two words (plus initial) over and over, trying to gather insight and meaning from them. I texted Jia and Casey, asking them to weigh in.

Maybe she wants to reconcile after you ran past her like Sonic the Hedgehog at the gala, Jia offered.

She hates you and wants you to know why, Casey suggested.

My gut twisted into knots as my mind filled with the last moments I'd hung out with her a decade ago. Memories of countless concerts, parties, and brunch meet-ups scrolled through my head. The weight of sadness was like having sandbags on my chest when I remembered waiting out in the cold because I'd shown up past the agreed-upon meeting time and was stuck outside the venue, unable to get into a sold-out show. There were memories of standing in the very back of her performances because I didn't get there early enough to get a seat. I hadn't taken enough time to critically examine my fallout with Naomi. Was it all these things adding up, or one big grievance, that ended our friendship?

Honestly, I didn't know.

Jia came back into the apartment with a stack of mail. She spoke softly. "Hey, I think this is a good thing. Your app was conceived so you could give people the opportunity of some kind of closure, right? To validate hurt and anger, so they can let those feelings, and those people, go?"

"It's funny, sending out those messages by mistake let me express my regrets and also opened up the possibility of repairing our friendship. Maybe this is what needs to happen. To meet with Naomi and hash it all out."

I let out a heavy sigh and pulled out my phone to set up a time and place to meet. To get our much needed closure.

* * *

The corners of my bankers box were crushed, and the cover didn't fit snugly: it was lopsided and rested askew, like someone wearing an ill-fitting hat a size too small. Umma and Appa were thrifty, so it didn't surprise me at all to find the word "Hymns" scribbled on one of the sides. They'd clearly gotten this carton from their church. Hopefully it had been offered to them, and they hadn't rummaged through the storage closet and dumped out hymnals. It seemed wrong to steal hymn boxes from a church, yet I could also see my parents doing it without a second thought.

The box was lighter than I expected. Lifting the top, I uncovered keepsakes that had been preserved for close to two decades. Treasures from high school that had no monetary value, but were priceless to me. Unfinished friendship bracelets intricately woven by hand with embroidery thread that I'd made for Naomi, and ones she'd given me too. Birthday cards, both store-bought and handmade. There were lots of photos too, from my awkward braces years and my awkward nonbraces years. Flipping through the pictures, there was a clear takeaway from my childhood: aside from looking tired in every shot, probably from so much studying and cramming, I'd loved being part of my friend group. Many of my buddies back then were extroverts and socially inclined. Looking back, I was lucky to have even been invited to parties and events. Naomi was one of the integral members of the little community I'd been a part of, and I was on the periphery. She was in the hub, and I was a spoke. It never occurred to me then that I needed her more than she needed me. Even though I was a fringe member of our friend group, Naomi had never made me feel second best. It wasn't in her nature.

A few trinkets had fallen to the bottom of the box. Happy Meal toys from McDonald's mostly, souvenirs from concerts and fairs, and some dumb things I'd won at the school carnival.

There were stacks of handwritten notes too. And thumbnail sketches. Some silly cartoons drawn by Naomi and other friends I'd lost touch with over the years. A surprising number of them were authored and illustrated by Harry. These were the exchanges I'd saved because they were what made me fall in love with him in the first place. At the time, I thought his words and jokes were so special, with his quirky humor, puns, and clever turns of phrases. Reading them now, they weren't as magical as I'd recollected. Yes, he was clever, cute, and charming, but he'd used jokes from comedians he admired. Many of the funny drawings were like modern-day memes and clearly things he'd copied from the internet. His words to me were not actually very personalized. One might even argue that he could have sent these same words and pictures to anyone.

Was Harry not as perfect as I thought? And was our closeness back then not as meaningful as I'd recalled? And if that was true, what other parts of our history were exaggerated or misremembered?

A tattered, timeworn letter was the very last thing I pulled out of the box. It was a thank-you note from Naomi, for letting her stay over a few nights in a row when her parents were fighting. She'd drawn little stick figures of my family: my parents, little Jia, our kitty named Kat (RIP), and me. She added a stick person with her name written beneath it. She'd stayed over at our house all the time our senior year, and my parents used to set out an extra place setting for dinner hoping Naomi would join us.

I smiled to myself. She'd been like a second sister, and for my parents, a third daughter. Tears welled in my eyes as I read all about how her mom and dad had agreed to a divorce, and how she'd decided to stay with her mom because she wanted to stay at the same school and live close to us. Because we were just as much her family as her own.

I set the letter down on my bed and let tears fall. We had been through so much together and I couldn't believe we weren't on speaking terms. Naomi and I had a relationship worth saving. Was it still possible? We had drifted, but maybe there was a way to pull us back together.

I had to try.

Chapter Sixteen

One of the best things about being pals with Casey was that he and I had compatible and complementary tastes in food. He loved eating pizza but hated the crust, which I enjoyed more than the saucy and cheesy parts. He liked the filling in a croissant or danish and let me eat the bready end sections. He also hated sugar and cake cones, abhorred pie crusts, and picked out the rye crisps in Chex Mix and happily offered them to me. He jokingly called me his food compost companion. In all ways platonic, we were meant for each other.

So when he knocked on Jia's apartment door with a flyer from the café across the street advertising two-for-one breakfast pastries, I immediately threw on my coat, grabbed my backpack, and followed him outside. The timing worked well—the landlord's security deposit and rent return had just hit my bank account. "We also have to work, but first we stuff our faces," he clarified as we jaywalked to the other side.

Casey caught me up on office gossip while we waited in line. Tyler and Anne, friends from work, were hooking up (which we all saw coming), one of my former managers who never did any work had been recruited to a start-up with bigger pay and a better title (yeah, good luck to that company), and my position had recently been filled by *two* people. A few employees had been laid off due to sluggish company quarterly performance. Most of them were recent hires.

It was nice to chat with Casey. Socializing and commiserating were some of the things I missed about my previous job. Eating lunch with coworkers and taking coffee breaks were the highlights of working in an office setting, and splitting my time between Jia's apartment and the coworking space didn't offer me any camaraderie. Jia often went to work during the day, Casey mostly helped me on nights and weekends, and the coworking space patrons had no interest in social interactions. For the most part, I was alone. The closest I had to a coworker was Harry. And my surprisingly thriving succulent plant.

But there were things I didn't miss about my last office. Booking meetings when everyone's schedules were full. Sitting in stuffy, unventilated conference rooms. Commuting. Poor thermostat control. Fluorescent lighting. There was much to be said about working from home in comparison.

And, of course, the worst of it all was having my ideas shut down and dismissed by upper management, simply because I'd been pigeonholed as a day-to-day operations person and had plateaued in middle-management purgatory.

Casey stroked his beard as he chose his pastry and coffee. After I ordered, he tapped his card on the payment screen. "You have to give me a bite of your cookie. I swore off circular sweets but I can't deny myself those chocolate pecan sandies!"

Before I could ask him about why he was no longer consuming round desserts, someone in line said, "Hey Sara."

It was Harry, wearing a fitted T-shirt and joggers, pulling off a low-maintenance "gym chic" look.

Casey tapped down his sunglasses.

I elbowed him and whispered, "Shit, it's Harry. Play it cool." Casey stood straighter and cleared his throat.

I panicked and threw him a *don't you dare say anything else* glare.

"Hi, Harry," I said.

The barista called out "Sara? Large iced Americano! And one London Fog latte, nonfat, with extra whip!"

In one swoop, Casey grabbed our drinks and ran over to the milk and sugar station without saying a word, leaving Harry and me at the counter together.

Harry ordered a plain drip coffee. After paying, he said to me, "I heard from Stan that you'll be on the show soon! Congrats! I can grab us a table if you're sticking around."

His coffee came quickly and he waited for a table near the window to clear out, hovering, or rather, stalking. Casey frantically waved his hands from the corner of the room, motioning me to come over.

He hissed, "He's so handsome I got all flustered and didn't say anything. I was *not* expecting Harry to be this *hot*! See, I'm accidentally rhyming. That means I'm super-nervous! But don't worry, I'm ready to play boyfriend."

Boyfriend? "Wait . . . Casey!"

He shoved my iced drink into my hand along with a wad of napkins and then marched over to Harry, who had finally claimed a table. I trailed a few steps behind.

"So you're Harry. Nice to meet you." Casey held out his hand, which Harry grabbed and shook with a firm grip. Casey used handshakes as litmus tests. He'd spent countless happy hours going on and on about how it was like a personality assessment. Fullness of grip, temperature, moisture level, strength, duration, vigor, and quality of eye contact were the characteristics he used to determine if someone was worth his time. As soon as Harry let his hand go,

Casey pursed his lips and raised an eyebrow at me. It was Casey's not-so-subtle way to signal *please go hump this man.*

Harry exclaimed, "Likewise. Any friend of Sara is a friend of mine."

I couldn't help but notice he said that last part with sincerity in his eyes and brightness in his tone. Like he really did trust my judgment.

Casey cleared his throat. "Uh. Thanks." He tugged his jacket closed and snapped the buttons of his stylish varsity outerwear.

I tried to find ways to change the subject as Casey offered Harry short answers to all his questions. But then Harry shifted to a new topic of conversation. For the worse.

"So you're Sara's boyfriend? I didn't catch your name. And I'm sure you heard I borrowed Sara on the night of the gala at the museum. My ex was there and it really helped having Sara around that night to support me."

Casey laughed nervously. "I'm Casey. And it was no big deal, you can have her anytime."

I kicked him under the table.

Casey coughed into his London Fog latte. "For any future galas, that's what I mean."

Harry looked down at his cup, took a sip, then lifted his gaze. "How long have you two been together?"

"Three months," I blurted.

"Six months," Casey offered at the same time, glancing at me. He gave me a mischievous, sly smile while I glared at him. "Well, she only counts three months, but a true romantic would think all of our little get-togethers as being meaningful."

Harry gave a restrained smile. "That's sweet."

Casey grinned. "I added in the additional months we were having bed relations."

Choking on my coffee, I was at a loss for words. Casey had taken the fake relationship to a weird, sexual place and he was going rogue. Most likely to teach me a lesson. And Casey wasn't the type who could be reeled in easily. Judging by his naughty grin, it was clear he was enjoying this improv and was testing his boundaries with me.

"Okaaay, Casey . . . that's enough," I said through gritted teeth. I looked at Harry. "I'm sorry, I—I have a lot to explain."

Casey's upper lip tugged upward even more. "You know better than anyone that anytime there's an opening for a dirty joke, I take it. Every time. So shame on you for leaving me vulnerable. And I said BED RELATIONS to keep it classy. Nothing kinky or taboo, which you *know* I'm capable of doing. You're welcome."

He popped the lid off his tea and took a long sip, savoring the whipped topping. After helping himself to a piece of my cookie, his gaze ping-ponged between Harry and me. Neither of us said a word.

He tried to secure the top back on his cup, but some of his tea spilled onto the table and spattered on the cuff of his jacket.

"Shit. This is dry-clean only and the stain could set. It's only my second time wearing it. That's what happens when someone spills the tea, I suppose." Casey looked at me and pouted. "Can I connect with you later about work? Tonight? I need to buy stain remover."

I nodded. His new jacket was his latest prized item, and he'd spent months searching for it. It meant a lot to him and he needed to get the stain out, stat. Plus, it was better for me to keep him far away from Harry. Who knew what he'd say next.

Casey pushed in his chair. "It really was nice to finally meet you!"

Leaving his nearly empty drink on the table, Casey walked out of the café waving his cell phone in the air. His way of telling me to call him later.

It was time to come clean before Harry could ask more questions. The next time Casey saw Harry he might say something much more salacious than his snarky quip about our fictitious "bed relations."

Time to end this charade once and for all. "So he and I are obviously not a couple," I admitted. "I'm sorry I wasn't being honest with you. I pretended I was dating someone because it was easier than explaining why I'm perpetually single. There are no bed relations, despite the impression Casey tried to give you of me being a total sextrovert."

Harry raised an eyebrow and nodded slowly. Then his head stopped bobbing. "I'm not sure I—you made up the whole thing?"

My face heated as words lodged inside my throat, not wanting to come out. "Yes. And it's weird I carried on the ruse as long as I did. I really am sorry."

The blank look on Harry's face suggested he needed time to process this information. His long pause made my skin itch.

I explained, "I asked him a while back to play the role of boyfriend if I needed him to, and he thought the day had finally come and rose to the challenge. We go way back . . . I met Casey at work because HR launched their Diversity, Equality, Inclusion committee and I was asked to be the rep for women of color, and Casey was head of the LGBTQ-plus group. We ended up working together after a reorg, so we went from committee acquaintances to teammates to best friends. There were times when I thought my ideas and vision for the app would exceed his abilities, but he's proved me wrong every time. There really is no better coder than Casey. So if anyone is my work husband, it's him." I lowered my head, letting my hair tumble forward, partially hiding my shame. "I guess it was easier than admitting I wasn't dating anyone and had no discernible social life. I was embarrassed then, but am even more so now."

Harry's eyes were unblinking, and he sat completely still.

I blurted, "It's hard for me to let people in and be honest about my feelings. I did it to guard myself. To protect my heart, like I've done my whole life."

He moved Casey's drink aside so he could reach for my hand. "There's nothing to be ashamed of." Harry's voice dropped low, and a ripple of electricity roared through me. His stare was so intense that I was worried he could see all my inner thoughts.

If he could, he would know his closeness, his deep gaze, his face . . . it was all a complete turn-on. Throughout my teenage years, I'd spent countless hours lying in bed, thinking about what it would be like if he and I could ever be more than friends. Even when I'd pictured him all grown up, I couldn't have imagined that he would look even better than my daydream version of him. His gorgeous, soulful dark eyes. That playful smirk. The thick wavy hair that he always cut fairly short overall but kept longer on top. He'd know how much I loved it when that stubborn lock fell into his eyes, and how he pushed it back, only so it could drop again.

I looked away, my cheeks flushed with searing heat.

Harry scooted his chair forward, moving both hands to rest on top of mine. "I remember that day, when you told me you were spoken for when I was building up the nerve to ask to see you again. It was the first time since I'd split with Claudia that both my heart and head told me I'd found someone special." He sighed. "It was like you'd knocked the wind out of me when you'd told me you were already with someone."

I bit my lip. "Really?" Debating whether to be completely honest, I opted for going all in. "I got flustered and didn't want to look like I had nothing in my life other than work. You know I had a crush on you back in high school, right? There's no way you missed that."

I didn't add that it had never actually gone away.

"Really?" He echoed me, smiling wide and leaning in more.

"Yes," I barely whispered. Where did my breath go?

He confessed, "High school was such a hard time for me. I'd been dating Claudia since freshman year. And everyone just assumed we were meant to be together, forever, and there was a lot of pressure to stay a couple. For a long time I believed it too—we looked like a couple, we did couple-y things, and had the same friends. We were homecoming king and queen. Our lives were not only intertwined, they were fused."

He continued. "There was a time we broke up back then, and I don't know if you remember, but it was right before prom. You and I were in PE together and I was about to get slammed in the face by Dylan with the dodgeball—"

I cringed. "And I jumped in the way and took the ball to the stomach."

He laughed. "It was the wildest power move I'd ever seen. Because you caught the ball, remember? And he was the other team's best player! It was the first and only time Dylan had ever been stopped."

I didn't remember that part. I could recall only having the breath knocked out of me, kind of like I was feeling right now. Dizzy. Light-headed. Winded.

"You were, like, half his size and won that game for our underdog team. And I saved face, literally, because he would have mauled me with that ball and for sure given me two black eyes, and somehow you intercepted it like it was no big deal. That day you wowed me, Sara."

"By *wow*, you mean you're into girls who can take cannonballs to the abdomen? Very sexy," I said dryly.

"No. I mean, yes. I mean . . . no." He ran his hand through his hair. "I'd always enjoyed being around you and we hung out a lot, but I don't know—" His face turned beet red as he took a sip of Casey's drink.

I'd never seen him this nervous in my entire life.

He said in a low tone, "I always worried that you only saw the best of me, and I really liked that about you, but I also didn't want to let you down or ruin what we had." He let out a breath. "If Claudia hadn't asked me to prom during lunch in front of all our friends, I wonder if we could have . . . back then . . . I don't know—" His sheepish gaze averted to the floor. "It was hard to see good things right in front of me. I regret a lot of decisions. And lack of decisions. My timing is never great, and even now, things are complicated. With our mentor-mentee relationship, and those Blindr gossipmongers, it's not like we could have gotten involved the last few weeks without it getting messy. But . . . then isn't now."

His eyes lifted and searched mine. With brightness in his voice, he said, "If you're not dating anyone, real or fake, does that mean there's a chance for . . . us to . . . you know—"

My dream romantic scenario was unfolding right before my eyes. Harry, gazing at me, caressing both my hands, asking if we could be more than friends. All while alarm bells rang in my head. He was actively dating (a LOT) and had admitted to not wanting to be saddled with marriage again. Those were huge red flags. How could I get involved with anyone who had no intention of being serious? The guy sitting across from me, the one who sent tingles down my body with a single look, was an unattached, forever bachelor. Logically, I knew all of that, and being this close to him was not a good idea.

But it was Harry Shim. The Harry Shim I'd wanted to date my whole life. Harry Shim who wanted me. And now that the mentorship period with him had ended, the timing was finally right. Getting clarity was more important now than ever. It was time to tell him exactly what I wanted, so that there would be no misunderstandings. "I don't want a fling. I'm looking for something meaningful," I confessed.

"I understand. And . . . I want to try. Would that be okay with you?" His knee pressed against mine under the table, and I turned my palms up so I could stroke his hands with the lightest touch of my thumbs. His eyes sparkled as he leaned forward. "Do we need to ask Casey for his blessing?"

"He's officially dumped. Worst boyfriend ever," I joked.

He said, "We've gone to a gala, your dad's hwangap, and now we're sort of having coffee. What's next?"

"Well . . . if you're a three-date rule kind of guy, I think those count. We could hang out at my place," I offered. "Jia's place, actually."

"I'd love that." He jumped up from his seat with so much energy that the chair almost toppled over. It wobbled back and forth and then fell into place. After bussing our table, he placed his hand on the small of my back as we left the café in a hurry.

* * *

The good news was that Jia had been out of town on a work trip and wasn't scheduled to come back until later that evening. The bad news was that I had taken liberties in being alone in her apartment while she was gone. I wasn't expecting her to return for a while, nor had I anticipated any company coming over. These liberties included and were not limited to: using her couches and coffee table as my temporary filing cabinet, piling her bed with clothes I'd tried on but not put away, and air-drying bras on every available doorknob.

That left only one place for Harry and me to go.

I flicked on the overhead light in the master closet, relieved to find the mattress free of stray underwear, bras, and pajamas.

"Well, it's better than the back seat of a compact car," Harry quipped, peering over my shoulder. "In comparison, this twin air mattress is much more luxurious."

I laughed. "More comfortable than lying on a beach too, I'm guessing. The bed has a memory-foam top, so be prepared for ultimate comfort."

He sat on the mattress and pulled me down to join him. The force sent us toppling backward. His strong hands took hold of my waist and eased me on top of him. My chest pressed onto his, and I released a tiny sigh as his lips met mine. I'd waited so long for this.

Harry pressed slow, tender kisses down my neck. While my mind should have been completely in the present—*Harry Shim is kissing me, holy shit! It's what I've dreamed about for so many years!*—I wondered if he could like me nearly as much as I liked him. Doubt crept into my mind, but Harry pulled me out of my thoughts when he tugged at the loose collar of my shirt and placed soft, warm kisses on my shoulder. Electricity rippled through me and a low moan escaped from the back of my throat.

I pulled his shirt over his head and threw it over my shoulder. As his clothing fell away, he tugged my hips to lock into his, and I could feel his muscles tightening and hardening under me. My hands slid down his chest, gliding to his taut stomach.

Our eyes locked, then his gaze traveled down from my face to my chest. I untied the drawstring of his pants with one hand while his palms slid up my thighs. Finding the top of my elastic waistband, he tugged and pulled. Leggings were not exactly sexy, but at least they made for quicker access. His hands stroked the length of my back, and I felt a surge of excitement between my thighs as his fingers explored my body, slowly and deliberately.

Pausing to kiss him on the lips, I surrendered to him as our bodies moved in rhythm together, sending my world spinning.

Harry abruptly created some distance between us. "Is that someone knocking?"

"I didn't hear any—"

Thud.

Thud, thud, thud.

THUD.

THUD, THUD.

There it was. Someone rapping at the door, to the tune of "Shave and a haircut, two bits."

Only one person I knew knocked that way.

I rolled off of Harry and gave him a quick peck on the cheek. "I'll be right back."

He patted the spot next to him. "I'll be waiting."

Chapter Seventeen

Wrapping myself in a plush hotel bathrobe that Jia had stolen on her last business trip, I peeked through the peephole to confirm my suspicions.

Yes. It was Casey, sans varsity jacket.

He hollered, "Are you ignoring me, Sara? Is it because I said all that stuff in front of your hunka-hunka-burning love Harry? Are you sulking and binging *Single's Inferno* while eating a tray of mochi ice cream again? I'm sorry! But I need to talk to you, it's urgent!"

Flinging open the door, I whispered sharply, "Can you keep it down?" I glanced over my shoulder and stepped outside. "How'd you get into the building without me buzzing you in?"

"I trailed a lady coming in with one of those doodle poodles. Wait, did you and—oh my God. This is huge! And I'm sorry to be here to bring down the mood, but there's a problem. A big one. And you know I'd normally get the fuck out of here if you and Harry are getting down and dirty and ask for details later, but this is actually important."

I took in a breath and exhaled. "Can you tell me what the problem is? As you can see—"

He exhaled and shook out his shoulders. "Okay, remember when you got all drunk with Jia and those messages got sent out?"

I scoffed. "Yes, that day will forever be burned into my memory. And I'd rather not speak of it ever again." I tightened the belt on the robe as I waited for him to finish chatting.

"Well, I had some time to go over the performance logs, reviewing user history and all those relevant metrics. I'm thorough and good at interpreting data, you know that, right?"

I nodded. Casey was one of the few people I'd ever work with or hire without double-checking his work.

He blew out his cheeks. "Those messages weren't sent out by mistake. It was no accident. Yes, our program crawled the obituaries and news that day and came across the other now deceased Sara Chae, may she rest in peace. But it didn't trigger the messages to automatically release. They were being held in a queue and were scheduled to send later by an administrator. You or me."

None of this made sense. The robe didn't have pockets, which meant I didn't have access to my phone to check the app data myself. Casey handed over his device and I clicked around and confirmed everything he'd said.

I checked the sent and unsent mail folders.

I saw nothing notable when I reread the note I sent to my parents, although there was a section at the end I didn't remember writing about treating their children unfairly, favoring one over the other, which Jia had already told me she'd added. The communication to Naomi was similar, it all looked how I remembered it from that night, except with an appended paragraph stating that she had been like a sister to Jia and me.

The original message I'd drafted to Harry was still sitting in the outbox. My sister had admitted that she'd replaced my pathetic, embarrassing confession of my love to Harry with Taylor Swift lyrics.

Jia was the last person to edit all the messages.

And someone, logged in as admin, manually scheduled their release.

Jia?

But why?

Casey said, "There's no one else that day who had access to the app other than you and me. I'm not one to tattle, but given the severity of this, today I have resting snitch face. You need to check with your messy girl Jia and ask her WTF."

I swallowed hard, too stunned to speak.

He asked, "Snitches only get stitches in prison and on TV right? Jia's wild, but she's not, like, dangerous, right?"

Shit. "I'll talk to her and find out what happened," I croaked, my stomach turning sour at the thought of confronting my sister. "I'm sure there's an explanation." For the life of me though, I couldn't think of a logical one. She'd read all my vulnerable words and knew how risky it would be for any of the messages to be exposed. Why would she sabotage me like that?

Casey reached out his hands and fluffed both sides of my hair. "I'm so sorry. But if it helps at all, you are *glowing* right now. I've never seen you look better."

I shrugged, and he offered me a snuggly hug. "You know I'm here for you, right? Jia and you are at a crossroads now and I do think you should hear her out. Not everyone has family who gives a shit about their lives, let alone gets along with them . . . take it from someone who has a wonderful found family for emotional support. Give her a chance to explain herself and dig deep to understand why."

"Thanks, Case. You know I'm here for you too if you need me."

We said our goodbyes and I closed the door gently behind me, pressing my forehead against the cool wooden surface.

"Everything okay?" a deep voice behind me asked. I turned to see Harry fully dressed, hair wild and messy.

The turn of events canceled out my euphoria. One of the best days of my life had just turned into a nightmare. Without wanting to divulge what I'd just learned, I explained to Harry that there was a work emergency that needed my immediate attention, and I would reconnect with him as soon as it blew over. I offered him a long, deep kiss, just to let him know this was a temporary setback, and we would need to pick up exactly where we left off.

Jia was on a plane heading home, and she would land in LAX in a few hours. It gave me time to say bye to Harry without pushing him out the door, and to mentally prepare my questions for my sister. I didn't know what she would say, or how I would react.

She'd been lying this whole time. To my face. She was my little sister, and I loved her. Why had she betrayed me?

Chapter Eighteen

Jia missed her connecting flight that afternoon. When she finally landed, there was astronomical surge pricing with all the rideshare companies at her new arrival time, so she opted to wait another extra hour at LAX airport for the fare to come down. Every second of postponement made me dread our confrontation even more, especially knowing that I'd be talking to her after a rough day of travel.

Casey texted me a few seconds before Jia's car arrived. If she kicks you out, or you voluntarily leave, you can sleep on my pullout couch if Harry won't take you.

A wave of nausea hit as I thought about asking Harry if I could crash at his place, especially after our closet session. No, I would take Casey up on his temporary housing offer if it came to that, and I'd need to figure out something else for the longer term.

Stuffing my phone in the back pocket of my jeans, I walked to the front door when I heard Jia rattling her keys on the welcome mat.

It was time to face the music.

You can do this, Sara. It's important and can't wait. "Hi. Can we talk?" I asked as soon as she opened the door.

"No 'How was your trip?' or 'I missed you so I cleaned your house!' sis? Geez." She rolled in her black hard-shell suitcase and set her large caramel-colored leather shoulder bag down with a thump.

With crossed arms and a face absent of cordiality, I didn't reply with my usual sisterly quip.

Her face fell. "Shit, did you find out I put you on that dating site, Pour Over? It's a new one and I thought if I got you in early, you'd have an advantage. It's Coffee Meets Bagel, but for nerds who are coffee and food snobs."

Well, this was not the start to the discussion I had anticipated. At all.

My scowl shifted as confusion blanketed my face. "Wait, you put me on a dating site without my consent?"

"Sort of. I posted your photo but no other info yet, and within twenty-four hours you were getting a ton of replies from that alone. I hadn't sifted through the messages yet to see if any of them were worth your time. But I figured it was something you could try while you suffered silently, pining away for Harry."

Something shifted in me. "Look, there's no more pining because he and I—"

Her eyes lit up. "Are you two a thing? Or completely over him? I'd be ecstatic for either one, actually!"

My whole goal was to have control of the conversation and steer it in a way to get answers about our drunken night, but it was already slipping away from me. "Harry and I are kind of a thing, but that's not what I need to talk to you about." I handed her printouts of the app messages sent to my parents and to Naomi. "Can you read the lines I highlighted?"

Her eyes searched the page. "Are these the notes that were sent to Umma and Appa? And Naomi?" She mumbled as she read the sections of interest. "You were hard on me, and Jia too. She tried to live up to your expectations, and you always held Sara as a benchmark."

Her eyes met mine.

"Those aren't my words," I said. "Look at the next page."

It was the message to Naomi, with only one line added that I'd almost missed. "Naomi, you were like a sister to me, and also to Jia."

"You wrote those sections? And did *you* also schedule send the messages out?" I asked.

She looked down at the floor, her body posture slumping forward. "Yes."

My breath hitched.

"You probably hate me right now." She chewed her bottom lip, contemplating her words. "We were both drunk that night and seeing you writing those messages, putting all your emotions out there and stepping out of your comfort zone—I hadn't seen you like that since you were a teenager. You are so rigid in your ways now, but finally, after a bit of liquid courage and a lot of my support, you were liberated. Probably because you thought it would have no consequences if the messages never left the server." She sat on the couch and sighed. "Nothing was holding you back, not even yourself this time. When you went to sleep, I edited your notes and I added in a few sentences here and there, selfishly, for me. So I could get a word in edgewise, because I wanted my truth spoken too. You started to stir from your sleep when I was reading your message to Harry, and usually once you're awake you're up for good, so I drafted a new one and put in those song lyrics. As soon as you fell back asleep peacefully, I scheduled your messages to send later. At the time I was still a little drunk, but deep in my bones I knew it was the right thing to do. Sisterly tough love, or so I thought."

I had plenty to be mad about, but I couldn't ignore the pit growing in my stomach, knowing she'd customized the notes and sent everything out *without* my permission. And that she'd replaced the message to my crush. Balling my fists, I tried to steady my breath. "Why was the note to Harry different? Why not just send the original?"

Shaking her head, she said, "Because in the original note you went on and on about how wonderful and perfect he was and how lucky you would be if you were together, and that you'd been crushing on him your entire life." She dropped the pages on the floor. "It pissed me off so much, because you couldn't see that he would have been lucky to have YOU. You deserve the world, Sara. And if he couldn't see that, back in high school or as a grown-ass adult, he needed to fuck off. He had plenty of chances to date you." She added, "You also have a tendency to think there are these formal rules for courting, but they're arbitrary. Opportunities pass you by and you let them, because you have no desire to change or adapt. When things get hard, you avoid confrontation and don't speak up. You're lucky I replaced your message with Taylor's lyrics, can you imagine if your OG note was sent out as is?"

I threw my hands in the air. "My original message wouldn't have been sent out though! You overrode the system to release them! Can you not see that none of this would have been set in motion if you hadn't meddled? Most of the time I appreciate your good intentions, but it's one thing to edit the messages and keep them private, it's another to violate my privacy and actually send them out into the wild. Did you even think through what would happen? Do you ever think of consequences?"

She raised her voice. "Okay, maybe not all the way through because I was pretty drunk, but I thought it was better than the status quo. Yes, I knew you'd have to deal with some awkward aftermath. But it was better than seeing you live your life enveloped in bubble wrap. It's worse than living in regret . . . you weren't really living at all. You have unrealistic notions of what romance and relationships are like, and I didn't want you to go through life without experiencing them."

I closed my eyes and took in deep breaths. "But that was my decision to make, not yours. Ruin your own carefree life, not mine!"

I stormed off to the closet. She followed me. "What's that supposed to mean? You think I live the way I do only because of what *I* want? You don't think your decisions and your relationships affect mine? That Mom and Dad's harsh opinions don't weigh on my mind all the time?"

I turned on my heel to face her. "What does the way you live even have to do with me?"

Jia sighed loudly. "Umma and Appa had me so late, and you were out of the house by the time I hit puberty. They put so much time and energy into you." She choked up. "Everything you accomplished, they held all of it over my head. What summer programs I got into, where I applied for college, it always came back to what you had done, and why your way was better."

I furrowed my brow. "That's not how I remember it. You were the youngest, and Mom and Dad were more lenient on you. They came down on me so hard and said I had to be your role model." I'd always seen Jia as my little sister, the one who got babied by the family, the one who got away with everything and was never under scrutiny.

She shook her head. "When you ended up with a job in tech, they wanted me to do the exact same thing, because that's where the money was. And even when I ended up doing well in marketing and branding, something they didn't approve of at all and didn't bother to try to understand, even when I got my MBA, they didn't congratulate me. The business side paid well, but not as well as your tech jobs, and they always mentioned that to me, that it wasn't too late to be like my older sister. So in the message to them I added a few lines to include me, so it wasn't only about you. They needed to hear that their way of parenting affected me too."

She wiped away tears that had just formed. I wanted to reach out and hug her, to apologize for being so unaware and not recognizing her pain, but I could tell Jia was just getting started and had much more to unload.

"Naomi was like another big sister to me. Sometimes when you went to your bedroom to study when she was spending the night at our house, she and I would hang out in the living room. We'd watch movies or work on crafts. Talk about boys. Talk about you. She helped me with viola sometimes."

The way she recounted her memories, it was like Naomi was the big sister she'd always wanted. I swallowed my hurt and let her continue.

"When you two had a falling-out, Naomi disappeared from my life too. It wasn't fair. I wanted her to know I missed her too. And that she meant a lot to the family. I know you two are maybe beyond the point of letting bygones be bygones, but I wanted her to know that she was special to me."

What was I supposed to do now? As different as Jia and I were, I knew she was coming from a place of well-meaning. Deep down I knew she wanted me to be happy and had been willing to do something drastic to make that happen. Was I happy before? Not really. Was I happier now, after she'd unleashed this shitstorm?

So much had happened. With my job. With Harry. My parents. But probably yes.

I closed my eyes and tried to calm my racing heart. Jia was unconventional in her problem-solving, always reacting before thinking, while I did the exact opposite. It was hard to believe she and I were from the same genetic pool. She was reckless too, and it was unbearable to witness sometimes, but hearing her explanation made it clearer why the messages sent from my app were just as much for her as they were for me.

Was I angry? Yes. Did I need time away to decompress and unpack

all of this shit? Also yes. Did I kind of hate my sister but also love her
for what she'd done?

Yes, but it was hard to see everything clearly. I needed some time,
and possibly distance, to be able to forgive her.

I let out a deep sigh. "I see where you're coming from, and I'm
sorry, Jia. But you turned my life upside down when you released
those messages, and I'm still dealing with the aftershocks, along
with getting my business off the ground. I wish you'd talked to me
earlier, especially because we've become closer since I've been living
with you. But you didn't." I dipped my chin and looked at the glossy
hardwood floor. "And I wish I had picked up on your distress. But
I didn't."

Her chin quivered as she looked at me. "I didn't mean to turn
your life into a nightmare. It wasn't on purpose. I hope you know
I'd never do that to you. I wanted you to move on with your life. To
grow up and communicate more. Please know that I did it for your
benefit." She sniffed. "Okay, and a little bit for my benefit too. Like
ninety-nine percent you, one percent me."

I raised an eyebrow and shook my head. "Are you serious? One
percent?"

"Okay, fine, eighty percent you, twenty percent me. I'm truly
sorry for all of this," she conceded, plopping down on her bed. "I
know this is a bratty thing to ask right now, but where does that
leave you and me? I don't want you to hate me and move out, at least
not yet." Jia looked around her room. "There's not much room in my
apartment to give you a ton of space though."

"Well, Casey offered me a place to crash, but I'm still not sure
I'll take him up on it. I might spend more time away from here
though, just to give us a little space." My watch buzzed with a notification. "Oh! I have a meet-up planned with Naomi tomorrow. So
some good might come out of your terribly hatched plan after all. At

the very least, I can get some closure on another part of my life. And then, as you hoped, I can move on."

She beamed. "Want me to come? Or I can send her flowers to let her know we missed her! Isn't she allergic to everything except calla lilies? Maybe a cookie assortment instead—"

I groaned. "Whoa there, you've done enough. It's my turn now to handle the rest of this, without any intervention from my scary godmother."

"Am I really that scary?" she asked.

I snorted. "Yes! I promise that at the very least I'll let Naomi know that my scary, meddling little sister, who means well, most of the time, misses her."

"Well, that alone should be enough to win her back," she joked.

I nodded. "I really hope so."

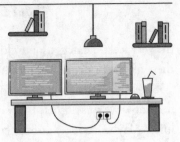

Chapter Nineteen

Naomi was sipping a Mexican Coke from a glass bottle at the bar and didn't see me come through the door, even though she was staring off in my direction. She looked up with surprise when I pulled up a stool and sat down.

"Sorry! I didn't see you. Just miles away, as usual," she said.

Naomi had always been the kind of person who gazed into the distance, thinking, hoping, and dreaming. It was a familiar sight, and I was happy to see that that part of her hadn't changed over the years.

She pretty much looked exactly the same. Up close I could see a few silver strands on her head and some small creases near the eyes, but they gave her character. As for me, no concealer in the world could hide those deepening dark circles under my tired eyes.

The bartender came over with a food menu. "The drink specials are on the board," he said, pointing behind his head.

Naomi said, "The carne asada fries are good here. And the kale salad."

I laughed. "Those seem like they shouldn't go together, but they kind of do. Want to share?"

She nodded. "Sure."

This meant she was willing to sit through a meal with me. That was a good sign.

I placed the order and asked for a Coke too. Thanks to the landlord's reimbursement, I could afford little treats for myself.

She took a sip from her bottle. "So . . . regarding your messages to me out of the blue, you appear to not, in fact, be dead."

Her deadpan had always made me laugh, but this time there was something a little more biting in her commentary. Not like she wanted me to be dead, per se. But for that to be the first thing she said to me after all these years—knowing she hadn't responded to my messages until after she'd spotted me in person—her sharp words were like little daggers to the chest.

"I regret a lot of things," I said to Naomi as the bartender popped the top off my bottle. "I'm sorry that the message was sent to you in the first place, and I'm especially sorry that I lost touch after all these years."

She tapped her fingers on the counter. "It was more than just losing touch though. We were best friends, and it's like we're strangers now." More puncture wounds to the heart. But Naomi was right, there was something deliberate about the way we had stopped communicating. We weren't even Christmas card friends. Or posting "Happy Birthday!" once a year on social media buddies. I didn't know she'd left the West Coast to go to Boston, and had no idea she'd returned to LA. How long had she been living in the same city as me, performing all around town?

We used to be attached at the hip in high school and a lot of people had assumed we were sisters. Admittedly, some of it was because of racism—I was Korean and she was Japanese, and some people didn't know the difference—but we also had overlapping classes and shared a goofy sense of humor. We swapped kimbap and Spam musubi from our lunches and shared vending machine snacks. I knew her crushes and she knew mine. She was there for my first period and I was there for hers. We were each other's people. Being completely honest with myself, what hurt the most was knowing that so much time had passed without any attempt at reconciliation from either of us, and we weren't the kind of people who would give up on a good friend.

She looked at me. "I wish I was above keeping score, but I'm not. The last time we communicated was nine years ago. I reached out to you. It was my birthday, and I was having a party to celebrate that and the fact that I'd just gotten into an MFA program in Boston. I announced the news at the party. But you were working late that night, and you said you'd make a late-night appearance. Do you remember making that promise, and then being a no-show?"

"That was the night before an investor meeting." I nodded, confirming everything she'd said. "I fell asleep at my desk. I called you but you didn't pick up."

The server delivered our food, along with a wicker basket lined with red-and-white-checkered cloth. Naomi peeled it back and helped herself to a hot roll. "The party started at seven and you called me close to ten. By then pretty much everyone had left and I was too wasted to have it out with you on the phone. The point is . . . it was the last straw. I couldn't keep being your ditchable pal."

"You weren't my ditchable pal," I argued, my stomach queasy. "We went out a lot! To movies, brunch, an occasional show." But as I scrolled back through my catalog of memories to firm up my position of being a good friend, the sinking feeling became deeper. It was true. I had canceled on her. A lot.

"You're only recounting the things you want to remember. I recall as early as college there were several study dates when I was at UCLA—you'd said you'd meet up, and you abandoned me. Then there were those nice dinners with reservations that you bailed on because you were working late. All the invitations to clubs, parties, and gallery openings you said no to, one after another. Did you even notice I eventually stopped asking you to come with me to anything?"

I frowned as flashes of those memories whipped through my mind. The bitter truth was . . . I hadn't. Not at the time. If anything, I remember being relieved I didn't have to turn down things or cancel plans that conflicted with my studying or my long work hours. I didn't like abandoning plans; being the flaky friend was never something I wanted to be, but now it made sense why I had nothing on my calendar.

When Jia and I talked the night before, it became clear that I was very set in my ways, so determined to avoid confrontation, and be all work with no time for play, that she felt like she had to do something drastic to make my life better. And now Naomi was informing me of the same problem, me not wanting to do things differently, or do different things, and that was precisely why our relationship fell apart. The entire time I thought Naomi had ghosted me, but it was actually *me* who had been the ghoster.

"You were obsessed with schoolwork, and then when you graduated, nothing could pull you away from your job. The only things you cared about were getting the highest grades in the class and then getting yearly promotions and raises, and you took me for granted. You didn't seem to care about me. Or about us. I didn't want to beg you to hang out with me. Even I have limits." Her voice wavered. "I hated that you chose your work over me. And I hated that I even wanted you to choose."

"Oh God, I am so sorry," I whispered. This truth hit me like a sucker punch to the face. A jolt of nausea made me woozy in the head. To keep from tipping over on my stool, I steadied myself by grabbing the bar counter with both hands. "I did care about you. I *do* care about you. I worked so hard so I could have time to coast and have free time later, but then I got laid off. I had to start all over again from the bottom. None of that is an excuse though; I should have been a better friend. I needed better work-life balance then, and I still do now."

"All that said, I know I could have been a better friend too," she admitted. "Most of the time it was me just inviting you to shows and events, not really hanging out and talking, not having real conversations when we needed them. I feel terrible about that. I know the indie music scene wasn't your favorite. One-on-one time is important in friendships, and it should have been something we both tried to make time for, but we didn't. Back then, our friendship felt like so much work." She ate a few fries and then pointed one at me. "I'll be honest, I was surprised to see you at the gala, looking fancy and being social with your new friends. When I got home I searched my inbox to see the last time I'd heard from you, and that's when I saw your messages."

So she hadn't been ignoring me, she'd never even seen my emails. That's good.

A light fluttering in my chest signaled a future of hope and optimism. Then Naomi explained, "I'll admit, I'd set up a rule in my inbox a while ago to move your messages to a separate folder because I didn't want to see them."

Ouch.

I rocked back a little, shocked by her confession. Then again, I would have set up email rules to block messages if I had given up on someone too.

She continued. "I was surprised to hear from you. I thought the whole thing might be a hoax and there was no way you could have died since I could have sworn I saw you at that event. I looked you up and found a press release about how you were recently accepted into some elite Silicon Beach start-up program for your app. Jia had also posted a photo of you two at dinner on social media the day you sent me your death notice, and I'd seen you with my own two eyes at the gala, but I still couldn't be too sure it was you." She sipped her drink. "But I read and reread your words, and even though there was a lot in there I disagreed with, especially about how I'd ghosted you, there was that part about how I was like family—practically a second sister to Jia—and my heart softened more than I expected. That's why I replied. That's why we're meeting now, because I missed that. I missed . . . us. Maybe it was a bad idea, who knows."

My eyes filled with tears. "I'm glad you did, and I'm happy we're here. I'm so happy we're talking about this." Thanks to Jia, I had a second chance with my former best friend. I'd wanted to strangle her yesterday, but now all I wanted to do was hug her and ugly cry on her shoulder.

"If I hadn't seen you at the gala, and you hadn't written me through your app, you would have never heard from me. It was too much of a coincidence to ignore it though. You know me, I'm very much not an optimist—at best I'm a realist—but I had to think this was all a sign from the universe. Kismet? Serendipity? Destiny maybe? Whatever it is, we need to appease whatever forces or deities or spirits that wanted us to reunite."

"Maybe we both needed an opportunity for . . . I hate to say it . . . last words," I said with a cringe face.

She cracked a smile and scooped some salad onto her plate. "Maybe you should change your app name to Some Last Words and an Epilogue."

A laugh burst out of me. "It's a catchy name. Like *Four Weddings and a Funeral.*"

While we ate, I showed her the app interface. She offered constructive feedback about the layout, design, and functionality that was insightful, both artistically and functionally. Harry had asked me to add a bunch of new capabilities, but Naomi was pointing out where there were areas of "features bloat": places where way too much was going on, so the user could be confused or abandon the app altogether. Or worse, look for a competitor who did it better.

"You're pretty great at this UX and design stuff. You've always had a good eye for that kind of thing," I said.

Naomi nodded. "I minored in design in college." She shifted the conversation back to our weighty past. "Lately I've been thinking about where my career is heading, and how I left a life of partying and admittedly bouts of substance abuse behind me, but even with all that in the past I'm still living paycheck to paycheck as a musician, doing random UX and sound engineer consulting gigs on the side to be able to have some savings for retirement. Sometimes I wonder if you had the right idea all along, going down a demanding career path with good pay, tucking away money every year. I thought by now I'd have more direction, but it seems like my professional life is headed nowhere." She chewed a fry and swallowed. "It's kind of depressing."

I cocked my head. "I hope you don't think I have my life figured out. On the contrary, I quit my very secure job and I have plenty of my own regrets, trust me."

Her eyebrows shot up. "Really? But you were at that fancy gala, draped on Harry Shim's arm! I remember that guy, he was like your Prince Charming." She paused. "I was at the gala as a favor to Claudia, his ex. She's mentioned to me before that she didn't see him as a fairy-tale prince at all. Remember her from high school? It's hard to believe she and I ended up being friends."

Uneasiness rippled through my gut, suppressing my appetite. Naomi had a stronger friendship with Claudia than with me. I couldn't believe it. "She seems nice I guess," I barely managed to say.

"She's very into philanthropy. At first I thought it was just for show, but I think it's something she actually enjoys. She used to be an event planner for different finance firms, so that's the perfect career for her. She's with some really nice guy now who's on the board of that wildlife foundation. Personally, I think he's a much better fit for her than Harry ever was."

"Who do you think would be a better fit with someone like Harry?" I asked, fishing for the answer I wanted to hear.

"Honestly, someone like you," she said without hesitating.

I blushed. Before I could say thank you, she added, "It's not a good thing, Sara. He's a workaholic. From what I hear, he was married to his job first and his wife second. They tried to make it work with vacations and some Hail Mary therapy, but it was hard for him to make any adjustments and meet somewhere in the middle. It was always her compromising."

My mouth opened and then immediately shut. It was not the right time to open up—telling her that he didn't know if he was cut out for marriage again, which was something I might want. And I kept it close to my chest that I was already in deep with him, thanks to our closet rendezvous. Were these things I could even share with her anymore?

Her eyebrows drew together with concern. "I know we haven't been close for a while, but please be careful. To be successful in the tech world, it seems like you need to choose work over personal life, and you can't have both unless you fight for it. I know you didn't ask for my opinion, but you also know I'll give it to you anyway because that's who I am. Maybe for your company, you can do things differently. Set things up so that before you launch, you establish your mission and key values, including work-life balance. You might get a more diverse talent pool if you establish that early."

God, I missed her. She had always had a perspective worth hearing.

And I didn't know how much I longed for that until now. "Your opinions are always welcome," I said with a sincere smile. "Even when they're painful to hear sometimes."

"Well, if that's the case I have one more opinion for you."

I literally braced myself by grabbing the counter again. Naomi was not someone who chose words with care. But whatever came out of her mouth would be direct, and also deserved.

She pushed forward on her stool and landed on her feet. "I think we need to hug."

YES, please. I slid off my seat so fast I almost fell to the ground. With my arms open wide, I pulled her into an embrace, and she squeezed me back. Our familiar, warm, snuggly hug whisked me back in time, to when we were best friends in high school and college. It was so nice to be with her again.

We didn't say anything for a long time. Finally, after the bartender plunked down our bill in front of us, she spoke. "Let's do this again sometime."

Still holding her, I said, "I'd like that a lot. And if it's not too much trouble, I think Jia would like to come too."

"My girl Jia? Hell yeah. I can't wait!"

We practically arm wrestled over the payment, but she managed to yank the merchant copy out of my hand and Frisbeed her credit card at the bartender, who laughed at us.

"I'll get the next one," I said. And I meant it. Because there would most definitely be a next time.

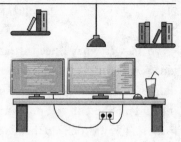

Chapter Twenty

*H*arry sent a string of texts.

How about dinner?

Dessert?

Hang out in my closet or yours?

Yes, I wanted to do all those things, especially the last one. But was this a good time? A day before the big competition?

I didn't need my Magic 8 Ball to tell me the right answer. *Outlook not so good.*

I replied. Sorry I've been quiet, got a lot on my mind, and the competition is so soon

To that, he answered quickly. Okay, making sure you're not mad at me

I need to concentrate on a few things due tonight, how about after The Bullpen is over?

Focus was what I needed right now. I still had to upload more videos, turn in additional paperwork requested by the undisclosed judges, and practice nailing my pitch. For some people, public speaking and off-the-cuff self-promotion was easy, but I had to memorize lines so I could deliver them while exuding confidence, trying to look at ease with carefully planned pauses and smiles. None of this came naturally to me. At best, I appeared soft-spoken and modest. At worst, I looked uncomfortably constipated. There was much room for improvement and not much time to prepare.

Over the course of several hours, I wrote, rewrote, and edited my elevator pitch, then read it aloud with as much enthusiasm and passion as I could muster. Next was memorization. Then rehearsing and recording. But even with all that practice, I still stumbled, stuttered, and blanked, blowing raspberries with every new video take. My phone was filled with a graveyard of useless videos, none of which were good enough to share publicly, even with heavy editing.

Jia had kept her promise by keeping her distance, leaving her own apartment for chunks of days and evenings to give me some quiet time, which I appreciated. And when she was home, I escaped to the coworking space and Casey's place. But it was during those long moments of solitude when I was left all alone with my thoughts that my destructive inner voice told me that this was all pointless and I needed to find another career. A job that was a more natural fit. An easier one that required less thinking. That I wasn't cut out for any of this.

I needed a break.

Arms stretched high above my head, I stood and walked around the living room, coming across the succulent plant that my old coworkers had given to me. Surprisingly, it was still alive, even though I'd watered it only once, the first week I got it. That was nearly three months ago. I grabbed my reusable bottle from the coffee table and poured a small amount of water into the pot. It sucked into the dirt immediately, with barely any trace of moisture. *Well, with that hydration boost it will live a few more weeks at least.* My work friends had been wise to give me something that required so little from me.

I picked up the accompanying note card and read the messages from my old colleagues. The words hit me even harder the second time around. My chest ached and I fought tears as I remembered how my work friends believed in me. In my app. In pursuing my dreams. Seeing this reminder offered me the exact motivation I needed to get the videos finished before the next-day deadline.

"Thanks, bud," I said to my succulent friend, while I fanned my eyes to keep from crying. After stabilizing my emotions, I blotted my face with a tissue and sank back down on the couch, readying myself for another around of recording.

Late that afternoon, I uploaded everything to the shared drive for my mentor, Stan, to review before submitting it to *The Bullpen*. My eyes opened wide with surprise when a text from Harry arrived just minutes after posting the new materials.

> Hope you don't mind that I peeked at your videos. They were perfect! Any chance you have time for one drink to celebrate? And a quick bite? I promise I'll have you back home at a reasonable time, no funny business

It was a milestone worth celebrating. In less than twenty-four hours, I would be on the set of *The Bullpen*, pitching my app to a panel of judges. I could leave the show with funding. It was exhilarating and terrifying at the same time, and like when I tried anything new, it left me with a combination of good and bad feelings.

But mostly good.

Mostly.

And how did I feel about having a celebratory drink with Harry? Good, mostly.

The longer I considered his offer, the more time I spent mentally playing reverse Uno cards of my opinions about Harry.

Maybe showing me attentiveness wasn't really part of any plan to be more intimate. Maybe it was just him being social.

Maybe he did care a lot. And what we have is special.

Or maybe not—Harry had always been this way. He was always "on"—making you feel special with even just a glance or a smile—and if anything, he'd gotten more practice in the fifteen or so years since high school.

Stop wasting brain cells on this, Sara. It's just a drink! Not a whimsical elopement proposal.

A calendar notification popped up on my phone. It was a reminder that Naomi had a solo performance at a club nearby. She hadn't told me about it; I'd found it on her website and was thinking about stopping by quickly to surprise her.

I messaged Harry back. One drink nearby? Only one

Opening the fridge and seeing nothing inside it, I added also a bite to eat. Starving.

Swinging by in twenty

Nineteen minutes later, the intercom buzzed.

I pressed the button on the hallway speaker and yelled, "Heading down!" Not quite twenty minutes had given me enough time to take a quick shower, put on a cute outfit, and apply a base level of makeup. My entire life I'd wondered why anyone would need a shower cap, but it made sense now. Thank goodness Jia had a drawer full of hotel toiletries she'd brought home from her business trips.

When I opened the front door of the apartment building, Harry, who had been leaning against the brick facade, pushed himself forward and stood up straight. "Just one drink, I promise!"

He gave me a melt-me-in-the-center-till-I-get-all-gooey smile. All I wanted to do was kiss him and take him upstairs again, but that was my body talking. My head was telling me to not do anything stupid, especially the night before the show recording. Even having this drink was probably not the best idea. But it was just one drink.

Just one.

"Naomi's playing at the Bar Liquidity a few blocks away. We can walk there and get a drink plus dinner, then watch her set. If that's okay with you."

"Sounds like a plan." He held out his hand for me to grab, but I opted to hold on to his arm instead. He smirked a little but didn't seem to mind. Hugging his biceps as we walked was probably as much bodily contact as I could allow that night.

Even though we were both wearing coats, pressing into his woolen sleeve still aroused my senses. Electricity passed between us, intensifying my attraction to him. *Sara, no. A drink, a bite to eat, that's it. And then bedtime.*

I studied his face as we walked, appraising him like a curious gemologist studying a prize jewel.

Focus, Sara.

His clean, woodsy scent was impossible to ignore, even though he was bundled up. He smelled so good.

Stop that.

His proximity caused my breath to grow heavier with each step. *Turn around and go home. You need your head in the game. And the game we are referring to is not STRIP UNO with Harry.*

"Wow! It's crowded, good for Naomi!" Harry said loudly, clearing my thoughts. We stood in the line to get into the bar.

Glancing at others around us reminded me of why I rarely went to these venues to see Naomi play. Hipster artsy types dominated the music scene in LA, leaving me feeling like a walking, human-shaped yawn. With Harry here, at least I wasn't alone. There were plenty of times I'd stood in line to see my best friend perform and had no one to talk to. It had been just me and my Sudoku app. I hadn't even realized that was part of the discomfort when I went out to see Naomi perform. It had been even worse when she was surrounded by her cooler friends. I wasn't even a third wheel then, sometimes I was a ninth or tenth wheel. But I felt like a spare tire with a flat.

The line moved. At the door, the bouncer asked for my ID. After handing it over, he did a double take at my birthdate. His eyes bulged. "Whoa!"

As if I needed any further embarrassment, he said to the guy who was stamping people's hands, "These two lovebirds are way over twenty-one!"

Harry surprised me when he took his ID back. "Thank you, young lad. Here's a wrapped candy for your trouble!" he said in a warbling, geriatric voice, shoving his hand into his pocket to pull out a neon green Jolly Rancher.

The bouncer bared his teeth, but took the candy anyway. "Thanks."

I laughed as we entered the venue. "Your grandpa voice was amazing. And are we really *that* old?"

"Mid-thirties isn't young, but it's definitely not old. We're just entering the years where the twenty-one-year-olds think we're over the hill and math-wise, in a few years we could be really young grandparents, that's all."

We made our way to the broody bartender who was slinging drink specials down the counter. Two women wearing leather from head to toe slid off their stools and one of them said to us, "We're leaving now if you want to sit here," then carried away their drinks.

Two seats at a crowded bar! That kind of luck never happened to me. I texted Naomi to tell her we were at the bar (surprise!) and contemplated taking a selfie with Harry, as this was our first full-fledged, not-fake date. Looking around, I got self-conscious and decided against it. We already looked like tourists in this sea of tat-tooed, pierced, and dyed trendsetters.

Harry asked for an old-fashioned. I ordered their Holy Molotov Mule and a plate of wings. Our ornery barkeep asked me, "I only use real ginger beer, none of that lightweight ginger ale garbage. Is that okay?"

I replied, "I wouldn't have it any other way. I prefer the spicy burn. Puts hair on my chest."

He snorted. "Got that right. I'll upgrade you to top-shelf vodka too, just because you got your priorities straight."

After he mixed our drinks and let us take our first sips, I remarked, "Wow, mine's like spicy liquid fire."

The bartender winked at me. "That's a compliment if I ever heard one. Should I open a tab for you two?"

Harry cleared his throat and handed him three twenties. "I think it's just one drink each tonight, plus the wings. Keep the change."

"Big spender," I observed.

"He deserves a good tip. He was funny and he made these drinks so potent they're basically a two-in-one." Harry glanced down at me. "You don't have to finish or anything, I know you have a big day tomorrow. After which, I hope you can celebrate with a nice dinner with me. Cheers, by the way."

We clinked glasses.

He sipped and grinned while he set his glass down on a napkin.

"What's so funny?" I asked.

"I was just thinking back to high school, how we were back then . . . and what we're like now." He took off his coat and placed it in his lap.

I tilted my head and smirked. "You mean, how nerdy we were? We used to spend so much free time discussing whether raccoons and pigeons were actually government spy tools because you never saw their babies."

"Yes!" He coughed out a laugh. "And remember when we were obsessed with figuring out why we had eyebrows? I think you did a report in biology for extra credit."

I grinned. "Yeah, I remember now. It was to keep out sweat and protect your eyes, but that seemed like BS. Maybe when the Cro-Magnons had different head shapes and forehead ridges, but eyebrows are questionably useful now." I waited for more jokey banter from him but he didn't offer any additional commentary. "I'll assume by your jaw hanging open that you're weirded out or have nothing more to say regarding the evolution of eyebrows."

He rolled his sleeves, putting his toned forearms on display. "Your brain amazes me, how your mind works . . . I find that so attractive," he finally said.

"Thank you." I blushed. Heat rushed to my cheeks from both the compliment and the vodka in the spicy cocktail.

After taking another sip, he mentioned, "By the way, do you need anything else from me for tomorrow? I'm not your mentor anymore, but I'm happy to do anything you need me to do."

"You mean in a business sense or a personal sense?" I asked coyly.

"Well, financial modeling, pitching, and shoulder massaging are a few of my best skills." He lowered his hand to my knee.

A current ran through my body when he made contact. *How is he able to flip my on switch every time he touches me?*

"You're also great at the grandpa voice," I deflected. I needed to de-escalate this situation because attraction was intensifying between us by the second.

"It's the sexiest grandpa voice you'll ever hear, I promise you that." His hand slid to my thigh. *Holy hell.*

I blurted, "You're sexy all right. Sexy grandpa voice. Sexy mentor. Sexy divorcé."

He abruptly pulled his hand off my leg, like he'd gotten too close to a hot burner on a stove.

What was that all about? Okay, yes, it was a bad joke, but was it libido-killing bad?

Perhaps it was.

My hand reached for his. "It was a string of bad jokes. I was just being dumb. I really do find you attractive, sexy to a fault, to a point I can't even stand it." I couldn't believe those words had come out of my mouth. No more Molotov Mules for me.

He grimaced.

Whatever I'd done must've been bad. A misstep even worse than I'd thought.

"It's not you, Sara, it's me." He exhaled out of his nose and stared at his drink without additional explanation.

What kind of cliché broody bullshit line was that? I wanted a de-escalation, not a complete shutdown. I steadied my voice. "Care to elaborate?"

Keeping his eye on his drink, he confessed, "I haven't been entirely truthful with you. But maybe this isn't the best time to talk about it."

My entire body went numb. What sort of truth bomb would he unleash with that kind of setup? My mind jumped to a million places, like a time machine going haywire. He was moving to another city. Maybe he had a secret baby. He was in love with

another woman? Did he have a third or fourth nipple? Wait, I'd
seen him shirtless and there was nothing to suggest it was anything
like that—

"Honestly, I shouldn't have said anything. Let's drop it for now so
you can focus on your big day tomorrow."

I stiffened. "Are you serious? You can't leave me hanging like
that, you *have* to tell me now." Feeling came back to my fingers
and toes, and the warm tingles coursing through my body had all
but disappeared. I opened and closed my fists as if I were manually
pumping my blood back to my heart. It was all I could do, because
whatever he was about to say might make it stop beating.

When his eyes finally met mine, a worried look flashed in them.
I swallowed hard and braced myself.

"I'm not technically divorced." His gaze briefly dropped back
down to his drink. After taking a sip, he looked at me again, eyes
even more apologetic than before.

"What do you mean by *technically*?"

Open, close. Open, close. My fingers lost all sensation as soon as
he dropped the I'm-still-married bomb.

The lights dimmed and the first music act began their set: a sub-
dued duo on acoustic guitars. They strummed and crooned while
Harry formulated a reply.

"Claudia and I are separated, and we have been for a long time.
Like, a really long time. It'll be four years next month."

Four years? Quickly doing the math, I realized when I saw the
two of them at the last high school reunion, they were barely hanging on as a couple. Why was he waiting so long?

He bit his bottom lip. "She and I haven't lived in the same place
for that entire time. We sold our house and used the money to buy
separate townhomes. Over the years, we've divided our finances and
created our own independent social circles."

"So why don't you—" I whispered, "Wait, are you still in love with her? Is that why—"

"What? No! I'm not in love with my ex anymore."

I chugged the rest of my drink. *Is she actually his ex though? Ex what? Not ex-wife. Technically speaking.* "So you're delaying for a reason?"

His shoulders slumped. "Well, I guess there are tax benefits for being married that aren't the same when you're divorced, plus the legal fees, and division of assets that has been taking some time to sort fairly . . ."

As he continued to rattle off all the monetary reasons to stay married, I reeled. Not from the alcohol, but from the words pouring from his mouth. They were devoid of any emotion, and all focused on money. I'd rather have heard him say he was a romantic, a dreamer, an optimist—rather than it being in a marriage that he and his wife didn't want anymore and it being purely for financial reasons. This was not the Harry I remembered from high school. Jia was right, that Harry didn't exist anymore.

Just as I thought things couldn't get worse, he added, "I'd be lying if I said my relationship with Claudia didn't affect my ability to commit to relationships. It's been hard."

This was all too much. And not what I needed the day before my big event. Harry was sure as hell right about that.

I grabbed my bag. "I really need to go. Thanks for the drink. You can eat the wings."

He downed the rest of his old-fashioned. "Let me walk you back."

"No, please don't. I need time to think." Actually, I didn't need time to think. I needed time to NOT think. I needed to purge. To get my mind clear for tomorrow and not have images of Harry and Claudia holding bags of money popping in and out of my head.

With haste, I committed the biggest faux pas one could make at a music performance—I crossed the front of the stage while the emcee introduced the next act to reach the closest exit. It was Naomi's band up next, not the Museum Maestros quartet but her indie rock group, Apocalyptic A-Holes. Naomi gaped as I offered an apologetic wave while scurrying past. Pushing through a side door, I discovered it was an emergency exit and rigged with a noisy alarm. But I got out of there so fast it barely triggered the shrill siren.

Down the alley behind the building, I could hear the band playing in the distance. It was a lively, upbeat, and fun song, one that could easily be a commercial hit given the right timing and opportunity. It was a shame to have to enjoy the performance from outside the bar.

I waited until I made it back to Jia's apartment before texting Naomi an apology.

> Sorry I had to leave early. You looked great and sounded amazing from the alley btw. Can I make it up to you with brunch this weekend?

Naomi had always been obsessed with brunch and it would surely be the best way to apologize. After all, she hadn't even been expecting me to come to her performance in the first place, and she went on thirty minutes later than scheduled. Hopefully she wouldn't see this as a snubbing situation and instead could offer some grace, seeing as how I truly tried to see her performance and had been there for an hour the night before the *Bullpen* event.

Peeling off my jacket, my thoughts drifted to Harry and his nonexistent divorce. Was he relaxing at home, relieved that he'd finally revealed his big secret after all this time, or was he overwrought with feelings like me, unsure of what this disclosure meant for his future and mine?

My mind continued buzzing and would not relax. I tried taking a bath. Dimming the lights. Meditating. Deep breathing. Finally, I nodded off while reading a business book about entrepreneurship, but woke up at one in the morning, unable to fall back asleep.

I grabbed my phone and fought the urge to doomscroll on social media, but lost. One of the first photos in my feed was a post from Naomi. I'd checked my messages and she hadn't written back about my brunch offer. I thought she was too busy to reply, but if she had time to post a photo, she had time to reply with a quick thumbs-up or -down, a Y or N. I wasn't asking for much given that we were both trying to make our friendship work this second time around.

What concerned me wasn't necessarily her posting the photo, at least not at first. It was a blurry photo of Naomi, not unlike a few of the images already present on her account. It was artistic and eye-catching, but deeply melancholy. But her words were what grabbed my attention. "Maybe this world isn't for people like me." Taken figuratively, I could see her offering commentary about how mainstream society's conventions weren't her thing, or something along those lines. But taking this literally, it was, possibly, her needing help.

I texted her. I'm coming over. Requesting a rideshare car, I ran outside with a puffy coat over my pajamas. The driver was close by in Santa Monica, and I was able to arrive at Naomi's within ten minutes. I leaped out of the back seat, praying that she was okay as I buzzed up to her apartment.

I tried again a second time when she didn't respond.

And a third time.

"Hello?" a muffled voice croaked over the crackling speaker.

It sounded like her, but it was hard to tell. She'd mentioned before that she had a roommate. It could be her instead.

"Naomi? It's me. Sara."

Just as I was about to buzz a fourth time, the apartment building door unlocked, and the humming sound from the locking mechanism continued as I walked through the tempered-glass door.

I made my way up the stairs to the second floor and knocked on the door to apartment 204. It was my first time visiting her home and I wasn't positive I had the correct place, but this was the number associated with her last name on the mailboxes on the ground floor.

The heavy wooden door creaked open and Naomi stood there, still in the same leather jacket and cap she was wearing onstage from earlier in the evening. With smudged eyeliner, her face was red and puffy. No doubt she'd been crying.

"Why are you here? Don't you have a big thing tomorrow?" she asked with dejection in her voice. After glancing at her watch, she added, "I mean . . . today?"

"You mean, why am I standing on your doorstep in my mismatched pajamas, the day I need to be at the studio? Because I was worried about you. Did you see my texts?"

She motioned for me to come inside. "You came all this way because you didn't get an answer about brunch? Forget me, are YOU okay?"

"I'm declaring this a brunch-adjacent emergency." I took off my shoes and followed her to the living room. "I also saw your latest post and wanted to check in on you." Pulling it up on my phone, I showed her my feed.

"Oh." That's all she said at first after sitting down. "That."

Naomi looked at me with a hint of melancholy in her face. "I'll admit, I was excited, then confused, when I saw you at my performance tonight and you didn't stay through my set. I didn't know how to address that with you. Then you texted and I figured I'd wait until the morning to respond since I felt so down after my show."

"It sounded great from outside, I heard your opening song out there. You sounded amazing from the alley. I'm sorry if I ruined all of that for you."

A hint of a smile appeared. "Oh, you didn't do that. The performance went fine for the most part. It's just that I've been doing this for fifteen years, and my career has plateaued. A record label rep was there, and he wanted to sign another band. Did you hear the acoustic duo, the guys with the matching mohawks who went up before us? They had a good set, and great onstage personas, and when they saw the label rep there they offered to take him out to dinner, the kind of place that's booked out a year in advance for reservations."

I nodded. The duo was good, but Naomi and her group were better. I hated how life was so unfair at times, and that practice and skills sometimes didn't amount to success. So much of it was about things out of your control. Like connections. Timing. Luck. Having a sellable, marketable look. And other people playing a little dirtier than you by bribing decision-makers with exclusive dinner reservations.

I said, "I have two things to say to that. First, you're an incredible musician. You have credentials, awards, and a ton of fans. Second, I don't think you're stuck at all, you have so much talent. You might need to look beyond what you're used to and look for new opportunities. For example, we need to add music options to our app, and I can't think of anyone who understands user design and music better than you. I'd love to have you help with that once I fundraise, which you know I'm determined to do."

She wiped away a tear. "You really mean it? You'd hire me for something like that? It would seriously be my dream job!"

"And it would be my dream to work with you. We've been using placeholder music up to this point but Harry said it's something we need to build a catalog for as soon as I can secure funding. I'll email you more information once I have that. Which I guess could be as early as today if I can get an investor on board from *The Bullpen*."

She looked at her watch. "Shit, Sara. You need to get some sleep! You want to crash here? My sofa has a pullout bed."

It was a tempting offer since I was barely able to keep my eyes open. I wouldn't be able to sleep well anyway because of my nerves, but being in a new place in an unfamiliar bed seemed like it could be worse than staying at Jia's. I couldn't believe this was my conclusion . . . preferring to sleep in Jia's closet. A windowless chamber without any substantial airflow was a better choice for me because it was less of an unknown.

"I think I'll head back to Jia's tonight but thank you for the offer."

The wait time for a car was only two minutes, which left no time for lengthy goodbyes. She pulled me into a warm embrace. "Thanks for coming over, it really meant a lot to me. And yes, let's have brunch. I love brunch!"

Our friendship was proving to be salvageable, but our connection could only grow stronger if I made more of an effort to make this relationship a priority. "No problem. I'm glad I came by. Oh, one more thing."

From my coat pocket, I pulled out a multicolor friendship bracelet. "My parents found this in my old belongings. It was only halfway done, but over the last few nights I had some time to finish it." After I tied it on her wrist, she gave me another hug.

"These are back in style, you know. It's the best gift I've been given in a long time." Opening the front door, she sent me on my way.

I nodded off in the car, which was actually a good sign. It meant I was not only tired, but able to sleep after all. After such a depressing discovery about Harry, it was nice to know that something was going right with Naomi back in my life. Too bad it was at the expense of getting rest. Casey had agreed to help me with my hair and makeup in the morning, and I'd have to warn him he would need to pull off a miracle.

The car pulled into a red zone to let me out. I trudged up the stairs and crashed on the couch in the living room as soon as I got into the apartment, falling face-down into the cushions with my coat still zipped. In only a few hours, One Last Word would debut on *The Bullpen*.

But first, sleep.

As I fell onto my bed, I got a text from Naomi. Thank you, my friend.

I reread her message a few times. Clutching my phone tightly, I conked out with a grin on my face.

Chapter Twenty-One

In *The Bullpen*'s contestant waiting room, there were pastries, packets of gourmet nuts, and carafes of coffee. Free food and drinks would normally distract me, but the only thing I was preoccupied with was my stubborn cowlick that would not stay down, no matter how much product Casey put in my hair. He secured a bobby pin to force the wayward wisps into submission. "Let's hope this works. But other than the rogue stalk of hair sprouting from your part, you look stunning!"

On a macro level, I had to admit he was right. He had blended, highlighted, matted, and glossed me into a camera-ready version of myself, and after he finished, Casey recorded me on his phone without any filters to prove he'd rid me of my perpetual forehead shine. "Can you please do your best to not sweat?" he joked.

"I don't think my sweat glands got your memo. I'm already dying."

He spun me in my chair and took photos from all angles. "I flat-ironed the shit out of your hair. It's so shiny!" He showed me the images on his phone and beamed.

Movement in the doorway caught my eye. Jia entered the room carrying a bouquet of flowers, with both of my parents in tow. They were all wearing bright blue shirts with "WE LOVE ONE

LAST WORD! #SaraSquad" across their chests. Jia beamed when she walked over to me.

"You all came?" Tears welled in my eyes, as Casey grabbed the show schedule from a nearby table and fanned my face.

"Don't you dare cry. I see those juicy tears forming in your eyes. And your forehead wrinkles are developing, NO Shar-Pei Sara allowed! Keep it together!" Casey demanded.

I laughed. Leave it to him to reverse my sentimental mood. "I love all the blue shirts. You look like one of those reunion families who go to theme parks together. Or a low-end bowling team."

Jia said, "I can't believe Umma and Appa agreed to wear them. And they weren't the only ones!"

Naomi's head popped out from around the doorframe. She smiled and walked in wearing her matching electric blue shirt. Then, to my surprise and horror, Casey pretended to do a strip-tease, unbuttoning his flannel shirt while showing off exaggerated dance moves. Underneath his long-sleeved shirt was a thematic bright blue tee.

Naomi put her hand on my shoulder. "I'm so proud of you, my friend. Sorry again for ruining your night's sleep."

"Thank you," I replied. "And I was already wide awake, you don't need to apologize for anything!"

Dad pulled a card out of Mom's purse and handed it to me. The last time I'd gotten one from my parents was college commencement. And before that, high school graduation.

Jia said, "Just so you know, they spent over an hour in the greeting card sections in various stores, trying to find the perfect words they wanted to convey, in a language they don't know fluently. I know this, because I was the one who drove them all around town to buy it."

I slid the card out from the bright pink envelope. Mom apologized. "Sorry, we forgot to lick closed."

"That's okay," I said, amused that my mom had apologized for depriving me of her saliva. The card, with a shiny red rose bouquet on the front, read "Congratulations to our daughter. We are so proud of you. We've watched you follow your dreams and decide who you are and who you want to be. We're excited for you, thinking about everything you'll be doing and all the dreams you'll be fulfilling. You are strong, smart, and beautiful inside and out. We love you so very much."

I tried my best to fight the tears, but I couldn't hold them back. Jia and Naomi both pulled out tissues from their purses and Casey pressed them under my eyes to keep my makeup from running.

I could barely get any words out. "Thank you, Umma. Thank you, Appa."

My dad looked at my mom and said, "We are sorry."

Thirty-four years of existence, and I'd never heard those words uttered from either of their mouths before.

I asked, "For what? I love the card."

But maybe it wasn't about that. There could be hundreds of reasons for an apology. Years of missed opportunities for meaningful reconciliation and healing had long passed us by, and I had written off my parents as being incapable of any personal growth: the fact that something would spur them into an apologetic state left me practically speechless. This admission of regret was not only out of character, it was also out of place. My hands turned clammy with the realization that something bad could have caused this shift in accountability. A change in financial circumstances. Health problems. Or worse. My mind jumped to a bad place.

Umma's shoulders slumped as she took in a large breath and exhaled deeply. "We wearing your shirt, but don't know about your company, Jia explain to us today. We try to leave you alone because you grown up and don't listen anyway, and you mad we don't care enough. Then when we get your message, we try to call you and you don't like that either." She let out a frustrated sigh and looked at Appa. "We try and try but whatever we do it's not good."

My dad added, "We don't know how to be parent of thirty-two-year-old woman."

"I'm thirty-four," I corrected, blotting my face with a fresh Kleenex.

Umma nodded. "See, same problem. We say something and you argue."

My voice grew louder. "Mom, it's not an argument, it's a fact. I'm thirty-four. This is not a debate."

Jia stepped between us. "Time out. What I'm hearing is that Umma and Appa don't know how to parent grown-ups, is that right?"

They nodded. My dad opened his mouth, but wisely shut it again.

I looked at both of my parents. "Sometimes you treat me like a child when you're worried, and I don't need you to parent your old way anymore. I'm a grown, independent woman. What I would love from you is your support when I need it. That's what's best now, you giving me room to let me figure out who I'm meant to become." I gestured toward their blue shirts, then proudly held up their greeting card. "And by showing up today, making me feel special on my big day, you did exactly that. Wearing those hashtag SaraSquad shirts lifted me up when I needed it the most. Thank you!"

Jia added, "Same goes for me. Please don't ask about why I'm not married, or having kids, or why I eat the way I do. I'd love for you to support me and assume I'm trying my best to make my life great."

My dad muttered to Mom, "Maybe we nagging too much?"

Nagging was my parents' primary love language, and it didn't work for Jia or me anymore. I don't know if it ever had.

"Maybe every day calling is too much?" Mom asked.

"Yes!" Jia and I said in unison.

My parents belly laughed at our earnest, fraught outburst. Jia and I looked at each other and erupted into a fit of giggles too, the best kind, where you think you've stopped and then start hysterically laughing again and again.

I debated whether to push my parents any further or to be content with how things were going, but I decided to take this as far as I could, while they were being receptive. "Do you think that instead of jumping in with offering advice, you could try asking instead, 'How can I help you?' I think it is a way to show support as parents, but in a different way."

Appa nodded along while Umma said, "Okay. We try."

I flipped the greeting card so it faced them. "I know you want me to be like these red roses. Pretty. Crowd-pleasing. Perfect. They are delicate and smell good and love sunny days. But that's not me. I'm more like a dandelion. Dandelions survive even in unfavorable conditions. They're resistant to a lot of pests. They can grow and thrive in the most unexpected places, like in cracks of sidewalks and driveways. I'm a dandelion, not a rose."

My mom responded, "We don't need rose or want rose. We proud of you no matter what."

Dad reached out and squeezed my hand. "Go be dandelion."

I pressed my lips together and nodded. "Thank you," I whispered.

The production assistant popped her head into the room. "Sara? We need to put a mic on you now. Are you ready?"

I wasn't. I'd barely recuperated from the overwhelming emotions, and it was almost time to go onstage.

Thanks to my family, I hadn't noticed who still hadn't made an appearance. I wholly expected Harry to come. Seeing my face fall as I glanced at the door, Jia read my mind and whispered, "He said he'd be here. I emailed him and delivered a shirt. He probably hit traffic."

Naomi rubbed my shoulder. "We're here to support you. We'll cheer extra loud."

I bit my lip. This was not the time to get emotional. One, because Casey would kill me if I shed any more tears, and two, I couldn't afford to look weak, not now. It was game-face time, only minutes away from pitching my business to big-name investors. I took a deep breath and told the production assistant I was ready to go.

"Good luck!" Casey yelled.

Jia cheered, "Make us proud!"

My parents yelled, "Daebak!"

I thanked everyone for coming and reminded them to not embarrass me during the broadcast. Umma asked everyone, "Why she think we doing that?" and Jia shot me a look that made me cackle.

I followed the PA to the holding area: the official bullpen. It was where the contestants gathered, waiting for their turn to go onstage. Before the show started, *The Bullpen* aired snippets of people waiting backstage, showing some participants chatting, wearing headphones, and rehearsing their pitch, while others paced around the room, trying not to bump into one another given the small space. The cameraman had finished securing the footage as I entered, so I could relax a little without worrying about any filming.

The PA said, "I'm Nancy by the way. I don't know if I mentioned that earlier. I need to slide the wire under your shirt and attach it to this little box that I'll clip to your pants. If you have to go to the bathroom, please let me know so we can mute you. We've had a few nervous contestants who went to the restroom without alerting us and, well, let's just say no one wants to hear what happens in there."

"Got it. I'll refrain from trash-talking into the mic too," I said with a laugh.

She smiled. "Oh, we'd love that actually! It adds to the excitement. And believe me, we've heard it all! You can manually turn off the switch if you want, until we're ready for you onstage."

She had trouble connecting the mic wire, so I pulled up my shirt, exposing my belly and back while she reattached the cord. When her icy fingers brushed my skin, I shivered and shimmied.

Behind me, a familiar voice deadpanned, "Nice moves. People relieve their stress in the weirdest ways."

Harry. Standing next to me, looking more disheveled than usual. With wild hair, day-old stubble, and wearing an ill-fitted black bomber jacket coupled with a rugged leather backpack. Not very Harry-like. But damn, still attractive.

I pulled my shirt down, yanking the mic along with it. My face flushed as I apologized to Nancy. "I'm so sorry, I wasn't expecting company."

She said, "No problem, it wasn't working anyway. Maybe you can try to pull this other cord through for me and I'll connect it to the battery on your pants." Following her orders, I was finally rigged with a mic.

"I'm scared I might detonate," I quipped.

"Ha! Please don't." Nancy's walkie-talkie beeped. "Shoot, I'm wanted on set. Good luck, Sara!"

As she scurried off, I turned to Harry. "Do you think sweat will cause the mic to short-circuit? Asking for a heavily perspiring friend."

He handed me a tissue. "I think they'd have figured out the right technology by now to prevent electrocution of public speakers. And sorry I'm late, I had a bunch of urgent things happen today, of all days. I'm here now and you have my full attention. How are you feeling?"

Now that he was here, a lot better, even though the last time I'd seen him things weren't exactly great between us. "I'm nervous. They still haven't revealed who the judges are."

He replied, "You have nothing to worry about. Your pitch is strong, you know your features inside and out, and you understand both the technical and business side." Harry offered me an assuring smile. "We can walk through a business exercise if you want. Tell me, what do you think is the worst product on the market. It can be tech, food, electronics, anything."

With no hesitation, I answered, "Chips Ahoy! cookies. Who even eats those things when there are so many better cookie options on the market? They're like the American version of biscotti because they're so dry and dusty. Are they even baked? Or molded out of cookie-flavored air clay?"

He laughed. "That's a perfect example. So let's walk through that business model. Someone at their holding company believes in those cookies. You can buy them in practically any grocery store or chain drugstore, so they have strong distribution, and they've been around forever. And now they have snack-size packs that are easy to travel with or pack in a lunch. Who's buying them and why? Honestly, I have no idea. Moms who like to eat dry, chalky discs that don't spoil quickly. But there's clearly a market for them. Just like there's a market for your app. It might not be fully realized yet, but it's there."

I nodded. This was a helpful way to think about everything.

His phone buzzed but he ignored the call. "You'll do great, I know it. You have a desirable product. A fantastic pitch. You're brilliant, fun, and wonderful. Should I continue?"

I blushed. "By all means . . . yes."

His phone buzzed again. This time he pulled it out of his pocket and glanced at the screen.

"You want to get that?" I asked with a tiny hint of annoyance in my voice. Couldn't he just silence it?

"Sorry," he said, matching my tone. "Let me put it on Do Not

Disturb mode." But before doing that, it buzzed again. He texted a one word reply and turned off the notifications.

Stuffing his device into his coat pocket, he continued. "As I was saying, you'll do great. And I'll be rooting for you. Oh! One more thing." He unzipped his outer layer to reveal his blue shirt. "I'm a SaraSquad member too! The shirt they ordered is an XXL, not L, so I needed to wear an oversize jacket to hide it and surprise you. It's Stan's coat, who wishes you luck, by the way."

My irritation melted away. His phone fell to the floor, and he placed it on the table next to us. "You need anything before I head to the studio audience?"

"Did you see any bottles of water by any chance?" My throat was parched, and the last thing I needed was for my voice to catch and then to go into a coughing fit on air.

"I passed by a cooler in the hallway. Let me grab a drink for you."

He turned around and headed out the door. I stared at him like I was watching a cowboy ride off into the sunset.

His phone screen lit up in the corner of my eye. I tried my best to ignore it, but the glow was persistent, and curiosity got the best of me. Peering closer, I discovered that it was Claudia sending him multiple messages in a row.

And like a moth to a flame, I read his messages. I couldn't help myself.

> If you need anything else from me today, I'm here for you

> Thank you so much for being such a doll! Will let you know when it arrives

> You're an amazing man <3 TY!

What did all that mean? Was he back with his ex? My stomach squeezed and a wave of nausea hit me hard. Was this why he was late? Because he was meeting up with Claudia?

Harry walked through the door, smiling as he carried two dripping-wet bottles of water. "They were floating in melted ice and I couldn't find a towel. I used my pants and now I look like I peed on myself." After taking in my reaction, he said, "You look pale, like you might throw up. Do you need a trash can? Is it stage fright? Are you okay?"

It wasn't stage fright.

It was unrequited love and cheater fright.

And no, I wasn't going to be okay. I had no choice but to focus on the show now and compartmentalize my work and love life. Because if I didn't, I would cry.

I muttered, "Your wife has been texting." His *wife*. Not ex-wife. Because they were still married. And apparently, still very friendly.

"Oh no." His face blanched. "You saw the messages? I can explain."

Nancy came bursting back into the room with her crackling walkie-talkie in hand, shooing Harry away before he could offer me an explanation as to why he and his ex were so chummy. Their friendliness was especially suspicious, given how he'd shown up late looking tousled and scruffy. Damn it, how did I not see the signs?

Nancy cleaned the room of all nonparticipants but as Harry reached the exit, he held on to the doorframe and refused to leave. She announced, "We're on air in ten minutes. All audience members need to be in their assigned seats." Nancy looked at him with narrowing eyes and said, "I need to deliver you to the audience right now, or you won't be let in."

He turned to me and pleaded, "I'll explain everything later. Good luck! You'll be great!"

The TV monitors on each wall of the waiting room flickered and a livestream of *The Bullpen*'s studio appeared on every display. The stage was crowded with personnel and crew preparing the set and making sure the lighting and sound were all working as planned. Cameras had been placed in various areas around the space, and three of them were directed at the stage from different angles, with two more covering the studio audience. Jia, my parents, Casey, and Harry all appeared on-screen, unaware of the surveillance around them. Jia pointed to the judge panel while chatting with my parents and Naomi. Casey and Harry huddled and talked before the camera switched to another vantage point, focusing on other audience members.

The biggest screen in the room showed the online livestream broadcast activity, which included the number of active viewers (5K, 6K, then 10K, rapidly growing by the second) and comments pouring in from around the globe. The show had rabid fans who couldn't wait to see which judges would dole out money to budding entrepreneurs. The free-flowing critical commentary suggested that the audience was inclined to be harsh and cynical rather than lighthearted and optimistic. I'd have to make sure I didn't look at the comments before walking onstage; I was already rattled enough without having random people from cyberspace weighing in with their opinions.

A producer entered our waiting area and called out three participants' names that weren't mine. They were the ones who'd been randomly selected to be the first to pitch the judges.

My blood was pumping so hard I could hear thumping in my ears. *Only a few minutes more.* I pushed down my feelings for Harry and focused on running through my pitch in my head.

As the first three competitors walked over to the stage door, the front center camera revealed the five judges' faces, one by one.

Mandy and Tom, two naysayers who had interviewed me virtually for the Pitch Warriors VC program, were on the stage.

Worse, sitting next to them were Bryce and Marcus, the two cofounders at my previous company who had canceled my project. The ones who had watched me storm out of their conference room and never look back. At the end of the judging section was a fifth spot, an empty chair.

"Shit! Not them!" I said out loud. My heart raced and my body turned ice cold.

Nancy flailed her arms to get my attention and pointed at her mic, then at me. She mouthed, "It's on now!"

Which meant everyone had heard what I said.

Overhead, a speaker clicked on and a booming voice broadcasted, "Rolling in three."

"Two."

"One."

Chapter Twenty-Two

What was the point of pitching now? Four out of the five judges had already expressed in the past that they hated my business idea, or hated me, or worse . . . both. The probability of getting funding had dropped dramatically, to zero. When the announcer disclosed all the judges on the show, my ears were ringing and my brain couldn't process any words spoken by him. I didn't even catch the unknown judge's name.

I watched backstage as the first two competitors were grilled hard by the panel and left the stage without any funding offers. The fifth judge was reticent, rarely looking up at the camera, so I spent my time analyzing the four judges who disliked me, wondering how badly they would treat me during my pitch session.

When the third contestant took the stage, the participants behind me chatted away, like they had no worries in the world. Tuning them out was impossible, so I shifted my attention from the panel to eavesdropping on my peers instead, hoping it was a better expenditure of time and energy.

The guy behind me boasted. A LOT. "I worked at Hillman and Goldstein in private equity for a number of years and made a lot of connections there. Mandy wanted me in the mentorship program, pulled some strings, but they ended up giving the last spot to some chick with a mediocre idea. Luckily, I was able to get on this show because my dad went to college with one of the producers."

"Oh, is it Jerry? My dad plays tennis with him," the other guy asked while I fumed.

"Yeah, Jerry! He went to college with my dad. They rowed together."

My eyes widened as they continued talking about preferential treatment so casually. Was that not a taboo subject among strangers? Or were old boy network situations now so normalized that they weren't a secret anymore?

I had the opposite of partiality going for me at the moment. There were four people on that stage who would absolutely *not* be showing any favoritism toward me on the show. It was almost impressive how the odds were so stacked against me during such a pivotal career inflection point of my career. Hundreds of thousands of viewers would see me go down in flames, in real time, and others who didn't would be able to watch the recorded version.

There was still a chance I could feign food poisoning or consume an apple peel from the snacks table, which would instantly give me swollen eyes and neck hives. I couldn't go on camera like that. It was no chickenpox, but it would be enough. Sure, I'd forgo my spot, but I wouldn't leave myself open to scrutiny by the judges or the online community tuning in to the program.

Or . . . I could rise to the occasion and go on stage, pitch my business, try to field questions without crumbling under pressure, and jet as soon as they finished filming my segment.

I looked over at the table. In the fruit bowl, a shiny, waxy Granny Smith apple with a barcode sticker beckoned me. All it would take was one bite. Apples were not always associated with auspicious events: ask Eve or Sleeping Beauty. A little nibble was all it would take.

Deep breaths, Sara.

I knew what needed to be done. If I could handle myself on *The*

Bullpen, I could do anything. And the truth was, even after a decade working in tech, and spending hours upon hours planning for this moment, I wasn't only nervous, I was heartbeat-pounding, queasy-to-the-point-of-vomiting terrified.

Nancy the PA jogged up to me. "You're next, and they'll be calling you up in a few seconds." She studied my face. "You'll do an amazing job. And you're in the best spot. Statistically speaking, the third and fourth slots get a warmer reception from the judges."

I couldn't help but sputter out a laugh. *Not this time.*

She splayed her fingers, pushing her hand forward to demonstrate the universal signal to stop. She tapped her earpiece and waved me on. "They're ready for you now. Good luck!"

I walked to the side of the stage, where the head producer smiled and nodded at me while pointing to the stage. "Walk over to the spot marked with an X. Deep breaths, okay? Inhale. Exhale. And don't forget to smile."

Head held high, I marched onto the stage, poised and grinning with confidence. *Be a dandelion.*

While the audience clapped, I wondered why the production team hadn't warned me that the lights would be so bright that my eyes would water, and that I wouldn't be able to see past the first row of the studio audience due to the glare.

I'd never quite understood the deer-in-headlights idiom until now. Other than the judges right in front of me, I couldn't see a damn thing.

"Girl, you got this!" Jia screamed. "Hwaiting!" Jia's Korean decree to cheer me on, for me to do my best.

"One! Last! Word!" Casey yelled from somewhere in the front middle section.

I stood on the red X. It was the only thing I could remember to do from the producer's instructions.

Pushing through my discomfort, I stood like a Buckingham soldier in front of the judges, arms at my sides, chin up, but then I remembered to smile and offered an awkward showing of teeth that I hoped looked more smiley than snarly on camera.

The man wearing horn-rimmed glasses seated in the fifth chair returned my smile. "Sara Chae. Welcome to the show. Why don't you tell us a little bit about your app, One Last Word."

"I'd be happy to do that." My company's logo appeared on the screen to my right, and then the demo rolled. "One Last Word helps solve the problem we all think about as we get older, 'what would you say to people in your life if your time on this Earth was limited and you had nothing left to lose?'"

I described the app for about five seconds before I was interrupted by Bryce. "Yes, but we've all seen tech like this before. It's just an email platform really, wrapped in a cheap new bow. Why do you think this has viability?"

Marcus chimed in. "We've had a chance to review the numbers. I don't see much growth potential."

It was the exact same argument they'd challenged me with that day in the conference room, the day I quit and ventured off on my own three months ago. If they couldn't see how the market could grow, it meant (1.) they weren't listening then (or now), or (2.) they didn't believe the numbers in the projections and forecasts, or (3.) they just didn't give a damn. Looking at their smug faces, it was potentially all three.

"The market size is significant, especially given the number of aging baby boomers, plus Gen Xers and millennials planning for their futures; for example, those who are buying life insurance or investing in 529 savings for their children," I explained.

"Speaking of significance, you don't appear to have a significant number of sign-ups. Not enough for me to take you seriously. Your subscriber base is woefully underwhelming," Mandy sniped.

"That's by design," I contested, thinking to myself how woefully underwhelmed I was by many things about Mandy too. "We recently came out of the user testing phase and have grown our current number of accounts simply by word of mouth. Yes, we have a limited number of users, but our product isn't in a stage where it's available to the masses yet. We have a high satisfaction rate among current customers, and we've built out the infrastructure optimizing for scalability and uptime. We're rolling out our marketing soon and will be hiring a full-time developer. Scaling, growing, hiring, and fundraising. That's what we are focusing on at this critical juncture."

The judges had my business plans in front of them on the table. Mandy flipped through the pages without reading anything and pushed the bound document away from her. "This product has no vision, and I wouldn't even use the product myself. It's a terrible idea. I'm out."

Tom made eye contact with her but had avoided looking directly at me. After he propositioned me at the gala, I hoped I would never cross paths with him again. Just thinking about that night sent a cold shiver running down my spine.

When he spoke, it was hard to even listen to him. "I agree one hundred percent with Mandy. None of this is convincing enough to become an investor or a partner. It's not only no, it's an absolutely never from me."

Not a surprise given our history, but did he have to say "absolutely never" on a livestream?

It was then open season for the co-CEOs to dump even more on the growing shit pile. "Also a no from us," Bryce added, smiling at me. "But Marcus and I would love to have you back at our company, as a mid-level product manager. The door is always open for nose-to-the-grindstone workers like yourself," he said with a hard-to-miss disparaging tone.

Marcus added, "I've had the displeasure of receiving a message from your app. You may remember one of our former employees, Marcia? She was let go recently and IT found an email she'd saved that they believe was intended for me, and they brought it to my attention. A glitch in your system, perhaps?" His know-it-all smirk . . . I wanted to punch it off his smug face.

Beads of sweat formed where my hairline met my forehead, but I didn't dare wipe them. That would show the judges, audience, and viewers that I was in distress, and I needed to show confidence. Or fake it at least. "Yes, we discovered the reason that early batch of messages was sent, and it wasn't faulty tech. They were released deliberately, and admittedly, the message never reached you due to my inability to spell." I remembered the words I'd written: *your company has lost its way and has stagnated. I'll gladly take this app elsewhere. When I succeed, I'll be sure to offer you a discount.* I was right though, it was the first time in five years that my old company posted a loss, and they had no new apps in the pipeline.

I added, "I made some predictions in the email about your company that were correct, and I'd happily provide business consulting services for a hefty fee. But back to the app itself, did you have any other questions? I'd also be happy to discuss other topics, such as innovation and talent retention."

Marcus cleared his throat. After a few seconds of silence, Bryce changed the subject. "Start-up life is hard on women, with all the long hours and demanding work. Are you sure you're cut out for this? I just don't see anyone working this long and hard unless they're fresh out of college."

My jaw dropped. Would they even be asking the same to a man? If they'd bothered to read my bio, or even past performance evaluations, they'd know what my work ethic was like, but I was also glad this topic came up. Given what I knew about the start-up world, and how I wanted my life to change, it was important to maintain balance for once in my life. If the last few months had taught me anything, it was that not only did family and friends matter to me more than I'd ever imagined, but creating boundaries and finding time for love did too. It would not be easy to make those a priority, but I would try. Starting now.

"I want to create a company where we value hard work, but also find balance, if that's what you're asking. Because I'm sure you're not asking a gendered question. That would not be a good look for someone in your position."

He squirmed. "No. Of course not. Thanks for your answer." Scooting forward in his chair, he added, "And it's still a no from me."

What was the point of all of this? Was I expecting any kind of different outcome? It wasn't just that the odds were stacked against me, but also most of these decision-makers were determined to sabotage this opportunity. It was like this was a rigged carnival game and I was dumb enough to keep handing over money, hoping to win.

Well, at a minimum, there were two things I wanted out of this experience.

One, to get through my entire business pitch, fighting hard and believing in myself without caving to their interruptions.

And second, somewhat related, to not cry.

As much as I was doing a good job at hiding my emotions up to this point—mainly because I was petrified due to sheer fear—hot tears were surfacing and I could tell they were on the verge of spilling. There was only one potential *yes* left in the room. Judge number five was my very last shot, so I turned to the horn-rimmed-glasses guy and said, "I'd love to finish my pitch without any more disruptions, if that works for you."

He replied, "Fire away."

So I did.

In less than twenty seconds, I managed to explain to him that the revenue would be from ads and product bundling, and that certain partners, such as will-making and insurance companies, were open to business opportunities. I explained how machine learning for our autocomplete prompt functionality was advanced enough to take the pressure off users who didn't know what to write, or were too afraid to speak their mind. By this point I had nothing to lose but to give it my all, even if it was a lost cause. Given the circumstances, I managed to deliver the best pitch possible. But was it enough? It upset me knowing that in general, women get less than 3 percent of venture capital funding, and I could very well be among the ones who try, but are excluded from this industry.

Tom cleared his throat, and Mandy offered him a surreptitious, approving glance. "Thank you, Sara, but it looks like you have noes across the board. We might ask you back in another season of the show in the future. A few contestants who lost out on funding will battle it out for another pitch opportunity in a future episode, and who knows, maybe one of us will reconsider, although it's not likely, if I'm being honest."

The producers had not told me about this. I asked, "There's a second-chance opportunity? And I'd go head-to-head pitching against other companies, like in a rap battle?"

This got a laugh out of the horn-rimmed-glasses guy.

Mandy clarified, "Even with a second chance, it's probably still no." She waved her hand dismissively and shot me a haughty, sly smile.

Bitch.

The judge with the glasses spoke. "Before we hastily move on, I'd like to take a turn to ask a few more questions."

The other judges quieted down. Way down. To the point of hushed silence, which made me wonder who this guy was.

He adjusted his glasses and lifted a copy of my business plan, which, when turned at a certain angle, revealed it was littered with colorful tabs and Post-its, not too different from how I annotated some of my favorite books. "I read the entire thing," he remarked. My heart thumped hard, this time with joy. But then he added, "And I don't agree with your vision."

My heart sank. *Sorry, Sara, you're not going to be a women-led start-up backed by venture capital.*

Then the vultures circled. Tom, Mandy, Marcus, and Bryce all chattered on about how they agreed with him.

Light-headed and demoralized, I felt like I was in a bad dream, their voices and words becoming fuzzy and distant. Through the mental fog I could hear complaints like "limited in scope," "lack of insights," and "questionable target market." All those concerns were addressed in the report, if they'd cared to read it.

One of the many reasons I had been scared to come on the show was the risk of humiliation; friends and family would learn my true value and worth, and it might be zero dollars. Everything was livestreamed and recorded for later viewing, which meant hundreds of thousands of people would see my downfall in real time and witness actual footage of me losing all of my dignity. Knowing what I did now, would I look back on this experience and think it was worth it?

Well, no.

Was I happy I did it anyway? Because it showed I had guts and grit?

Also no.

"May I speak?" The VC with the glasses immediately commanded their attention. "It's hard to get a word in edgewise with you all; your pile-on mentality leaves me perplexed. What I wanted to say, before I was interrupted by your uninformed commentary, was that I didn't agree with the vision of One Last Word, which is a product I stand by completely. And that's because I think it should be bigger. Bolder. And I can absolutely see this breaking through the clutter in the communications space with the right partner in place."

Wait.

What was happening?

Was he . . . on my side?

I held my breath, waiting for the big reveal . . . *but it's still a no for me.* He tilted his chin up and unexpectedly closed his eyes, like he'd decided it was the perfect time to catch some z's. I braced myself for the good and bad of what he could possibly say or ask next, assuming he wasn't napping.

The longer he kept his eyes closed, the more I lost faith. Female entrepreneurs had a harder time raising money for several reasons, one of which was the types of questions asked during pitch opportunities like this, because they were usually different in scope for men versus women. I'd watched the previous show, where the head of a seed fund asked seasoned female cofounders of an ad-tech start-up about a fair valuation for their company, stating that he couldn't invest without them showing annual growth of 75 percent or more, along with hundreds of "sticky" customers and consistent profits. On the same show, he offered seed investment in a company founded by two young serial start-up founder dudes with no customers with a valuation of $100 million, without any actual numbers to back that up.

A fifth "no" was a strong possibility. My stomach clenched, ready for the gut punch.

The bespectacled judge's eyes popped open and he finally spoke. "Could you please tell me why you created the app in the first place?"

It was such a basic question. Was it so simple that it was a trick of some kind? Setting me up to admit to something and then chastising my reasoning?

Before I could answer, he stated, "Let me rephrase that. You created the product for a reason. What was it? I read your pitch documents, which impressed me. But I want to know why you created this specific messaging opportunity right at this moment. What were you trying to accomplish that others before you hadn't?"

I offered the most straightforward answer I could. "I've grown a lot over the years, professionally and socially, and still, I've felt muted. Now I'm able to speak my mind. To tell people what I think. And I wanted to create an app that could empower others to know that if they had regrets and hadn't spoken up, that it wasn't too late to say something. Recently I've discovered the power of showing others appreciation, sometimes long overdue, and that's also something this communication tool can provide."

Scratching his brow, he asked, "And what do your beta users think of the product? Could you summarize the user data in a few short sentences?"

Pleased he was asking something right in my wheelhouse, and that it was a promising sign, I replied, "Simply put, they love getting in the last word. They plan to use it for all facets of their lives. Past employment. Family and friends. Romance." The urge was strong to look around for Harry, but I stopped myself.

He flipped to the front page. "One more area I want to touch on before I decide anything. Before, you mentioned wanting more work-life balance."

Oh no. I liked this guy, but I also didn't want to fall into a trap that pioneering women before me had faced. The question that boiled down to one thing: "Are you on the mommy track or not?" It wasn't a question men or future fathers ever had to answer. I stiffened and told myself, *Sara, if he implies you get a motherhood penalty just because of your gender, you can walk off this stage. There are other people whose opinions matter more, and they're all wearing cheesy blue shirts in the audience.*

After contemplation, I responded, "There are companies that pride themselves at making 'Best Companies to Work For' lists, and that would be the kind of business I would like to run: one that employees are excited about, that they can't wait to show up for each day, and that are loyal to and stay at for many years, doing their best work. I've never enjoyed working at companies with high attrition. Those places leave employees feeing undervalued and demoralized." I shot a look over at Bryce and Marcus, because how could I not?

I continued. "There has been a lot of media attention around women who are leaving high positions because of burnout. Women in mid-level and senior leadership face more challenges than men do in those same jobs, from everyday microaggressions, such as being questioned on their expertise, to carrying a greater responsibility in diversity and inclusion initiatives, to being overburdened by non-promotable, thankless work that their male peers somehow escape more readily. I want to create a fair company that prioritizes career advancement, flexibility, and employee well-being for everyone."

He adjusted his glasses and smiled at me. "I value the same things you do from a work culture perspective, so we're in alignment in a lot of ways. Also, an idea for your company just came to me, one that diversifies your portfolio but still retains what you want to do at your core. I'm envisioning related products that remind you about birthdays, anniversaries, and graduations. And holiday card reminders with ample lead time, which I could use myself. So what do you think about diversification further down the road? How does that sound to you?"

Here I was, on a livestream, with congratulations from viewers streaming on the large screen mounted above the announcer. Lots of party-hat and clapping emojis.

"Some of these diversification ideas have come up before, and they're definitely worth exploring."

"We can talk partnerships and percentage ownership if you're ready, and if you're serious about creating a culture that values the employee, then maybe we could chat about leadership structure too. Maybe you'd want to put yourself in a senior creative or product role but not CEO or president, yet still maintain majority ownership."

Was this a dream? Because this man was saying all the right things. I couldn't imagine a more ideal business investor pairing.

Earlier I'd scribbled on my hand "Ask for a quarter mil! Or more!" so I stood straight and stated, "The investment ask is for three hundred fifty thousand, with five percent equity."

He looked at the ceiling and tilted his chin upward again, this time keeping his eyes open, bobbing his head like he was mentally running through mathematical models in his head. "How about more with a ten percent stake? We can go higher if you're open to rolling out the other communications products we just talked about."

My gaze swept over to the audience and my eyes had adjusted to the light. I could see my family and friends leaning forward, waiting for my answer. Casey bobbed his head eagerly while Harry pressed his lips together to form a straight line, which he did when he was thinking hard. Then, ever so slightly, he tugged his ear, a move so subtle that I almost thought I'd imagined it.

Take the deal.

The judge asked, "Yes or no? We can talk specifics over the break if you'd like. You get the last word."

"Yes!" I said firmly.

The audience erupted into applause and the unnamed investor

stood so we could shake on it. Up close, I could see the white embroidered logo on his light blue shirt.

The Blackwell Group.

Blackwell was the largest early-stage venture capital fund on the West Coast. And then it hit me that this was Greg Peters, the CEO of the company. He specialized in swooping in at the company development stage: pre-product or pre-revenue.

It was no wonder everyone was so deferential to him. I found myself completely tongue-tied as soon as I took his hand in mine—this man was a legend! He was investing in big social media platforms when they were baby companies.

I breathed a sigh of relief for the first time. This was exactly what I wanted. A valued partner. Investment money. And expertise to take me to the next level.

The announcer repeated that we had a deal for the viewers at home, while Greg said, so only I could hear, "We'll chat more later, looking forward to working together." The closest camera to us panned out to the studio audience applauding before the show segment ended for a quick break.

Nancy was waiting in the wings to escort me off the stage. "I'm so excited this worked out for you! That was so suspenseful. When that last guy came in with a counteroffer, those other judges' faces were priceless! See, like I said, you had a great spot!"

I couldn't wait to see a replay of the show. I wanted to see the looks on the judges' faces too. Maybe I could frame the images or use them as my desktop or phone background.

Nancy whisked me away to a side room to fill out additional paperwork. I'd already signed waivers, releases, and NDAs for the show—this new pile of documents awaiting my signature were for my forthcoming deal with Blackwell. "Sorry, our network is down, so we need to go archaic and sign hard copies instead. Usually it's all digital."

"Could I look at these at home and send them back tomorrow? I think I need more time to look through the initial agreement and the proposed numbers." The truth was, my brain was exhausted and my body was so wound up that I needed a little time to get back to a steady, healthy state. The last thing I wanted was to sign important papers under any duress.

"You know, not enough people ask to do that. We've had other contestants review paperwork with their lawyers and return it to our legal staff within a couple of days. That's fine."

I gathered the mound of documents and walked to the waiting area, where the contestants and their invited guests were hanging out. Jia, Casey, Naomi, and my parents were there, and they whooped and cheered as soon as they saw me.

Jia squealed and hugged my tired body. "Over a quarter million in funding! With the possibility of more? Does this mean you'll be moving out of my closet soon?"

I laughed. "Yes, or maybe we both move into a larger place, with an even bigger closet for me!"

Jia checked over her shoulder before asking, "I know we should be all cheery and positive, but what was up with that Mandy woman? She was a spawn of Satan. Don't get me wrong, all of them seemed evil except for the last guy on the right, Mr. Moneybags."

"Yeah, she was particularly nasty today. She's the type of person who would go to a middle school theater production and blast them on social media for being too amateur and inexperienced, and then rate them with a one-star review, just to make all the kids cry," I complained.

Jia quipped, "So what if the Mandys of the world hate you? That's the game . . . the more successful you are, the more enemies you make."

Casey pulled me into an embrace next. "I can't wait to quit my job and work with you! It'll be like old times. And we can talk trash about all those haters when we eat lunch together."

Grinning my head off, I said, "You're my first hire!" then looked at Naomi as I said, "And you'll be my second!"

My mom said, "Appa and I happy for you! But you need to move out of closet right away. It's not a good place to live for CEO."

Appa shot her a look. "We supposed to support, Dangshin. Ask how we can help."

Umma nodded slowly. "*How* can we help you move out of closet?"

I groaned but Jia laughed. "Well, at least they're trying," she said. "I also loved what you said about work-life balance. It's what I've always wanted for you."

I nodded. "I know what kind of life I want now. And I need to have the courage to live it the way I want. Change will be hard, but it'll be good for me."

She leaned in and whispered, "Did you see him over there?" Jia jerked her head toward her left.

To my surprise, Harry was sitting at the table where I'd placed my personal belongings earlier that morning, staring hard at papers in a manila folder.

Jia announced, "Okay everyone, let's head out and grab an early dinner. And you're invited to come to my place later tonight to celebrate! Sara, join us as the guest of honor."

I thanked them for coming and waved as they exited the room. Then I walked over to where the tables were to greet Harry.

"Hey you," I said while readjusting the messenger bag strap sliding off my shoulder.

Harry's eyes lifted from the folder in front of him and he broke into a smile. "Oh, hi! You did great! And I take it you saw my suave signal to you?" He tugged his ear in an exaggerated way, as if he were checking that his lobes were securely attached to his head.

"Blackwell has a stellar reputation, and Greg is the best of the best. He's a nice guy who's been really vocal about the changing face of VC, how it shouldn't just be white tech bros funding a bunch of white tech bros. I'm not surprised he was so enthusiastic about your app. How exciting for you!"

"I couldn't have done it without your mentoring. Or your ear pulling," I joked.

"It's such a great opportunity, and I'm so glad you took this chance by being on the show. As the great Wayne Gretzky said, 'You miss one hundred percent of the shots you don't take.' And you just scored and won the game!"

He pulled together the papers spread out in front of him, like the opposite of a magician spreading out a deck of cards. Then he stuffed everything in the folder and gave me his full attention. "You're Stan's biggest success story from the Pitch Warriors program. I texted him and he's thrilled too!"

Still on the high from the successful appearance on the show, I didn't want to get bogged down in an investigation of whatever he was doing with his own stack of paperwork, with tabs and sticky notes affixed to so many pages. It looked like a business contract, probably something important for work. Important enough to bring backstage to *The Bullpen*.

"Jia's having a get-together later tonight if you want to come. I couldn't have gotten this far without you. Thank you for everything." *Keep it formal, Sara. Protect your heart and don't get dragged down in drama on one of the best days of your life.*

"You're welcome," he said with a quavering smile, his eyes glistening.

"Are you okay?" I asked, now curious about what was going on with him.

"I am, don't mind me. Do you have a pen by the way? Mine

ran out of ink at the worst possible time, and I need to sign something."

I fished out a pen from the bottom of my tote. "It's swag from *The Bullpen*. I hope it's decent quality."

Staring at the branded ballpoint, he said, "I don't think Claudia would mind. She'd be relieved just to have these documents finally signed, sealed, and delivered, even if the ink is spotty. She's been texting me nonstop today, making sure I had everything needed to sign the papers. Her lawyer is like ninety years old and wants this done in writing and not over DocuSign."

Confusion clouded my face as he opened the file folder and stared at the top page. My gaze swept from Harry's handsome face down to the stack of papers. I'd just had a mentally grueling day and had signed a lot of paperwork myself, so my brain wasn't fully cooperating to figure out what he was talking about. This wasn't going to be a moment of showcasing my brilliant deductive reasoning. "And what exactly is it that you're signing?" I finally asked.

With the swag pen, he scribbled a couple of times on the page with blue glittery gel ink. "Signed. It's done. I'm officially divorced. Well, in California it takes six months to go into effect, but that shouldn't be an issue."

My jaw dropped. "You signed your divorce agreement? Here? Backstage?"

He dipped his chin and gave me a sheepish look. "Yes. The papers were supposed to be delivered by courier last night, but they showed up right when I was leaving my condo today, and I was late because of it." He looked at me with apologetic eyes. "For years I dragged my feet because I thought that signing these papers meant I was quitting something that was a huge part of my life. And a huge part of my identity. And I thought I'd end up just like my parents, jaded about marriage and stigmatized by divorce by my family back in Korea."

His eyes filled with tears. "My parents were pressured into marrying each other and never truly experienced romance. I thought that would also be my fate and had resigned myself to it, but then after reconnecting with you again, something changed inside me. You gave me hope and helped me see that I was simply letting go of something that wasn't working anymore."

Just when I was thinking how enamored I was by everything he'd just said, because it was so incredibly thoughtful and romantic, he added, "They say you can't win them all. In the words of Mike Tyson, 'Everyone has a plan until they get punched in the mouth.'"

I raised an eyebrow. "You have a lot of sports analogies for me today. First hockey, then boxing. What does that say about you? Or the two of us together?"

He stood from his chair and with his index finger, he gently lifted my chin.

"Well, these divorce papers have been sent to me a few times over the years, but I kept ignoring them. I stubbornly kept trying to rationalize the marriage, even though Claudia had moved on. You got so mad at me. Especially about the joint taxes part." He chuckled.

I said softly, "I wanted you to listen to your heart and not only to your accountant." I pressed my hand on his upper chest and asked, "What did *this* say?"

Harry took a step toward me. Then another. He closed the gap between us. "It said to be with you." He lifted his hand and stroked my cheek with the backs of his fingers. I closed my eyes and enjoyed his gentle touch.

I let out a soft sigh. "I've been tough on you, but I'm no expert. You have a life that's so different from mine. I have no personal experience with marriage or divorce, but I know this isn't easy for you." I looked into his eyes. "I have my own issues. I'm guilty of holding people up to an ideal standard, a level of perfection that doesn't allow room for any faults, flaws, or mistakes. And I haven't experienced meaningful love because of it. I hide my feelings and deflect to not get emotionally hurt. And I've always prioritized career above all else. While I can't completely relate to what you went through, I know what feeling like a failure in the love department feels like."

He asked, "And why do you think you're looking for something unattainable?"

I peered at him through my lashes. "Pistanthrophobia?"

He cocked his head. "Pistan-WHAT-bia?"

"It might be a made-up word. I saw it on Urban Dictionary once. The fear of getting hurt by someone in a romantic relationship. As I said, I have a lot to work through, including why I'm seeking love advice from Urban Dictionary."

Maybe it was time to admit Jia was right. That it was possible that all this time I didn't feel like I really deserved to be with anyone I wanted to date. If I was ever attracted to anyone, I would immediately give up out of fear of rejection or never pursue it fully, looking for reasons to reject him or telling myself it wasn't possible, so why bother trying.

He said, "I'm dealing with gamophobia myself." He paused a beat, struggling to fight a grin. "The fear of commitment or marriage. Also an Urban Dictionary find. Maybe we both need professional help." He laughed.

"Ah, yes. How's that gamophobia for you?"

"With therapy and time, I'd say it's going better than ever," he admitted. "I still need to work on a few things, like no longer putting career before everything, same as you."

"I want to change too. I admitted as much on the show today, that I want balance in my life and want to make it a priority. Striving for perfection all the time is exhausting and unhealthy." I held up my right hand. "I hereby swear that I will settle with the course my far-from-perfect life takes me and savor the small enjoyable moments along the way."

"Me too." Placing his hands on my shoulders, Harry asked, "So maybe we can get over our phobias together? And savor the little moments together?"

A wide grin spread across my face. "Yes please." Loving someone and giving him my heart was the bravest thing in the world, and I was ready to do that now.

He glanced around the room. It was mostly cleared out, aside from a few of the junior staff cleaning up. Wrapping his hands around my waist, he said, "Would you like to continue this riveting discussion at my place or yours? Before you choose, I need to confess that my place is being painted, so there are sheets of clear plastic drapes everywhere. It looks a lot like a meat freezer."

My eyes widened. "Well, that's not very romantic. Jia's place then. She's out right now, so we'll have the place to ourselves for a couple of hours if we leave soon."

"Then we better go, to maximize our alone time." Harry's gaze fell to my mouth, and he kissed me softly on the lips. "After you," he said, gesturing his hands at the open double doors.

Even after a tiring day, I moved quickly to the exit. We had no time to waste.

Chapter Twenty-Three

Before we entered my sister's apartment, I set the alarm on my phone.

"Is that a timer? Or are you counting this encounter as a workout session?" Harry asked.

"It's a ten-minute warning so we'll be ready when they all arrive. Jia texted that they'd be home in an hour. No surprises this time."

When I turned the doorknob, he pressed into me from behind and wrapped his arms around my waist. He whispered, "Mmmm timekeepers are sexy."

I playfully shifted my elbow to gently poke his ribs, making him jerk back. I'd inadvertently discovered a ticklish spot.

Once we were inside, I spun around and took in his tall, broad physique along with his handsomely boyish face. At the last reunion, I'd noticed that other high school classmates had physically changed so much that I would barely even recognize them if I passed them on the street. Yet Harry still managed to hold on to his youthfulness after all these years. He'd aged like fine wine.

"You look beautiful," he whispered.

"It's the hair and makeup from the show. To cover up my sleep deprivation." I needed to learn to accept a compliment without deflecting. "I mean . . . thanks."

He shook his head. "No, it's not just that. You look confident. And happy. More than ever before, and that includes high school."

Suddenly, I became self-conscious. Not just from being around Harry, but also because Jia's living room had large sliding doors that opened up to a patio that overlooked the street and she rarely closed the blinds. I didn't even know if the vertical blinds worked. And I needed them to close if we were going to be in here.

He peered down at me and then glanced at the patio area. He walked over and tugged on the metal chain, giving it a few tries, gently at first and then using more force, but then the conclusion we both feared came true. "It's stuck." Using his hands to cup his face on the window, he said, "There're a lot of people walking around and lots of surrounding buildings. Unless the CEO of One Last Word wants to go viral in the worst way possible, I think we might need to relocate elsewhere."

"To the bedroom?" Presumably he knew that meant the closet. This wasn't his first wardrobe rodeo.

"Yes please." As we walked down the hallway, he slid his hands from my waist to my hips, making my heart flutter wildly in my chest. By the time we reached the closet, his hands had moved farther down, exploring me in newly stirred places.

I turned on the light and pulled him into the room. Now that he was facing me, we locked eyes at first, and then his gaze slid downward slowly. His nearness alone sent me into a dizzying state. I inhaled sharply as he stepped forward and pulled my body closer to his.

His breath was warm, and my heart rate soared as his lips brushed against mine. "I've been waiting for this for so long, Sara."

I parted my mouth and raised myself on the balls of my feet to meet his next kiss. "Me too," I said as our lips drew apart. *I've waited more than fifteen years.*

His hands slipped down the curve of my spine. He gently tugged me forward, removing all the space between us. It was the most sensual experience I'd ever felt in my life.

"Come on vacation with me," he murmured into my hair.

I pulled away to look up at him. "But I'm still working through the Blackwell Group deal. And I need to meet with Greg next week . . . but I want to spend time with you. Let's do a weekend getaway, to start."

He smiled. "A staycation then! Los Olivos. Santa Barbara, San Luis Obispo." His brows furrowed. "Unless you're the nature type. Then we could go to Joshua Tree or Big Bear. All close by, but very different."

"No thanks to those. I'm not a camping type," I said, scrunching my nose.

He cocked an eyebrow. "Not even glamping?"

There was nothing glam about camping. Nope. "I'm more like gramping. Like your grandparents camping. I'd complain about all of it, not want to do physical activity, and go to bed early."

He barked out a laugh. "Then wine tasting it is! A quick weekend getaway to start. An initial small step toward a brave new balanced world."

"I love wine tasting. I'm a fan of tasting anything if food or drinks are involved. And I want to go to Hawaii sometime! For kalua pork, mai tai, and pineapple tasting with you." My body thrummed with excitement. When was the last time I went on a proper vacation? And how fun would it be to do all these things with Harry?

"I love the sound of that." He leaned down and kissed the side of my neck.

I ran my hands down the front of his chest, feeling his heart hammer hard against them. With a few tugs on his shirt, his blue tee was on the floor. I centered my hips against him and gripped his waist.

He whispered, grazing my earlobe with his soft lips, "Let's move this down to the bed."

Down we both went. With Harry underneath me, I unbuttoned his jeans and loosened the buckle while his mouth explored the base of my neck with a flurry of kisses, making my skin prickle. "Your turn," he said, pulling on the bottom hem of my blouse.

As I pulled off my top, his eyes raked over me. "I love everything about you."

Instead of making me blush, his words sent a hot current down my spine.

"I love everything about you too."

He trailed his hands up my thighs and with a firm grip, he pressed my hips down onto his. His body stirred beneath me as electricity pulsed, then surged between us. Desire took over, our bodies clenching and shuddering, as we moved together in perfect harmony.

And this time, we had no interruptions.

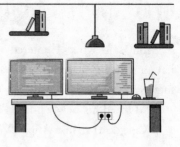

Chapter Twenty-Four

I bolted upright when I heard Jia's keys jangle.

Grabbing my phone, I noticed I had set the alarm for A.M. instead of P.M. "Oh no, they're here!" Harry didn't look startled at all. In fact, he wore a goofy, satisfied grin on his face as I pulled on the closest shirt I could find.

He asked, "You don't think it would be suspicious if you walked out there in my XXL electric blue tee?"

I rolled my eyes and tore it off. "So maybe I'm not thinking straight after our R-rated romp. My silk blouse is wrinkled, which is also a telltale sign of our sexcapade." I looked around Jia's work collection and pulled down a simple black cashmere sweater. "I'm going to head out there, could you please get dressed immediately and join us?" A quick peck on the lips let him know I was being playful and not angry. Even if my parents freaked out about Harry being here, I wouldn't let it bother me. After all, I'd just had the best day of my life.

My parents were sitting on the living room couch holding out wineglasses, waiting for Jia to pour them a Costco signature red blend. Judging by the large, empty cardboard boxes stacked in the hallway, they'd had a productive warehouse party food shopping trip.

Mom said when I entered the room, "Congratulations! If you have a new business can you get Umma and Appa executive Costco membership?"

Dad lifted his newly poured beverage. "Cheers!"

"Wait, don't drink, Appa! We all need glasses!" Jia cried out.

Casey and Naomi came out of the kitchen with fancy stemmed drinkware and handed them to Jia and me. I thanked them and said, "Actually, we're going to need one more."

Casey waggled his eyebrows. "Ohhhhh, is he coming soon? We have plenty of food and snacks for our celebratory soirée!"

The door to Jia's room opened, and Harry—with disheveled hair and that goofy grin still on his face, damn it—came strolling down the hall.

"Ohhh." Casey shot me a look. "You naughty minx."

Mom placed her wineglass down on the coffee table next to her coaster. "Hey, we know you! You're funny guy at Appa big hwangap party."

Harry sheepishly walked over to my side and shoved his hands into his pockets. "Nice to see everybody again."

Dad looked at Mom. Then he stared at Harry and pointed at me. "Are you . . . she . . . both . . ."

I opened my mouth to offer an explanation, but Mom steamrolled into the conversation by asking Harry, "You still dating my daughter?"

He didn't hesitate. "I wasn't actually dating her when I first met you at the party, but we might be dating now, although she hasn't actually confirmed it." A coy sideways glance over to me made me laugh. It was hard to believe that after so many years of dating avoidance, and unrealized fears of inferiority and inadequacy, I was now copiloting this relationship equally with Harry Shim.

Umma's eyes narrowed. "I have more question."

Jia whispered, "Remember, no nagging."

"I'm just asking question. Not nagging," Umma huffed. Crossing her arms, she scowled and pursed her lips. "Never mind."

Dad took a turn. "How old are you?"

"Same as Sara. Thirty-four."

"You want to get married?" His words came out more shaky than before.

Harry looked at me. "I've been married before and it didn't work out, but I would again, with the right partner."

Tipsy Casey filled his glass again. "Well, speaking of weddings, let's try something fun." Grabbing a spoon from the counter, he tapped it against the rim of his wineglass. "Kiss!"

Without any hesitation, Harry turned to me and planted a soft, sensual kiss on my lips.

Jia and Casey whooped and cheered. To my utter shock, my mom clapped. "I don't care if you married before. I'm so happy Sara is dating anybody. I never see anyone interested in her. Never. My whole life."

Dad added, "Me too. I never see. It's miracle."

"Thanks, Umma. Thanks, Appa," I said dryly.

Harry grinned. "Well, I'm happy to be that one person."

I elbowed him and laughed.

Dad held up his wine. "Now we can do toast!"

Jia poured Harry a glass while Casey cleared his throat. "May we all be showered with shards from Sara breaking more glass ceilings in tech and VC!"

I whispered, "That's kind of dark, Case."

"But very dramatic," he explained.

Harry said, "To love and romance," and lifted his drink.

"And to prioritizing relationships," I said.

"To rekindled friendships," Naomi said next.

"And no nagging," Mom promised, then added, "But wedding would be nice."

With drinks in our hands, we all yelled "Cheers!" then clinked our glasses.

Epilogue

One year later

As I passed Casey's office, he shouted, "Hey, can you grab a quick lunch?"

I double backed and paused at his door. "Not today, I just finished a string of press interviews and now I have the TECH TITANS luncheon. I finally get to meet everyone in person!"

A few weeks after *The Bullpen* aired, I was invited to join a networking support group, formed by women who worked in the tech and VC industries. In their mission statement, it said "Women do not always have the same access to deep, decades-durable old boy's club networks that many men have had, so we formed TECH TITANS to provide everyone who joins with access to resources, training, and mentorships to help them succeed." They'd asked me to be their keynote speaker at the annual fundraising dinner in a few months.

"Oh, that's today! Have fun!" Casey chirped, and then got back to programming. He had hired a developer and designer to work on his team, but he insisted on rolling up his sleeves and doing a lot of the work collaboratively.

I added, "But why don't you come over this weekend for dinner? With your new beau?"

He grinned. "Yes! Double date! Lance just revealed his family owns a small vineyard near Solvang. He hid that from me because he knew I wouldn't shut up about it, and of course I can't. The wine is actually pretty good, and that's from someone who thinks all wine tastes like Robitussin. We'll bring a few bottles."

"Sounds great!" I'd sworn to Casey that I would be his wing-woman when my mentorship was over, but then he met someone at *The Bullpen* before I could deliver on my promise. One of the handsome producers had complimented him on the blue #SaraSquad T-shirts while the audience was getting seated. Casey saw it as an invitation to push that door wide open, asking for his number and friending him on all his social media accounts.

Naomi was slowly walking toward the stairwell while looking at her phone. When I caught up with her, a smile lit up her face. "Oh hi! I'm headed down to the new Viet sandwich shop that just opened. Want anything?" Her phone buzzed. "That's Casey, asking for a veggie banh mi. I didn't even ask him yet, he just sensed I was going."

I told her about the luncheon. "You should join me next time. Maybe when it's not the day before release though." It was risky to step away for a couple of hours the day before our launch, but the rollout was in capable hands and there were people at the event to whom I needed to introduce myself. People whom I wanted to have the product launch on their radar, namely investors and heads of media in the greater LA area.

Naomi said, "Count me in for next time. Today, that banh mi is calling my name." Naomi had worked on all the UX, videos, and music for One Last Word on a compressed schedule with a senior designer. Together, they had recently won an industry award. The irony of all this was that Naomi was so busy that she was ditching all sorts of outings and events left and right. Luckily I saw her several times a week and had spent plenty of time with her both professionally and socially. We had gotten much closer over the last year.

Immediately after the luncheon, I resumed interviews with various media outlets about the release and before the workday ended, we had one companywide rally meeting. A long, exhausting, but exciting day.

Just before dinnertime, my phone rang. It was Harry.

"Hey! I was wondering if you wanted me to pick something up from your favorite sushi place or if you'd like to grab a bite to eat around your office. Or maybe near our home?"

It was so nice to hear him say "our" and "home." We'd been living together a few months now and I was still getting used to the sound of it.

I couldn't make up my mind at first, too exhausted to make even a simple dinner decision, but I figured in the end that I wanted to be home when the product officially released instead of here in the office. Barring any catastrophes, everything would go live at midnight on the East Coast, so nine o'clock Los Angeles time. It was six o'clock now.

Hearing a few knocks on the door, I glanced up to see Harry grinning in the hallway.

My mouth fell open. "Wait, you're here?"

From behind his back, he pulled out a small bouquet of flowers, the kind that looked thoughtfully and artistically curated. "These are for you."

I motioned for him to come in and leaned over the corner of my desk to hug him. He stole a quick kiss, then gazed into my eyes. "No rush to leave, I just wanted to surprise you and come home together. I got a good parking spot right in front!"

After answering a few last-minute emails from my investor, Greg, and his cohorts from his company, we headed home and ordered delivery. Within thirty minutes I had my spicy drunken noodles with shrimp, he had his pad see ew, plus thai iced teas for both of us. Sitting together on the couch, he worked while I checked the app admin dashboard.

Casey and Naomi were online, chatting away with the rest of the team. The PR team released the product announcement and press coverage hit in the Asian markets first, exactly as we planned. All systems go!

I opened my outbound mail folder in the app and pulled up letters of appreciation to Jia, Naomi, and my parents, for being there for me during one of the most stressful times of my life. Releasing One Last Word would have been so much harder without their unconditional support.

Glancing over at Harry, the love of my life, who was intensely engrossed in his Excel macro, I pulled up my drafted message to him and smiled to myself. We'd come so far since those Taylor Swift lyrics arrived in his inbox, and now it was time to take the next step. It read:

Dear Harry,

How do you feel about destination weddings in Hawaii?
Because I have a follow-up question for you . . .

The alarm buzzed on my phone. It was officially midnight on the East Coast.

One Last Word had officially launched.

Champagne and party emojis blew up in the company group chat.

And all my messages were sent.

Harry's inbox dinged with a notification, and a wide grin spread across his face as he read what I'd written. Glancing up from his screen, he stared at me with longing.

His whole face broke into a wide smile. Then he kissed me. "Yes! Let's go to Hawaii!"

Acknowledgments

*I*f you've reached this far, you'll know that *One Last Word* is heavy on themes of self-discovery and the challenges of "adulting." As with all my adult books, I wanted the story to center on women working in male-dominated workplaces, and with *One Last Word* it felt like the right next step to pull the curtain back on the venture capital world. All you have to do is Google "Women in VC" and you'll see so much coverage on how anti-woman and insular this industry is, and I was compelled to cast a spotlight on this—as comedically as possible—so others outside the tech and finance fields could see what that world is like. While the companies and people portrayed in the story are fictional, the hardships and struggles revealed in the book are all based on realities of the industry, all based on true stories and data collection. As usual, I did a lot of research (including attending virtual VC pitch meetings), and I didn't pull punches. Thank you so much to Dave Whelan, Holly Han, and Jeremy Miller for sharing your experiences about the VC, start-up and investing worlds. To Jennifer Pullen, I really appreciate the time you spent chatting with me about what the venture capital space is like for women.

I'm a huge fan of Jenny Han, and this book pays homage to her books and TV shows. *One Last Word* is millennial fiction loosely inspired by *TATBILB*. Authors like Jenny Han paved the way for writers like me. Thank you, Jenny, for all that you do for Asian American creators!

Asanté Simons and Carrie Feron, this book would not exist without you. It was my first time having two intense, full rounds of developmental edits, but it was well-worth the effort it took to get the story right. Asanté, I deeply appreciate how you took this project to the finish line like the champion you are. Thank you to the production, sales, and marketing teams for all your time and hard work, and to Decue Wu and Yeon Kim for the stunning cover.

Kathleen Carter, thank you again for working behind the scenes to make sure *One Last Word* got into the right hands. I can't imagine releasing this book without you.

Brent Taylor, thank you for your early feedback on the concept of this book. You saw the potential in this idea and were the best sensitivity reader for my Kettlebell King. I appreciate it so much.

Helen Hoang, you always give me the most honest and thoughtful advice and I love that our friendship has lasted so many years (we still need to write our publishing musical btw). Rosey Lim, thanks for your support and transparency during the highs and lows during my publishing journey. And for all the cat parenting advice.

To Julie Kim, I heart you for being my Korean language consultant and for driving me so many times to McDonald's. The next iced coffee and apple pie are on me.

To Kathleen, Kristin and Chelsea, my AZ retreat buddies, this book would have been delivered really late if it weren't for our retreat. And thanks to you, I know what my next book will be about. I heart you all.

Stephan Lee and Lindsey Kelk, thanks for always texting me back and finding time to have lunch or coffee when I need those breaks.

Ken, Michael, and Katrina, my MAPID writing group, I can't believe we've managed to meet so consistently. Sorry I broke the

EXPLORE MORE BY
SUZANNE PARK

"A fantastic, empowering second chance romance that combines wit and charm with an always insightful commentary on imposter syndrome, anxiety, and the challenge of finding ourselves. Suzanne Park wrote a true gem!"
— Ali Hazelwood, *New York Times* bestselling author

"A cinematic, charming heart-squeeze-of-a-book that has found its way to my Ultimate Comfort Reads shelf."
— Emily Henry, #1 *New York Times* bestselling author

"*Loathe at First Sight* bursts with humor, heart, and great energy. I loved it! Park is a hilarious new voice in women's fiction." — Helen Hoang, author of *The Kiss Quotient*

"Park gives us the story that only she could create. It's hilarious, smart, and the rom-com we need!"
— Alexa Martin, ALA Award-winning author of *Intercepted*

streak by getting Covid (*shakes fist angrily at sky*). I am so grateful we're still sharing and critiquing after all these years, I value your feedback and friendship so much.

To my family, thank you for your love and support, especially as I learn how to be comfortable with slowing down and enjoying the small, joyful moments.

To my bookish author and writer friends, thank you for your behind-the-scenes camaraderie. My Pitch Wars buds (Annette, Jenny, Alexa, Kellye, and Sarah), Asian Ma-fee-ya (Michelle, Julie, and Carolyn), and debut buddies (Alison, Liz), you are my lifeline!

To my bookstagram community near and afar (hi Nurse Bookie!), I light up every time I run into you at events and see your enthusiastic book posts on the interwebs. I appreciate your passion for books and your spotlighting of marginalized creators. Huge hugs for being so wonderful.

To all the booksellers and librarians who include me in your hand-selling and your curated recommendations, I appreciate you more than you'll ever know. I could not be where I am without you, thank you so much.

And finally, to my readers, thank you from the bottom of my heart. I hope you find this novel interesting and it makes you belly laugh in the funny parts. If you enjoyed this book or my previous ones, please tell your friends—it would make my mom and dad's day.